Mack Reynolds

The Adventures of Homer Crawford
(Illustrated Edition)

OK Publishing 2021

Mack Reynolds
The Adventures of Homer Crawford

(Illustrated Edition)

Published by
MUSAICUM
Books

- Advanced Digital Solutions & High-Quality book Formatting -

musaicumbooks@okpublishing.info

2021 OK Publishing

ISBN 978-80-272-7454-3

Contents

Black Man's Burden

"Take up the white man's burden
Send forth the best ye breed...."
—Kipling

BLACK MAN'S
BURDEN

I

The two-vehicle caravan emerged from the sandy wastes of the *erg* and approached the small encampment of Taitoq Tuareg which consisted of seven goat leather tents. They were not unanticipated, the camp's scouts had noted the strange pillars of high-flung dust which were set up by the air rotors an hour earlier and for the past fifteen minutes they had been visible to all.

Moussa-ag-Amastan, headman of the clan, awaited the newcomers at first with a certain trepidation in spite of his warrior blood. Although he hadn't expressed himself thus to his followers, his first opinion had been that the unprecedented pillars were djinn come out of the erg for no good purpose. It wasn't until they were quite close that it could be seen the vehicles bore resemblance to those of the Rouma which were of recent years spreading endlessly through the lands of the Ahaggar Tuareg and beggaring those who formerly had conducted the commerce of the Sahara.

But the vehicles traveling through the sand dunes! That had been the last advantage of the camel. No wheeled vehicle could cross the vast stretches of the ergs, they must stick to the hard ground, to the tire-destroying gravel.

They came to a halt and Moussa-ag-Amastan drew up his teguelmoust turban-veil even closer about his eyes. He had no desire to let the newcomers witness his shocked surprise at the fact that the desert lorries had no wheels, floated instead without support, and now that they were at a standstill settled gently to earth.

There was further surprise when the five who issued forth from the two seemingly clumsy vehicles failed to be Rouma. They looked more like the Teda to the south, and the Targui's eyes thinned beneath his teguelmoust. Since the French had pulled out their once dreaded Camel Corps there had been somewhat of a renaissance of violence between traditional foes.

However, the newcomers, though dark as Negro Bela slaves, wore Tuareg dress, loose baggy trousers of dark indigo-blue cotton cloth, a loose, nightgownlike white cotton shirt, and over this a *gandoura* outer garment. Above all, they wore the teguelmoust though they were shockingly lax in keeping it properly up about the mouth.

Moussa-ag-Amastan knew that he was backed by ten or more of his clansmen, half of whom bore rifles, the rest Tuareg broadswords, Crusader-like with their two edges, round points and flat rectangular cross-members. Only two of the strangers seemed armed and they negligently bore their smallish guns in the crooks of their arms. The clan leader spoke at strength, then, but he said the traditional *"La bas."*

"There is no evil," repeated the foremost of the newcomers. His Tamabeq, the Berber language of the Tuareg confederations, seemed perfect.

Moussa-ag-Amastan said, "What do you do in the lands of the Taitoq Tuareg?"

The stranger, a tall, handsome man with a dominating though pleasant personality, indicated the vehicles with a sweep of his hand. "We are Enaden, itinerant smiths. As has ever been our wont, we travel from encampment to encampment to sell our products and to make repair upon your metal possessions."

Enaden! The traveling smiths of the Ahaggar, and indeed of the whole Sahara, were a despised and ragged lot at best. Few there were that ever possessed more than a small number of camels, a sprinkling of goats, perhaps a sheep or two. But these seemed as rich as Roumas, as Europeans or Americans.

Moussa-ag-Amastan muttered, "You jest with us at your peril, stranger." He pointed an aged but still strong hand at the vehicles. "Enaden do not own such as these."

The newcomer shrugged. "I am Omar ben Crawf and these are my followers, Abrahim el Bakr Ma el Ainin, Keni Ballalou and Bey-ag-Akhamouk. We come today from Tamanrasset and we are smiths, as we can prove. As is known, there is high pay to be earned by working in the oil fields, at the dams on the Niger, in the afforestation projects, in the sinking of the new wells whose pumps utilize the rays of the sun, in the developing of the great new oases.

There is much Rouma money to be made in such work and my men and I have brought these vehicles specially built in the new factories in Dakar for desert use."

"Slave work!" one of Moussa-ag-Amastan's kinsmen sneered.

Omar ben Crawf shrugged in obvious amusement, but there was a warmth and vitality in the man that quickly affected even strangers. "Perhaps," he said. "But times change, as every man knows and today there no longer need be hunger, nor illness, nor any want-if a man will but work a fraction of each day."

"Work is for slaves," Moussa-ag-Amastan barked.

The newcomer refused to argue. "But all slaves have been freed, and where in the past this meant nothing since the Bela had no place to go, no way to live save with his owner, today it is different and any man can go and find work on the many projects that grow everywhere. So the slaves slip away from the Tuareg, and the Teda and Chaamba. Soon there will be no more slaves to do the work about your encampments. And then what, man of the desert?"

"We'll fight!" Moussa-ag-Amastan growled. "We Tuareg are warriors, bedouin, free men. We will never be slaves."

"*Inshallah*. If God wills it," the smith agreed politely.

"Show us your wares," the old chieftain snapped. "We chatter like women. Talk can wait until the evening meal and in the men's quarters of my tent." He approached the now parked vehicles and his followers crowded after him. From the tents debouched women and children. The children were completely nude, and the Tuareg women were unveiled for such are the customs of the Ahaggar Tuareg that the men go veiled but women do not.

* * * * *

One of the lorries was so constructed that a side could be raised in such fashion to display a wide variety of tools, weapons, household utensils, and textiles. Ohs and ahs punctuated the air, women being the same in every land. Two of the smiths brought forth metal-working equipment of strange design and set up shop to one side. A broken bolt on an aged Lebel rifle was quickly repaired, a copper cooking pot brazed, some harness tinkered with.

Of a sudden, Moussa-ag-Amastan said, "But your women, your families, where are they?"

The one who had been introduced as Abrahim el Bakr, an open-faced man whose constant smiling seemed to take a full ten years off what must have been his age, explained. "On the big projects, one can find employment only if he allows his children to attend the new schools. So our wives and children remain near Tamanrasset while the children learn the lore of books."

"Rouma schools!" one of the warriors sneered.

"Oh, no. There are few Roumas remaining in all the land now," the smith said easily. "Those that are left serve us in positions our people as yet cannot hold, in construction of the dams, in the bringing of trees to the desert, but soon, even they will be unneeded."

"*Our* people?" Moussa-ag-Amastan rumbled ungraciously. "You are smiths. The smiths have no people. You are neither Kel Rela, Tégehé Mellet, Taitoq, nor even Teda, Chaambra, or Ouled Tidrarin."

One of the smiths said easily, "In the great new construction camps, in the new towns, with their many ways to work and become rich, the tribes are breaking up. Tuareg works next to Teda and a Moor next to a former Haratin serf." He added, as though unthinkingly, even as he displayed an aluminum pan to a wide-eyed Tuareg matron, "Indeed, even the clans break up and often Tuareg marries Arab or Sudanese or Rifs down from the north ...or even we Enaden."

The clansmen were suddenly silent, in shocked surprise.

"That cannot be true!" the elderly chief snapped.

Omar ben Crawf looked at him mildly. "Why should my follower lie?"

"I do not know, but we will talk of it later, away from the women and children who should not hear such abominations." The chief switched subjects. "But you have no flocks with you. How are we to pay for these things, these services?"

"With money."

The old man's face, what little could be seen through his teguelmoust, darkened. "We have little money in the Ahaggar."

The one named Omar nodded. "But we are short of meat and will buy several goats and perhaps a lamb, a chicken, eggs. Then, too, as you have noted, we have left our women at home. We will need the services of cooks, some one to bring water. We will hire servants."

The other said gruffly, "There are some Bela who will serve you."

The smith seemed taken aback. "Verily, El Hassan has stated that the product of the labor of the slave is accursed."

"El Hassan! Who is El Hassan and why should the work of a slave be accursed?"

One of the tribesmen said, "I have heard of this El Hassan. Rumors of his teachings spread through the land. He is to lead us all, Tuareg, Arab and Sudanese, until we are all as rich as Roumas."

Omar said, "It is well known that the Roumas and especially the Americans are all rich as Emirs but none of them ever possess slaves. The bedouin have slaves but fail to prosper. Verily, the product of the labor of the slave is accursed."

"Madness," Moussa-ag-Amastan muttered. "If you do not let our slave women do your tasks, then they will remain undone. No Tuareg woman will work."

* * * * *

But the headman of his clan was wrong.

The smiths remained four days in all, and the abundance of their products was too much. What verbal battles might have taken place in the tent of Moussa-ag-Amastan, and in those of his followers, the smiths couldn't know, but Tuareg women are not dominated by their men. On the second day, three Tuareg women applied for the position of servants, at surprisingly high pay. Envy ran roughshod when they later displayed the textiles and utensils they purchased with their wages.

Nor could the aged Tuareg chief prevent in the evening discussions between the men, a thorough pursuing of the new ideas sweeping through the Ahaggar. Though these strangers proclaimed themselves lowly Enaden-itinerant desert smiths-they were obviously not to be dismissed as a caste little higher than Haratin serfs. Even the first night they were invited to the tent of Moussa-ag-Amastan to share the dinner of shorba soup, cous cous and the edible paste *kaboosh*, made of cheese, butter and spices. It was an adequate desert meal, meat being eaten not more than a few times a year by such as the Taitoq Tuareg who couldn't afford to consume the animals upon which they lived.

After mint tea, one of the younger Tarqui leaned forward. He said, "You have brought strange news, oh Enaden of wealth, and we would know more. We of the Ahaggar hear little from outside."

Moussa-ag-Amastan scowled at his clansman, for his presumption, but Omar answered, his voice sincere and carrying conviction. "The world moves fast, men of the desert, and the things that were verily true even yesterday, have changed today."

"To the sorrow of the Tuareg!" snapped Moussa-ag-Amastan.

The other looked at him. "Not always, old one. Surely in your youth you remember when such diseases as the one the Roumas once called the disease of Venus, ran rampant through the tribes. When trachoma, the sickness of the eyes, was known as the scourge of the Sahara. When half the children, not only of Bela slaves and Haratin serfs, but also of the Surgu noble clans, died before the age of ten."

"Admittedly, the magic of the Roumas cured many such ills," an older warrior growled.

"Not their magic, their learning," the smith named El Ma el Ainin put in. "And, verily, now the schools are open to all the people."

"Schools are not for such as the Bela and Haratin," the clan chief protested. "The Koran should not be taught to slaves."

El Ma el Ainin said gently, "The Koran is not taught at all in the new schools, old one. The teachings of the Prophet are still made known to those interested, in the schools connected with the mosques, but only the teachings of science are made in the new schools."

"The teachings of the Rouma!" a Tuareg protested, carefully slipping his glass of tea beneath his teguelmoust so that he could drink without his mouth being obscenely revealed.

Omar ben Crawf laughed. "That is what we have allowed the Roumas to have us believe for much too long," he stated. "El Hassan has proven otherwise. Much of the wisdom of science has its roots in the lands of Asia and of Africa. The Roumas were savages in skins while the earliest civilizations were being developed in Africa and Asia Minor. Hardly a science now developed by the Roumas of Europe and America but had its beginning with us." He turned to the elderly chief.

"You Tuareg are of Berber background. But a few centuries ago, the Berbers of Morocco, known as the Moors to the Rouma, leavened only with a handful of Jews and Arabs, built up in Spain the highest civilization in all the world of that time. We would be foolish, we of Africa, to give credit to the Rouma for so much of what our ancestors presented to the world."

The Tuareg were astonished. They had never heard such words.

Moussa-ag-Amastan was not appeased. "You sound like a Rouma, yourself," he said. "Where have you learned of all this?"

The smiths chuckled their amusement.

Abrahim el Bakr said, "Verily, old one, have you ever seen a black Rouma?"

Omar ben Crawf, the headman of the smiths, went on. "El Hassan has proclaimed great new beliefs that spread through all North Africa, and eventually, *Inshallah*, throughout the continent. Through his great learning he has assimilated the wisdom of all the prophets, all the wisemen of all the world, and proclaims their truths."

The Tuareg chief was becoming increasingly irritated. Such talk as this was little short of blasphemy to his ears, but the fascination of the discussion was beyond him to ignore. And he knew that even if he did his young men, in particular, would only seek out the strangers on their own and then he would not be present to mitigate their interest. In spite of himself, now he growled, "What beliefs? What truths? I know not of this El Hassan of whom you speak."

Omar said slowly, "Among them, the teachings of a great wise man from a far land. That all men should be considered equal in the eyes of society and should have equal right to life, liberty and the pursuit of happiness."

"Equal!" one of the warriors ejaculated. "This is not wisdom, but nonsense. No two men are equal."

Omar waggled a finger negatively. "Like so many, you fail to explore the teaching. Obviously, no man of wisdom would contend that all men are equally tall, or strong, or wise, or cunning, nor even fortunate. *No* two men are equal in such regards. But all men should have equal right to life, liberty and the pursuit of happiness, whatever that might mean to him as an individual."

One of the Tuareg said slyly, "And the murderer of one of your kinsmen, should he, too, have life and liberty, in the belief of El Hassan?"

"Obviously, the community must protect itself against those who would destroy the life or liberty of others. The murderer of a kinsman of mine, as well as any other man, myself included, should be subject equally to the same law."

It was a new conception to members of a tribal society such as that of the Ahaggar Tuareg. They stirred under both its appeal and its negation of all they knew. A man owed alliance to his immediate family, to his clan, his tribe, then to the Tuareg confederation-in decreasing degree. Beyond that, all were enemies, as all men knew.

One protested slowly, seeking out his words, "Your El Hassan preaches this equality, but surely the wiser man and the stronger man will soon find his way to the top in any land, in any tribe, even in the nations of the Rouma."

Omar shrugged. "Who could contend otherwise? But each man should be free to develop his own possibilities, be they strength of arm or of brain. Let no man exploit another, nor suppress another's abilities. If a Bela slave has more ability than a Surgu Tuareg noble, let him profit to the full by his gifts."

There was a cold silence.

Omar finished gently by saying, "Or so El Hassan teaches, and so they teach in the new schools in Tamanrasset and Gao, in Timbuktu and Reggan, in the big universities at Kano, Dakar, Bamako, Accra and Abidian. And throughout North Africa the wave of the future flows over the land."

"It is a flood of evil," Moussa-ag-Amastan said definitely.

* * * * *

But in spite of the antagonism of the clan headman and of the older Tuareg warriors, the stories of the smiths continued to spread. It was not even beyond them to discuss, long and quietly, with the Bela slaves the ideas of the mysterious El Hassan, and to talk of the plentiful jobs, the high wages, at the dams, the new oases, and in the afforestation projects.

Somehow the news of their presence spread, and another clan of nomad Tuareg arrived and pitched their tents, to handle the wares of the smiths and to bring their metal work for repair. And to listen to their disturbing words.

As amazing as any of the new products was the solar powered, portable television set which charged its batteries during the daylight hours and then flashed on its screen the images and the voices and music of entertainers and lecturers, teachers and storytellers, for all to see. In the beginning it had been difficult, for the eye of the desert man is not trained to pick up a picture. He has never seen one, and would not recognize his own photograph. But in time, it came to them.

The programs originated in Tamanrasset and in Salah, in Zinder and Fort Lamy and one of the smiths revealed that the mysterious waves, that fed the device its programs, were bounced off tiny moons which the Rouma had rocketed up into the sky for that purpose. A magic understandable only to marabouts and such, without doubt.

At the end of their period of stay, the smiths, to the universal surprise of all, gave the mystery device to two sisters, kinswomen of Moussa-ag-Amastan, who were particularly interested in the teachers and lecturers who told of the new world aborning. The gift was made in the full understanding that all should be allowed to listen and watch, and it was clear that if ever the set needed repair it was to be left untinkered with and taken to Tamanrasset or the nearest larger settlement where it would be fixed free of charge.

There were many strange features about the smiths, as each man could see. Among others, were their strange weapons. There had been some soft whispered discussion among the warriors in the first two days of their stay about relieving the strangers of their obviously desirable possessions-after all, they weren't kinsmen, not even Tuareg. But on the second day, the always smiling one named Abrahim el Bakr had been on the outskirts of the *erg* when a small group of gazelle were flushed. The graceful animals took off at a prohibitive rifle range, as usual, but Abrahim el Bakr had thrown his small, all but tiny weapon to his shoulder and *flic flic flic*, with a sound no greater than the cracking of a ground nut, had knocked over three of them before the others had disappeared around a dune.

Obviously, the weapons of the smiths were as great as their learning and their new instruments. It was discouraging to a raider by instinct.

Then, too, there was the strangeness of the night talks their leader was known to have with his secret *Kambu* fetish which was able to answer him in a squeaky but distinct voice in some unknown tongue, obviously a language of the djinn. The *Kambu* was worn on a strap on Omar's wrist, and each night at a given hour he was wont to withdraw to his tent and there confer.

On the fourth night, obviously, he was given instruction by the *Kambu* for in the morning, at first light, the smiths hurriedly packed, broke camp, made their good-byes to Moussa-ag-Amastan and the others and were off.

Moussa-ag-Amastan was glad to see them go. They were quite the most disturbing element to upset his people in many seasons. He wondered at the advisability of making their usual summer journey to the Tuareg sedentary centers. He had a feeling that if the clan got near enough to such centers as Zinder to the south, or Touggourt to the north, there would be wholesale desertion of the Bela, and, for that matter, even of some of his younger warriors and their wives.

However, there was no putting off indefinitely exposure to this danger. Even in such former desert centers as Tessalit and In Salah, the irrigation projects were of such magnitude that there was a great labor shortage. But always, of course, as the smiths had said, if you worked at the projects your children must needs attend the schools. And that way lay disaster!

The five smiths took out overland in the direction of Djanet on the border of what had once been known as Libya and famed for its cliffs which tower over twenty-five hundred feet above the town. Their solar powered, air cushion, hover-lorries, threw up their clouds of dust and sand to right and left, but they made good time over the *erg*. A good hovercraft driver could do much to even out a rolling landscape, changing his altitude from a few inches here to as much as twenty-five feet there, given, of course, enough power in his solar batteries, although that was little problem in this area where clouds were sometimes not seen for years on end.

This was back of the beyond, the wasteland of earth. Only the interior of the Arabian peninsula and the Gobi could compete and, of course, even the Gobi was beginning to be tamed under the afforestation efforts of the teeming multitudes of China who had suffered its disastrous storms down through the millennia.

* * * * *

Omar checked and checked again with the instrument on his wrist, asking and answering, his voice worried.

Finally they pulled up beside a larger than usual wadi and Omar ben Crawf stared thoughtfully out over it. The one they had named Abrahim el Bakr stood beside him and the others slightly to the rear.

Abrahim el Bakr nodded, for once his face unsmiling. "Those cats'll come down here," he said. "Nothing else would make sense, not even to an Egyptian."

"I think you're right," Omar growled. He said over his shoulder, "Bey, get the trucks out of sight, over that dune. Elmer, you and Kenny set the gun up over there. Solid slugs, and try to avoid their cargo. We don't want to set off a Fourth of July here. Bey, when you're finished with the trucks, take that Tommy-Noiseless of yours and flank them from over behind those rocks. Take a couple of clips extra, for good luck-you won't need them, though."

"How many are there supposed to be?" Abrahim el Bakr asked, his voice empty of humor now.

"Eight half-trucks, two armed jeeps, or land-rovers, one or the other. Probably about forty men, Abe."

"All armed," Abe said flatly.

"Um-m-m. Listen, that's them coming. Right down the *wadi*. Get going men. Abe, you cover me."

Abe Bakr looked at him. "Wha'd'ya mean, cover you, man? You slipped all the way round the bend? Listen, let me plant a couple quick land mines to stop 'em and we'll get ourselves behind these rocks and blast those cats half way back to Cairo."

"We'll warn them as per orders."

"Crazy man, like you're the boss, Homer," Abe growled. "But why'd I ever leave New Jersey?" He made his way to the right, to the top of the wadi's bank and behind a clump of thorny bush. He made himself comfortable, the light Tommy-Noiseless with its clip of two hundred .10 caliber, ultra-high velocity shells resting before him on a flat rock outcropping. He thoughtfully flicked the selector to the explosive side of the clip. Let Homer Crawford say what he would about not setting off a Fourth of July, but if he needed covering in the moments to come, he'd need it bad.

The chips were down now.

The convoy, the motors growling their protests of the hard going even here at the gravel bottomed wadi river bed, made its way toward them at a pace of approximately twenty kilometers per hour.

The lead jeep-Skoda manufacture, Homer Crawford noted cynically-was some thirty meters in advance. It drew to a halt upon seeing him and a turbaned Arab Union trooper swung a Brenn gun in his direction.

An officer stood up in the jeep and yelled at Crawford in Arabic.

The American took a deep breath and said in the same language, "You're out of your own territory."

The officer's face went poker-expressionless. He looked at the lone figure, dressed in the garb of the Tuareg, even to the turban-veil which covers all but the eyes of these notorious Apaches of the Sahara.

"This is no affair of yours," the lieutenant said. "Who are you?"

Homer Crawford said very clearly, "Sahara Division, African Development Project, Reunited Nations. You're far out of your own territory, lieutenant. I'll have to report you, and also to demand that you turn and go back to your origin."

The lieutenant flicked his hand, and the trooper behind the Brenn gun sighted the weapon and tightened his trigger finger.

Crawford dropped to the ground and rolled desperately for a slight depression that would provide cover. He could have saved himself the resultant bruises and scratches. Before the Brenn gun spoke even once, there was a *Götterdammerung* of sound and the three occupants of the jeep, driver, lieutenant and gunner were swept from the vehicle in a nauseating obscenity of exploding flesh, uniform cloth, blood and bone.

To the side, Abe Bakr behind his thorn bush and rock vantage point turned the barrel of his Tommy-Noiseless to the first of the half tracks. Already Arab Union troopers were debouching from them, some firing at random and at unseen targets. However, the so-called Enaden smiths were well concealed, their weapons silenced except for the explosion of the tiny shells upon reaching their target.

It wasn't much of a fight. The recoilless automatic rifle manned by Elmer Allen and Kenny Ballalou swept the wadi, swept it of life, at least, but hardly swept it clean. What few individuals were left, in what little shelter was to be found in the dry river's bottom, were picked off easily, if not neatly by the high velocity automatics in the hands of Abe Bakr and Bey-ag-Akhamouk.

Afterwards, the five of them, standing at the side of the wadi, stared down at their work.

Elmer Allen muttered a bitter four-letter obscenity. He had once headed a pacifist group at the University in Kingston, Jamaica. Now his teeth were bared, as they always were when he went into action. He hated it.

Of them all, Bey-ag-Ahkamouk was the least moved by the slaughter. He grumbled, "Guns, explosives, mortar, flame throwers. If there is anything in the world my people don't need in the way of *aid*, it's weapons."

"Our people," Homer Crawford said absently, his eyes-taking in the scene beneath them-empty, as though unseeing. He hated the need for killing, almost as badly as did Elmer Allen.

Bey looked at him, scowling slightly, but said nothing. There had been mild rebuke in his leader's voice.

"Well," Abe Bakr said with a tone of mock finality in his voice, as though he was personally wiping his hands of the whole affair, "how are you going to explain all this jazz to headquarters, man?"

Homer said flatly, "We were attacked by this unidentified group of, ah, gun runners, from some unknown origin. We defended ourselves, to the best of our ability."

Elmer Allen looked at the once human mess below them. "We certainly did," he muttered, scowling.

"Crazy man," Abe said, nodding his agreement to the alibi.

The others didn't bother to speak. Homer Crawford's unit was well knit.

He said after a moment. "Abe, you and Kenny get some dynamite and plant it in this wadi wall in a few spots. We'll want to bury this whole mess. It wouldn't do for someone to come along and blow himself up on some of these scattered land mines, or find himself a bazooka or something to use on his nearest blood-feud neighbor."

II

The young woman known as Izubahil was washing clothes in the Niger with the rest but slightly on the outskirts of the chattering group of women, which was fitting since she was both a comparative stranger and as yet unselected by any man to grace his household. Which, in a way, was passingly strange since she was comely enough. Clad as the rest with naught but a wrap of colored cloth about her hips, her face and figure were openly to be seen. Her complexion was not quite so dark as most. She came from up-river, so she said, the area of the Songhoi, but by the looks of her there was more than average Arab or Berber blood in her veins. Her lips and nose were thinner than those of her neighbors.

Yes, it was strange that no man had taken her, though it was said that in her shyness she repulsed any advances made by either the young men, or their wealthier elders who could afford more than one wife. She was a nothing-woman, really, come out of the desert alone, and without relatives to protect her interests, but still she repulsed the advances of those who would honor her with a place in their house, or tent.

She had come out of the desert, it was known, with her handful of possessions done up in a packet, and had quietly and unobtrusively taken her place in the Negro community of Gao. Little better than a slave or Gabibi serf, she made her meager living doing small tasks for the better-off members of the community.

But she knew her place, was dutifully shy and quiet spoken, and in the town or in the presence of men, wore her haik and veil. Yes, it was passing strange that she found no man. On the face of it, she was getting no younger, surely she must be into her twenties.

Up to their knees in the waters of the Niger, out beyond the point where the dugout canoes were pulled up to the bank, their ends resting on the shore, they pounded their laundry. Laughing, chattering, gossiping. Life was perhaps poor, but still life was good.

Someone pretended to see a crocodile and there was a wild scampering for the shore. And then high laughter when the jest was revealed. Actually, all the time they had known it a jest, since it was their most popular one-there were seldom crocodiles this far north in the Niger bend.

There was a stir as two men dressed in the clothes of the Rouma approached the river bank. It was not forbidden, but good manners called for males to refrain from this area while the woman bathed and washed their laundry, without veil or upper garments. These mean were obviously shameless, and probably had come to stare. From their dress, their faces and their bearing, they were strangers. Possibly Senegalese, up from the area near Dakar, products of the new schools and the new industries mushrooming there. Strange things were told of the folk who gave up the old ways, worked on the dams and the other new projects, sent their little ones to the schools, and submitted to the needle pricks which seemed to compose so much of the magic medicine being taught in the medical schools by the Rouma witchmen.

One of them spoke now in Songhoi, the *lingua franca* of the vicinity. Shamelessly he spoke to them, although none were his women, nor even his tribal kin. None looked at him.

"We seek a single woman, an unwed woman, who would work for pay and learn the new ways."

They continued their laundry, not looking up, but their chatter dribbled away.

"She must drop the veil," the man continued clearly, "and give up the haik and wear the new clothes. But she will be well paid, and taught to read and be kept in the best of comfort and health."

There was a low gasp from several of the younger women, but one of the eldest looked up in distaste. "Wear the clothes of the Rouma!" she said indignantly. "Shameless ones!"

The man's voice was testy. He himself was dressed in the clothing worn always by the Rouma, when the Rouma had controlled the Niger bend. He said, "These are not the clothes of the Rouma, but the clothes of civilized people everywhere."

The women's attention went back to their washing. Two or three of them giggled.

The elderly woman said, "There are none here who will go with you, for whatever shameless purpose you have in your mind."

But Izubahil, the strange girl come out of the desert from the north, spoke suddenly. "I will," she said.

There was a gasp, and all looked at her in wide-eyed alarm. She began making her way to the shore, her unfinished washing still in hand.

The stranger said clearly, "And drop the veil, discard the haik for the new clothing, and attend the schools?"

There was another gasp as Izubahil said definitely, "Yes, all these things." She looked back at the women. "So that I may learn all these new ways."

The more elderly sniffed and turned their backs in scorn, but the younger stared after her in some amazement and until she disappeared with the two strangers into one of the buildings which had formerly housed the French Administration officers back in the days when the area was known as the French Sudan.

Inside, the boy strangers turned to her and the one who had spoken at the river bank said in English, "How goes it?"

"Heavens to Betsy," Isobel Cunningham said with a grin, "get me a drink. If I'd known majoring in anthropology was going to wind up with my doing a strip tease with a bunch of natives in the Niger River, I would have taken up Home Economics, like my dear old mother wanted!"

They laughed with her and Jacob Armstrong, the older of the two, went over to a sideboard and mixed her a cognac and soda. "Ice?" he said.

"Brother, you said it," she told him. "Where can I change out of these rags?"

"On you they look good," Clifford Jackson told her. He looked surprisingly like the Joe Louis of several decades earlier.

"That's enough out of you, wise guy," Isobel told him. "Why doesn't somebody dream up a role for me where I can be a rich paramount chief's favorite wife, or something? Be loaded down with gold and jewelry, that sort of thing."

Jake brought her the drink. "Your clothes are in there," he told her, motioning with his head to an inner room. "It wouldn't do the job," he added. "What we're giving them is the old Cinderella story." He looked at his watch. "If we get under way, we can take the jet to Kabara and go into your act there. It's been nearly six months since Kabara and they'll be all set for the second act."

She knocked back the brandy and made her way to the other room, saying over her shoulder, "Be with you in a minute."

"Not that much of a hurry," Cliff called. "Take your time, gal, there's a bath in there. You'll probably want one after a week of living the way you've been."

"Brother!" she agreed.

Jake was making himself a drink. He said easily to Cliff Jackson, "That's a fine girl. I'd hate her job. We get the easy deal on this assignment."

Cliff said, "You said it, Nigger. How about mixing me a drink, too?"

"Nigger!" Jake said in mock indignation. "Look who's talking." His voice took on a burlesque of a Southern drawl. "Man when the Good Lawd was handin' out *cullahs*, you musta thought he said *umbrellahs*, and said give me a nice black one."

Cliff laughed with him and said, "Where do we plant poor Isobel next?"

Jake thought about it. "I don't know. The kid's been putting in a lot of time. I think after about a week in Kabara we ought to go on down to Dakar and suggest she be given another assignment for a while. Some of the girls, working out of our AFAA office don't do anything except drive around in recent model cars, showing off the advantages of emancipation, tossing money around like tourists, and living it up in general."

* * * * *

On the flight up-river to Kabara, Isobel Cunningham went through the notes she'd taken on that town. It was also on the Niger, and the assignment had been almost identical to the Gao one. In fact, she'd gone through the same routine in Ségou, Ké-Macina, Mopti, Gôundam and Bourem, above Gao, and Ansongo, Tillabéri and Niamey below. She was stretching her luck, if you asked her. Sooner or later she was going to run into someone who knew her from a past performance.

Well, let the future take care of the future. She looked over at Cliff Jackson who was piloting the jet and said, "What're the latest developments? Obviously, I haven't seen a paper or heard a broadcast for over a week."

Cliff shrugged his huge shoulders. "Not much. More trouble with the Portuguese down in the south."

Jake rumbled, "There's going to be a bloodbath there before it's over."

Isobel said thoughtfully, "There's been some hope that fundamental changes might take place in Lisbon."

Jake grunted his skepticism. "In that case the bloodbath would take place there instead of in Africa." He added, "Which is all right with me."

"What else?" Isobel said.

"Continued complications in the Congo."

"That's hardly news."

"But things are going like clockwork in the west. Kenya, Uganda, Tanganyika." Cliff took his right hand away from the controls long enough to make a circle with its thumb and index finger. "Like clockwork. Fifty new fellows from the University of Chicago came in last week to help with the rural education development and twenty or so men from Johns Hopkins in Baltimore have wrangled a special grant for a new medical school."

"All ... Negroes?"

"What else?"

Jake said suddenly, "Tell her about the Cubans."

Isobel frowned. "Cubans?"

"Over in the Anglo-Egyptian Sudan area. They were supposedly helping introduce modern sugar refining methods —"

"Why supposedly?"

"Why not?"

"All right, go on," Isobel said.

Cliff Jackson said slowly, "Somebody shot them up. Killed several, wounded most of the others."

The girl's eyes went round. "Who ... and why?"

The pilot shifted his heavy shoulders again.

Jake said, "Nobody seems to know, but the weapons were modern. Plenty modern." He twisted in his bucket seat, uncomfortably. "Listen, have you heard anything about some character named El Hassan?"

Isobel turned to face him. "Why, yes. The people there in Gao mentioned him. Who is he?"

"That's what I'd like to know," Jake said. "What did they say?"

"Oh, mostly supposed words of wisdom that El Hassan was alleged to have made with. I get it that he's some, well you wouldn't call him a nationalist since he's international in his appeal, but he's evidently preaching union of all Africans. I get an undercurrent of anti-Europeanism in general, but not overdone." Isobel's expressive face went thoughtful. "As a matter of fact, his program seems to coincide largely with our own, so much so that from time to time when I had occasion to drop a few words of propaganda into a conversation, I'd sometimes credit it to him."

Cliff looked over at her and chuckled. "That's a coincidence," he said. "I've been doing the same thing. An idea often carries more weight with these people if it's attributed to somebody with a reputation."

Jake, the older of the three said: "Well, I can't find out anything about him. Nobody seems to know if he's an Egyptian, a Nigerian, a MOR ... or an Eskimo, for that matter."

"Did you check with headquarters?"

"So far they have nothing on him, except for some other inquiries from field workers."

Below them, the river was widening out to the point where it resembled swampland more than a waterway. There were large numbers of waterbirds, and occasional herds of hippopotami. Isobel didn't express her thoughts, but a moment of doubt hit her. What would all this be like when the dams were finished, the waters of this third largest of Africa's rivers, ninth largest of the world's, under control?

She pointed. "There's Kabara." The age-old river port lay below them. Cliff slapped one of his controls with the heel of his hand and the craft began to sink earthward.

* * * * *

They took up quarters in the new hotel which adjoined the new elementary school, and Isobel immediately went into her routine.

Dressed and shod immaculately, her head held high in confidence, she spent considerable time mingling with the more backward of the natives and especially the women. Six months ago, she had given a performance similar to that she had just finished in Gao, several hundred miles down river.

Now she renewed old acquaintances, calling them by name-after checking her notes. Invariably, their eyes bugged. Their questions came thick, came fast in the slurring Songhoi and she answered them in detail. They came quickly under her intellectual domination. Her poise, her obvious well being, flabbergasted them.

In all, they spent a week in the little river town, but even the first night Isobel slumped wearily in the most comfortable chair of their small suite's living room.

She kicked off her shoes, and wiggled weary toes.

"If my mother could see me now," she complained. "After giving her all to get the apple of her eye through school, her wayward daughter winds up living with two men in the wilds of deepest Africa." She twisted her mouth puckishly.

Cliff grunted, poking around in a bag for the bottle of cognac he couldn't remember where he had packed. "Huh!" he said. "The next time you write her you might mention the fact that both of them are continually proposing to you and you brush it all off as a big joke."

"Huh, indeed!" Isobel answered him. "Proposing, or propositioning? If either of you two Romeos ever rattle the doorknob of my room at night again, you're apt to get a bullet through it."

Jake winced. "Wasn't me. Look at my gray hair, Isobel. I'm old enough to be your daddy."

"Sugar daddy, I suppose," she said mockingly.

"Wasn't me either," Cliff said, criss-crossing his heart and pointing upward.

"Huh!" said Isobel again, but she was really in no mood for their usual banter. "Listen," she said, "what're we accomplishing with all this masquerade?"

Cliff had found the French brandy. He poured three stiff ones and handed drinks to Isobel and Jake.

He knew he wasn't telling her anything, but he said, "We're a king-size rumor campaign, that's what we are. We're breaking down institutions the sneaky way." He added reflectively. "A kinder way, though, than some."

"But this ... what did you call it earlier, Jake? ... this Cinderella act I go through perpetually. What good does it do, really? I contact only a few hundreds of people at most. And there are millions here in Mali alone."

"There are other teams, too," Jake said mildly. "Several hundreds of us doing one thing or another."

"A drop in the bucket," Isobel said, her piquant sepian face registering weariness.

Cliff sipped his brandy, shaking his big head even as he did so. "No," he said. "It's a king-size rumor campaign and it's amazing how effective they can be. Remember the original dirty-rumor campaigns back in the States? Suppose two laundry firms were competing. One of them, with a manager on the conscience-less side, would hire two or three professional rumor spreaders. They'd go around dropping into bars, barber shops, pool rooms. Sooner or later, they'd get a chance to drop some line such as *did you hear about them discovering that two lepers worked at the Royal Laundry*? You can imagine the barbers, the bartenders, and such professional gossips, passing on the good word."

Isobel laughed, but unhappily. "I don't recognize myself in the description."

Cliff said earnestly, "Sure, only few score women in each town you put on your act, really witness the whole thing. But think how they pass it on. Each one of them tells the story of the miracle. A waif comes out of the desert. Without property, without a husband or family, without kinsfolk. Shy, dirty, unwanted. Then she's offered a good position if she'll drop the veil, discard the haik, and attend the new schools. So off she goes-everyone thinking to her disaster. Hocus-pocus, six months later she returns, obviously prosperous, obviously healthy, obviously well adjusted. Fine. The story spreads for miles around. Nothing is so popular as the Cinderella story, and that's the story you're putting over. It's a natural."

"I hope so," Isobel said. "Sometimes I think I'm helping put over a gigantic hoax on these people. Promising something that won't be delivered."

Jake looked at her unhappily. "I've thought the same thing, sometimes, but what are you going to be with people at this stage of development —*subtle?*"

Isobel dropped it. She held out her glass for more cognac. "I hope there's something decent to eat in this place. Do you realize what I've been putting into my tummy this past week?"

Cliff shuddered.

Isobel patted her abdomen. "At least it keeps my figure in trim."

"Um-m-m," Jake pretended to leer heavily.

Isobel chuckled at him in a return to good humor. "Hyena," she accused.

"Hyena?" Jake said.

"Sure, there aren't any wolves in these parts," she explained. "How long are we going to be here?"

The two men looked at each other. Cliff said, "Well, we'd like to finish out the week. Guy named Homer Crawford has been passing around the word to hold a meeting in Timbuktu the end of this week."

"Crawford?"

"Homer Crawford, some kind of sociologist from the University of Michigan, I understand. He's connected with the Reunited Nations African Development Project, heads one of their cloak and dagger teams."

Jake grunted. "Sociologist? I also understand that he put in a hitch with the Marines and spent kind of a shady period of two years fighting with the FLN in Algeria."

"On what side?" Cliff said interestedly.

"Darn if I know."

Isobel said, "Well, we have nothing to do with the Reunited Nations."

Cliff shook his large head negatively. "Of course not, but Crawford seems to think it'd be a good idea if some of us in the field would get together and ...well, have sort of a bull session."

Jake growled, "We don't have much in the way of co-operation on the higher levels. Everybody seems to head out in all directions on their own. It can get chaotic. Maybe in the field we could give each other a few pointers. For one, I'd like to find out if any of the rest of these jokers know anything about that affair with the Cubans over in the Sudan."

"I suppose it can't hurt," Isobel admitted. "In fact, it might be fun swapping experiences with some of these characters. Frankly, though, the stories I've heard about the African Development teams aren't any too palatable. They seem to be a ruthless bunch."

Jake looked down into his glass. "It's a ruthless country," he murmured.

* * * * *

Dolo Anah, as he approached the ten Dogon villages of the Canton de Sangha, was first thought to be a small bird in the sky. As he drew nearer, it was decided, instead, that he was a larger creature of the air, perhaps a vulture, though who had ever seen such a vulture? As he drew nearer still, it was plain that in size he was more nearly an ostrich than vulture, but who had ever heard of a flying ostrich, and besides —

No! It was a man! But who in all the Dogon had ever witnessed such a *juju* man? One whose flailing limbs enabled him to fly!

The ten villages of the Dogon are perched on the rim of the Falaise de Bandiagara. The cliffs are over three hundred feet high and the villages are similar to Mesa Verde of Colorado, and as unaccessible, as impregnable to attack.

But hardly impregnable to arrival by helio-hopper.

When Dolo Anah landed in the tiny square of the village of Irèli, the first instinct of Amadijuè the village witchman was to send post haste to summon the Kanaga dancers, but then despair overwhelmed him. Against powers such as this, what could prevail? Besides, Amadijuè had not arrived at his position of influence and affluence through other than his own true abilities. Secretly, he rather doubted the efficacy of even the supposedly most potent witchcraft.

But this!

Dolo Anah unstrapped himself from the one man helio-hopper's small bicyclelike seat, folded the two rotors back over the rest of the craft, and then deposited the seventy-five pound vehicle in a corner, between two adobe houses. He knew perfectly well that the local inhabitants would die a thousand deaths of torture rather than approach, not to speak of touching it.

Looking to neither right nor left, walking arrogantly and carrying only a small bag-undoubtedly housing his *gris gris*, as Amadijuè could well imagine-Dolo Anah headed for the largest house. Since the whole village was packed, bug-eyed, into the square watching him there were no inhabitants within.

He snapped back over his shoulder, "Summon all the headmen of all the villages, and all of their eldest sons; summon all the Hogons and all the witchmen. Immediately! I would speak with them and issue orders."

He was a small man, clad only in a loincloth, and could well have been a Dogon himself. Surely he was black as a Dogon, clad as a Dogon, and he spoke the native language which is a tongue little known outside the semi-desert land of Dogon covered with its sand, rocks, scrub bush and baobab trees. It is not a land which sees many strangers.

The headmen gathered with trepidation. All had seen the juju man descend from the skies. It had been with considerable relief that most had noted that he finally sank to earth in the village of Irèli instead of their own. But now all were summoned. Those among them who were Kanaga dancers wore their masks and costumes, and above all their gris gris charms, but it was a feeble gesture. Such magic as this was unknown. To fly through the air *personally*!

Dolo Anah was seated to one end of the largest room of the largest house of Irèli when they crowded in to answer his blunt summons. He was seated cross-legged on the floor and staring at the ground before him.

The others seemed tongue-tied, both headmen and Hogons, the highly honored elders of the Dogon people. So Amadijuè as senior witchman took over the responsibility of addressing this mystery juju come out of the skies.

"Oh, powerful stranger, how is your health?"

"Good," Dolo Anah said.

"How is the health of thy wife?"

"Good."

"How is the health of thy children?"

"Good."

"How is the health of thy mother?"

"Good."

"How is the health of thy father?"

"Good."

"How is the health of thy kinswomen?"

"Good."

"How is the health of thy kinsmen?"

"Good."

To the traditional greeting of the Dogon, Amadijuè added hopefully, "Welcome to the villages of Sangha."

His voice registering nothing beyond the impatience which had marked it from the beginning, Dolo Anah repeated the routine.

"Men of Sangha," he snapped, "how is your health?"

"Good," they chorused.

"How is the health of thy wives?"

"Good!"

"How is the health of thy children?"

"Good!"

"How is the health of thy mothers?"

"Good!"

"How is the health of thy fathers?"

"Good!"

"How is the health of thy kinswomen?"

"Good!"

"How is the health of thy kinsmen?"

"Good!"

"I accept thy welcome," Dolo Anah bit out. "And now heed me well for I am known as Dolo Anah and I have instructions from above for the people of the Dogon."

Sweat glistened on the faces and bodies of the assembled Dogon headmen, their uncharacteristically silent witchmen, the Hogons and the sons of the headmen.

"Speak, oh juju come out of the sky," Amadijuè fluttered, but proud of his ability to find speech at all when all the others were stricken dumb with fear.

* * * * *

Dolo Anah stared down at the ground before him. The others, their eyes fascinated as though by a cobra preparing to strike its death, focused on the spot as well.

Dolo Anah raised a hand very slowly and very gently and a sigh went through his audience. The dirt on the hut floor had stirred. It stirred again and slowly, ever so slowly, up through the floor emerged a milky, translucent ball. When it had fully emerged, Dolo Anah took it up in his hands and stared at it for a long moment.

It came to sudden light and a startled gasp flushed over the room, a gasp shared by even the witchmen, Amadijuè included.

Dolo Anah looked up at them. "Each of you must come in turn and look into the ball," he said.

Faltering, though all eyes were turned to him, Amadijuè led the way. His eyes rounded, he stared, and they widened still further. For within, mystery upon mystery, men danced in seeming celebration. It was as though it was a funeral party but of dimensions never known before, for there were scores of Kanaga dancers, and, yes, above all other wonders, some of the dancers were Dogon, without doubt, but others were Mosse and others were even Tellum!

Amadijuè turned away, shaken, and Dolo Anah spoke sharply, "The rest, one by one."

They came. The headmen, the Hogons, the witchmen and finally the sons of the headmen, and each in turn stared into the ball and saw the tiny men within, doing their dance of celebration, Dogon, Mosse and Tellum together.

When all had seen, Dolo Anah placed the ball back on the ground and stared at it and slowly it returned to from whence it came, and Dolo Anah gently spread dust over the spot. When the floor was as it had been, he looked up at them, his eyes striking.

"What did you see?" he spoke sharply to Amadijuè.

There was a tremor in the village witchman's voice. "Oh juju, come out of the sky, I saw a great festival and Dogon danced with their enemies the Mosse and the Tellum-and, all seemed happy beyond belief."

The stranger looked piercingly at the rest. "And what did you see?"

Some mumbled, "The same. The same," and others, terrified still, could only nod.

"That is the message I have come to give you. You will hold a great conference with the people of the Tellum and the people of the Mosse and there will be a great celebration and no longer will there be Dogon, Mosse and Tellum, but all will be one. And there will be trade, and there will be marriage between the tribes, and no longer will there be three tribes, but only one people and no longer will the headmen and witchmen of the tribes resist the coming of the new schools, and all the young people will attend."

Amadijuè muttered, "But, great juju come out of the sky, these are our blood enemies. For longer than the memory of the grandfathers of our eldest Hogon we have carried the blood feud with Tellum and Mosse."

"No longer," Dolo Anah said flatly.

Amadijuè held shaking hands out in supplication, to this dominating juju come out of the skies. "But they will not heed us. Tellum and Mosse have hated the Dogon for all time. They will wreak their vengeance on any delegation come to make such suggestions to them."

"I fly to see their headmen and witchmen immediately," Dolo Anah bit out decisively. "They will heed my message." His tone turned dangerous. "As will the headmen and witchmen of the Dogon. If any fail to obey the message from above, their eyes will lose sight, their tongues become dumb, and their bellies will crawl with worms."

Amadijuè's face went ashen.

At long last the headman of all the Sangha villages spoke up, his voice trembling its fear. "But the schools, oh great juju-as all the Dogon have decided, in tribal conference-the schools are evil for our youth. They teach not the old ways —"

Dolo Anah cut him short with the chop of a commanding hand. "The old ways are fated to die. Already they die. The new ways are the ways of the schools."

Amazed at his own temerity, the head chief spoke once more. "But, since the coming of the French, we have rejected the schools."

Dolo Anah looked at him in scorn. "These will not be schools of the French. They will be the schools of Bantu, Berber, Sudanese and all the other peoples of the land. And when your young people have attended the schools and learned their wisdom they in turn will teach in the schools and in all the land there will be wisdom and good life. Now I have spoken and all of you will withdraw save only the sons of the headmen."

They withdrew, making a point each and every one not to turn their backs to this bringer of disastrous news and leaving only the terror-stricken young men behind them.

* * * * *

When all were gone save the dozen youngsters, Dolo Anah looked at them contemplatively. He shrugged finally and said, pointing with his finger, "You, you and you may leave. The others will remain." The three darted out, glad of the reprieve.

He looked at the remainder. "Be unafraid," he snapped. "There is no reason to fear me. Your fathers and the Hogons and the so-called witchmen, are fools, nothing-men. Fools and cowards, because they are impressed by foolish tricks."

He pointed suddenly. "You, there, what is your name?"

The youth stuttered, "Hinnan."

"Very well, Hinnan. Did you see me approach by the air?"

"Yes ...yes ...juju man."

"Don't call me a juju man. There is no such thing as juju. It is nonsense made by the cunning to fool the stupid, as you will learn when you attend the schools."

Hinnan took courage. "But I saw you fly."

"Have you never seen the great aircraft of the white men of Europe and America go flying over? Or have none of you witnessed these craft sitting on the ground at Mopti or Niamey. Surely some of you have journeyed to Mopti."

"Yes, but they are great craft. And you flew alone and without the great wings and propellers of the white-man's aircraft."

Dolo Anah chuckled. "My son, I flew in a helio-hopper as they are called. They are the smallest of all aircraft, but they are not magic. They are made in the factories of the lands of Europe and America and after you have finished school and have found a position for yourself in the new industries that spread through Africa, then you will be able to purchase one quite cheaply, if you so desire. Others among you might even learn to build them, themselves."

Hinnan and the others gasped.

Dolo Anah went on. "And observe this." He dug into the ground before him and revealed the crystal ball that had magically appeared before. He showed to them the little elevator device beneath it which he manipulated with a small rubber bulb which pumped air underneath.

One or two of them ventured a scornful laugh, at the obviousness of the trick.

Dolo Anah took up the ball and unscrewed the base. Inside were a delicate arrangement of film on a continuous spool so that the scene played over and over again, and a combination of batteries and bulbs to project the scene on the ball's surface. He explained, in patient detail, the workings of the supposed magic ball. Two of the boys had seen movies on trips to Mopti, the others had heard of them.

Finally one, highly encouraged now, as were the others, said, "But why do you show us this and shame us for our foolishness?"

Dolo Anah nodded encouragement at the teen-ager. "I do not shame you, my son, but your fathers and the Hogons and the so-called witchmen. For long ages the Dogon have been led by the oldest members of the tribe, the Hogons. This can be nonsense because in spite of your traditions age does not necessarily bring wisdom. In fact, senility as it is called can bring childish nonsense. A people should be governed by the wisest and best among them, not by tradition, by often silly beliefs handed down from one generation to another."

Hinnan, who was eldest son of the head chief, said, "But why do you tell us this, after shaming our fathers and the old men of the Dogon?"

For the first time since the elders had left, Dolo Anah's eyes gleamed as before. "Because you will be the leaders of the Dogon tomorrow, most like. And it is necessary to learn these great truths. That you attend the schools and bring to the Dogon tomorrow what they did not have yesterday, and do not have today."

"But suppose we tell them of how you have deceived them?" the other articulate Dogon lad said.

Dolo Anah chuckled and shook his head. "They will not believe you, boy. They will be afraid to believe you. And besides, men are almost everywhere the same. It is difficult for an older man to learn from a younger one, especially his own son. It is vanity, but it is true." His mouth twisted in memory. "When I was a lad myself, on the beaches of an island far from here in the Bahamas, my father beat me on more than one occasion, indignant that I should wish to attend the white man's schools, while he and his father before him had been fishermen. Beneath his indignation was the fear that one day I would excel him."

"You are right," Hinnan said uncomfortably, "they would not believe us." Instinctively, the son of the head chief assumed leadership of the others. "We will keep this secret between us," he said to them.

Dolo Anah came to his feet, yawned, stretched his legs and began to pack his gadgets into the small valise he carried. "Good luck, boys," he said unthinkingly in English.

As he left the hut, he emerged into a respectfully cleared area around the hut. Without looking left or right he approached his folded helio-hopper, made the few adjustments that were needed to make it air-borne, strapped himself into the tiny saddle, flicked the start control and to the accompaniment of a gasp from the entire village of Irèli, took off in a swoop.

In a matter of moments, he had disappeared to the north in the direction of the Mosse villages.

III

The Emir Alhaji Mohammadu, the Galadima Dawakin, Kudo of Kano, boiled furiously within as his gold plated Rolls Royce progressed through the Saba N'Gari section of town, the quarter outside the dirt walls of the millennium old city. He rode seated alone in the middle of the rear seat and his single counselor sat beside the chauffeur. Before them, a jeep load of his bodyguard, dressed in their uniforms of red and green, cleared the way. Another jeep followed similarly laden.

They entered through one of the ancient gates and swept up the principal street. They stopped before the recently constructed luxury hotel in the center of town and the bodyguard leapt from the jeeps and took positions to each side of the entry. The counselor popped out from his side of the car and beat the chauffeur to the task of opening the Emir's door.

Emir Alhaji Mohammadu was a tall man and a heavy one, his white robed figure towered some six and a half feet and his scales put him over the three hundred mark. He was in his mid fifties and almost a quarter century of autocratic position had marked his face with permanent scowl. He stomped now into the western style hotel.

His counselor, Ahmadu Abdullah, had already procured the information necessary to locate the source of the Emir's ire and now scurried before his chief, leading the way to the suite occupied by the mysterious strangers. He banged heavily on the door, then stepped behind his master as it opened.

One of the strangers, clad western style, opened the door and stepped aside courteously motioning to the large inner room. The Emir strutted arrogantly inside and stared in high irritation at the second and elder stranger who sat there at a heavy table. This one came to his feet, but there was no sign of acknowledgment of the Emir's rank. It was not too long a time before that men prostrated themselves in Alhaji Mohammadu's presence.

He looked at them. Though both were of dark complexion, there seemed no manner of typing them. Certainly they were neither Hausa nor Fulani, there being no signs of Hamitic features, but neither were they Ibo or Yoruba from farther south. The Emir's eyes narrowed and he wondered if these two were Nigerians at all!

He barked at them in Hausa and the older answered him in the same language, though there seemed a certain awkwardness in its use.

Emir Alhaji Mohammadu blared, "You dare summon me, Kudo of this city? You presume —"

They had resumed seats behind the table and the two of them looked at him questioningly. The older one interrupted with a gently raised hand. "Why did you come?"

Still glaring, the Emir turned to the cringing Ahmadu Abdullah and motioned curtly for the counselor to speak. Meanwhile, the ruler's eyes went around the room, decided that the couch was the only seat that would accommodate his bulk, and descended upon it.

Ahmadu Abdullah brought a paper from the folds of his robes. "This lying letter. This shameless attack upon the Galadima Dawakin!"

The younger stranger said mildly, "If the charges contained there are incorrect, then why did you come?"

The Emir rumbled dangerously, ignoring the question. "What is your purpose? I am not a patient man. There has never been need for my patience."

The spokesman of the two, the older, leaned back in his chair and said carefully, "We have come to demand your resignation and self-exile."

A vein beat suddenly and wildly at the gigantic Emir's temple and for a full minute the potentate was speechless with outrage.

Ahmadu Abdullah said quickly, "Fantastic! Ridiculous! The Galadima Dawakin is lawful ruler and religious potentate of three million devoted followers. You are lying strangers come to cause dissention among the people of Kano and —"

The spokesman for the newcomers took up a sheaf of papers from the table and said, his voice emotionless, "The reason you came here at our request is because the charges made in that letter you bear are valid ones. For a quarter century, you, Alhaji Mohammadu, have milked your people to your own profit. You have lived like a god on the wealth you have extracted from them. You have gone far, far beyond the legal and even traditional demands you have on the local population. Funds supposedly to be devoted to education, sanitation, roads, hospitals and a multitude of other developments that would improve this whole benighted area, have gone into your private pocket. In short, you have been a cancer on your people for the better part of your life."

"All lies!" roared the Kudo.

The other shook his head. "No. We have carefully gathered proof. We can submit evidence to back every charge we have made. Above all, we can prove the existence of large sums of money you have smuggled out of the country to Switzerland, London and New York to create a reserve for yourself in case of emergency. Needless to say, these funds, too, were originally meant for the betterment of the area."

The Emir's eyes were narrow with hate. "Who are you? Whom do you represent?"

"What difference does it make? This is of no importance."

"You represent my son, Alhaji Fodio! This is what comes of his studies in England and America. This is what comes of his leaving Kano and spending long years in Lagos among those unbeliever communists in the south!"

The younger stranger chuckled easily. "That is about the last tag I would hang on your son's associates," he said in English.

But the older stranger was nodding. "It is true that we hope your son will take over the Emirate. He represents progress. Frankly, his plans are to end the office as soon as the people are educated to the point where they can accept such change."

"End the office!" the Emir snarled. "For a thousand years my ancestors —"

* * * * *

The spokesman of the strangers shook his head wearily. "Your ancestors conquered this area less than two centuries ago in a jehad led by Othman Dan. Since then, you Fulani have feudalistically dominated the Hausa, but that is coming to an end."

The Emir had come to his feet again, in his rage, and now he towered over the table behind which the two sat as though about to physically attack them. "You speak as fools," he raged.

"Are you so stupid as to believe that these matters you have brought up are understandable to my people? Have you ever seen my people?" He sneered in a caricature of humor. "My people in their grass and bush huts? With not one man in a whole village who can add sums higher than those he can work out on his fingers? With not one man who can read the English tongue, nor any other? Would you explain to these the matters of transferring gold to the Zürich banks? Would you explain to these what is involved in accepting dash from road contractors and from politicians in Lagos?"

He sneered at them again. "And do you realize that I am church as well as state? That I represent their God to my people? Do you think they would take your word against *mine*, their Kudo?"

In talking, he had brought a certain calm back to himself. Now he felt reassured at his own words. He wound it up. "You are fools to believe my people could understand such matters."

"Then actually, you don't deny them?"

"Why should I bother?" the Emir chuckled heavily.

"That you have taken for personal use the large sums granted this area from a score of sources for roads, hospitals, schools, sanitation, agricultural modernization?"

"Of course I don't deny it. This is my land. I am the Kudo, the Emir, the Galadima Dawakin. Whatever I choose to do in Kano and to all my people is right because I wish it. Schools? I don't want them corrupting my people. Hospitals for these Hausa serfs? Nonsense! Roads? They are bad for they allow the people to get about too easily and that leads to their exchanging ideas and schemes and leads to their corruption. Have I appropriated all such sums for my own use? Yes! I admit it. Yes! But you cannot prove it to such as my people, you who represent my son. So be-gone from Kano. If you are here tomorrow, you will be arrested by the same men of my bodyguard who even now seek my son, Alhaji Fodio. When he is captured, it will be of interest to revive some of the methods of execution of my ancestors."

The Emir turned on his heel to stalk from the room but the older of the two murmured, "One moment, please."

Alhaji Mohammadu paused, his face dark in scowl again.

The spokesman said agreeably, "It is true that your people, and particularly your Hausa serfs, have no understanding of international finance nor of national corruption methods such as the taking of *dash*. However, they are susceptible to other proof." The other man raised his voice. "John!"

From an inner room came another stranger, making their total number three. He was grinning and in one hand held a contraption which boasted a conglomeration of lenses, switches, microphones, wires and triggers. "Got it perfectly," he said. You'd think it had all been rehearsed.

While the Emir and his counselor stared in amazement, the spokesman of the strangers said, "How long before you can project?"

"Almost immediately."

The other young man left the room and returned with what was obviously a movie projector. He set it up at one end of the table, pointed at a white wall, and plugged it in to a convenient outlet.

Before the Emir had managed to control himself beyond the point of saying any more than, "What is all this?" the cameraman had brought a magazine of film from his instrument and inserted it in the projector.

The photographer said conversationally, to the hulking potentate, "You'd be amazed at the advances in cinema these past few years. Film speed, immediate development, portable sound equipment. You'd be amazed."

Someone flicked out the greater part of the room's light. The projector buzzed and on the wall was thrown a re-enactment of everything that had been said and done in the room for the past ten minutes.

When it was over, the lights went on again.

The spokesman said conversationally, "I assume that if this film were shown throughout the villages, even your Hausa serfs would be convinced that throughout your reign you have systematically robbed them."

Emir Alhaji Mohammadu, the Galadima Dawakin, Kudo of Kano, his face in shock, turned and stumbled from the room.

* * * * *

The gymkhana, or fantasia as it is called in nearby Morocco, was under full swing before Abd-el-Kader and the camel- and horse-mounted warriors of his Ouled Touameur clan came dashing in, rifles held high and with great firing into the air. The Ouled Touameur were the noblest clan of the Ouled Allouch tribe of the Berazga division of the Chaambra nomad confederation-the noblest and the least disciplined. There were whispered rumors going about the conference as to the identity of the mysterious raiders who were preying upon the new oases, the oil and road building camps and the endless other new projects springing up, all but magically, throughout the northwestern Sahara.

The gymkhana was in full swing with racing and feasting, and storytellers and conjurers, jugglers and marabouts. And in the air was the acrid distinctive odor of *kif*, for though Mohammed forbade alcohol to the faithful he had naught to say about the uses of *cannabis sativa* and what is a great festival without the smoking of *kif* and the eating of *majoun*?

The tribes of the Chaambra were widely represented, Berazga and Mouadhi, Bou Rouba and Ouled Fredj, and there was even a heavy sprinkling of the sedentary Zenatas come down from the towns of Metlili, El Oued and El Goléo. Then, of course, were the Haratin serfs, of mixed Arab-Negro blood, and the Negroes themselves, until recently openly called slaves, but now-amusingly-named servants.

The Chaambra were meeting for a great ceremonial gymkhanas, but also, as was widely known, for a *djemaa el kebar* council of elders and chiefs, for there were many problems throughout the Western Erg and the areas of Mzab and Bourara. Nor was it secret only to the inner councils that the meeting had been called by Abd-el-Kader, of Shorfu blood, direct descendent of the Prophet through his daughter Fatima, and symbol to the young warriors of Chaambra spirit.

Of all the Ouled Touameur clan Abd-el-Kader alone refrained from discharging his gun into the air as they dashed into the inner circle of khaima tents which centered the gymkhana and provided council chambers, dining hall and sleeping quarters for the tribal and clan heads. Instead, and with head arrogantly high, he slipped from his stallion tossing the reins to a nearby Zenata and strode briskly to the largest of the tents and disappeared inside.

Bismillah! but Adb-el-Kader was a figure of a man! From his turban, white as the snows of the Atlas, to his yellow leather boots, he wore the traditional clothing of the Chaambra and wore them with pride. Not for Abd-el-Kader the new clothing from the Rouma cities to the north, nor even the new manufactures from Dakar, Accra, Lagos and the other mushrooming centers to the south.

His weapons alone paid homage to the new ways. And each fighting man within eyesight noted that it was not a rifle slung over the shoulder of Abd-el-Kader but a sub-machine gun. Bismillah! This could not have been so back in the days when the French Camel Corps ruled the land with its hand of iron.

The djemaa el kebar was already in session, seated in a great circle on the rug and provided with glasses of mint tea and some with water pipes. They looked up at the entrance of the warrior clan chieftain.

* * * * *

El Aicha, who was of Maraboutic ancestry and hence a holy man as well as elder of the Ouled Fredj, spoke first as senior member of the conference. "We have heard reports that are disturbing of recent months, Abd-el-Kader. Reports of activities amongst the Ouled Touameur. We would know more of the truth of these. But also we have high interest in your reason for summoning the djemaa el kebar at such a time of year."

Abd-el-Kader made a brief gesture of obeisance to the Chaambra leader, a gesture so brief as to verge on disrespect. He said, his voice clear and confident, as befits a warrior chief, "Disturbing only to the old and unvaliant, O El Aicha."

The old man looked at him for a long, unblinking moment. As a youth, he had fought at the Battle of Tit when the French Camel Corps had broken forever the military power of the Ahaggar Tuareg. El Aicha was no coward. There were murmurings about the circle of elders.

But when El Aicha spoke again, his voice was level. "Then speak to us, Abd-el-Kader. It is well known that your voice is heard ever more by the young men, particularly by the bolder of the young men."

The fighting man remained standing, his legs slightly spread. The Arab, like the Amerind, likes to make speech in conference, and eloquence is well held by the Chaambra.

"Long years ago, and only shortly after the death of the Prophet, the Chaambra resided, so tell the scribes, in the hills of far away Syria. But when the word of Islam was heard and the true believers began to race their strength throughout all the world, the Chaambra came here to the deserts of Africa and here we have remained. Long centuries it took us to gain control of the wide areas of the northern and western desert and many were the battles we fought with our traditional enemies the Tuareg and the Moors before we controlled all the land between the Atlas and the Niger and from what is now known as Tunisia to Mauritania."

All nodded. This was tribal history.

Abd-el-Kader held up four fingers on which to enumerate. "The Chaambra were ever men. Warriors, bedouin; not for us the cities and villages of the Zenatas, and the miserable Haratin serfs. We Chaambra have ever been men of the tent, warriors, conquerors!"

El Aicha still nodded. "That was before," he murmured.

"That will always be!" Abd-el-Kader insisted. His four fingers were spread and he touched the first one. "Our life was based upon, one, war and the spoils of war." He touched the second finger. "Two, the toll we extracted from the caravans that passed from Timbuktu to the north and back again. Three, from our own caravans which covered the desert trails from Tripoli to Dakar and from Marrakech to Kano. And fourth" —he touched his last finger —"from our flocks which fed us in the wilderness." He paused to let this sink in.

"All this is verily true," muttered one of the elders, a so-what quality in his voice.

Abd-el-Kader's tone soured. "Then came the French with their weapons and their multitudes of soldiers and their great wealth with which to pursue the expenses of war. And one by one the Tuareg and the Teda to the south and the Moors and Nemadi, yes, and even the Chaambra fell before the onslaughts of the Camel Corps and their wild-dog Foreign Legion." He held up his four fingers again and counted them off. "The four legs upon which our life was based were broken. War and its spoils was prevented us. The tolls we charged caravans to cross our land were forbidden. And then, shortly after, came the motor trucks which crossed the desert in a week, where formerly the journey took as much as a year. Our camel caravans became meaningless."

Again all nodded. "Verily, the world changes," someone muttered.

The warrior leader's voice went dramatic. "We were left with naught but our flocks, and now even they are fated to end."

The elderly nomads stirred and some scowled.

"At every water hole in the desert teams of the new irrigation development dig their wells, install their pumps which bring power from the sun, plant trees, bring in Haratin and former slaves —our slaves-to cultivate the new oases. And we are forbidden the water for the use of our goats and sheep and camels."

"Besides," one of the clan chiefs injected, "they tell us that the goat is the curse of North Africa, nibbling as it does the bark of small trees, and they attempt to purchase all goats until soon there will be few, if any, in all the land."

"So our young people," Abd-el-Kader pressed on, "stripped of our former way of life, go to the new projects, enroll in the schools, take work in the new oases or on the roads, and disappear from the sight of their kinsmen." He came to a sudden halt and all but glared at them, maintaining his silence until El Aicha stirred.

"And —?" El Aicha said. This was all obviously but preliminary.

Abd-el-Kader spoke softly now, and there was a different drama in his voice. "And now," he said, "the French are gone. All the Rouma, save a handful, are gone. In the south the English are gone from the lands of the blacks, such as Nigeria and Ghana, Sierra Leone and Gambia. The Italians are gone from Libya and Somaliland and the Spanish from Rio de Oro. Nor will they ever return for in the greatest council of all the Rouma they have decided to leave Africa to the African."

They all stirred again and some muttered and Abd-el-Kader pushed his point. "The Chaambra are warriors born. Never serfs! Never slaves! Never have we worked for any man. Our ancestors carved great empires by the sword." His voice lowered again. "And now, once more, it is possible to carve such an empire."

He swept his eyes about their circle. "Chiefs of the Chaambra, there is no force in all the Sahara to restrain us. Let others work on the roads, planting the new trees in the new oases, damming the great Niger, and all the rest of it. We will sweep over them, and dominate all. We, the Chaambra, will rule, while those whom Allah intended to drudge, do so. We, the Chosen of Allah, will fulfill our destiny!"

* * * * *

Abd-el-Kader left it there and crossed his arms on his chest, staring at them challengingly.

Finally El Aicha directed his eyes across the circle of listeners at two who had sat silently through it all, their burnooses covering their heads and well down over their eyes. He said, "And what do you say to all this?"

"Time to go into your act, man," Abe Bakr muttered, under his breath.

Homer Crawford came to his feet and pushed back the hood of the burnoose. He looked over at the headman of the Ouled Touameur warrior clan, whose face was darkening.

In Arabic, Crawford said, "I have sought you for some time, Abd-el-Kader. You are an illusive man."

"Who are you, Negro?" the fighting man snapped.

Crawford grinned at the other. "You look as though you have a bit of Negro blood in your own veins. In fact, I doubt if there's a so-called Arab in all North Africa, unless he's just recently arrived, whose family hasn't down through the centuries mixed its blood with the local people they conquered."

"You lie!"

Abe chuckled from the background. The Chaambra leader was at least as dark of complexion as the American Negro. Not that it made any difference one way or the other.

"We shall see who is the liar here," Homer Crawford said flatly. "You asked who I am. I am known as Omar ben Crawf and I am headman of a team of the African Development Project of the Reunited Nations. As you have said, Abd-el-Kader, this great council of the headmen of all the nations of the world-not just the Rouma-has decided that Africa must be left to the Africans. But that does not mean it has lost all interest in these lands. It has no intention, warrior of the Chaambra, to allow such as you to disrupt the necessary progress Africa must make if it is not to become a danger to the shaky peace of the world."

Abd-el-Kader's eyes darted about the tent. So far as he could see, the other was backed only by his single henchman. The warrior chief gained confidence. "Power is for those who can assert it. Some will rule. It has always been so. Here in the Western Erg, the Chaambra will rule, and I, Abd-el-Kader will lead them!"

Homer Crawford was shaking his head, almost sadly it seemed. "No," he said. "The day of rule by the gun is over. It must be over because at long last man's weapons have become so great that he must not trust himself with them. In the new world which is still aborning so that half the nations of earth are in the pains of labor, government must be by the most wise and most capable."

In a deft move the sub-machine gun's sling slipped from the desert man's shoulder and the short, vicious gun was in hand. "The strong will always rule!" the Arab shouted. "Time was when the French conquered the Chaambra, but the French have allowed their strength to ebb away, and now, armed with such weapons as these, we of the Sahara will again assert our birthright as the Chosen of Allah!"

Abe Baker chuckled. "That cat sure can lay on a speech, man." As though magically, a snub-nosed hand weapon of unique design appeared in his dark hand.

El Aicha's voice was suddenly strong and harsh. "There shall be no violence at a djemaa el kebar."

Homer ignored the automatic weapon in the hands of the excited Arab. He said, and there was still a sad quality in his voice. "The gun you carry is a nothing-weapon, desert man. When the French conquered this land more than a century ago they were armed with single-shot rifles which were still far in advance of your own long barrelled flintlocks. Today, you are proud of that tommy gun you carry, and, indeed, it has the fire power of a company of the Foreign Legion of a century past. However, believe me, Abd-el-Kader, it is a nothing-weapon compared to those that will be brought against the Chaambra if they heed your words."

The desert leader put back his head and laughed his scorn.

He chopped his laughter short and snapped, more to the council of chiefs than to the stranger. "Then we will seize such weapons and use them against those who would oppose us. In the end it is the strong who win in war, and the Rouma have gone soft, as all men know. I, Abd-el-Kader will have these two killed and then I shall announce to the assembled tribes the new jedah, a Holy War to bring the Chosen of Allah once again to their rightful position in the Sahara."

"Man," Abe Baker murmured pleasantly, "you're going to be one awful disappointed cat before long."

El Aicha said mildly, "Such decisions are for the djemaa el kebar to make, O Abd-el-Kader, not for a single chief of the Ouled Touameur."

The desert warrior chief sneered openly at the old man. "Decisions are made by those with the strength to enforce them. The young men of the Chaambra support me, and my men surround this tent."

"So do mine," Homer Crawford said decisively. "And I have come to arrest you and take you to Columb-Béchar where you will be tried for your participation in recent raids on various development projects."

El Aicha repeated his earlier words. "There shall be no violence at a djemaa el kebar."

The Ouled Touameur chief's eyes had narrowed. "You are not strong enough to take me."

* * * * *

In English, Abe Baker said, "Like maybe these young followers of this cat need an example laid on them, man."

"I'm afraid you're right," Crawford growled disgustedly.

The younger American came to his feet. "I'll take him on," Abe said.

"No, he's nearer to my size," Crawford grunted. He turned to El Aicha, and said in Arabic, "I demand the right of a stranger in your camp to a trial by combat."

"On what grounds?" the old man scowled.

"That my manhood has been spat upon by this warrior who does his fighting with his loud mouth."

The assembled chiefs looked to Abd-el-Kader, and a rustling sigh went through them. A hundred times the wiry desert chieftain had proven himself the most capable fighter in the tribes. A hundred times he had proven it and there were dead and wounded in the path he had cut for himself.

Abd-el-Kader laughed aloud again. "Swords, in the open before the ascan."

Homer Crawford shrugged. "Swords, in the open before the assembled Chaambra so that they may see how truly weak is the one who calls himself so strong."

Abe said worriedly, in English, "Listen, man, you been checked out on swords?"

"They're the traditional weapon in the Arab *code duello*," Homer said, with a wry grin. "Nothing else would do."

"Man, you sound like you've been blasting pot and got yourself as high as those cats out there with their *kif*. This Abd-el-Kader was probably raised with a sword in his hand."

Abd-el-Kader smiling triumphantly, had spun on his heel and made his way through the tent's entrance. Now they could hear him shouting orders.

El Aicha looked up at Homer Crawford from where he sat. His voice without inflection, he said, "Hast thou a sword, Omar ben Crawf?"

"No," Crawford said.

The elderly tribal leader said, "Then I shall loan you mine." He hesitated momentarily, before adding, "Never before has hand other than mine wielded it." And finally, simply, "Never has it been drawn to commit dishonor."

"I am honored."

Outside, the rumors had spread fast and already a great arena was forming by the packed lines of Chaambra nomads. At the tent entrance, Elmer Allen, his face worried, said, his English in characteristic Jamaican accent, "What did you chaps do?"

"Duel," Abe growled apprehensively. "This joker here has challenged their top swordsman to a fight."

Elmer said hurriedly, "See here, gentlemen, the hovercraft are parked over behind that tent. We can be there in two minutes and away from —"

Crawford's eyes went from Elmer Allen to Abe Baker and then back again. He chuckled, "I don't think you two think I'm going to win this fight," he said.

"What do you know about swordsmanship?" Elmer Allen said accusingly.

"Practically nothing. A little bayonet practice quite a few years ago."

"Oh, great," Abe muttered.

Elmer said hurriedly, "See here, Homer, I was on the college fencing team and —"

Crawford grinned at him. "Too late, friend."

As they talked, they made their way to the large circle of men. In its center, Abd-el-Kader was stripping to his waist, meanwhile laughingly shouting his confidence to his Ouled Touameur tribesmen and to the other Chaambra of fighting age. No one seemed to doubt the final issue. Beneath his white burnoose he wore a gandoura of lightweight woolen cloth and beneath that a longish undershirt of white cotton, similar to that of the Tuareg but with shorter and less voluminous sleeves. This the desert fighter retained.

Crawford stripped down too, nude to the waist. His body was in excellent trim, muscles bunching under the ebony skin. A Haratin servant came up bearing El Aicha's sword.

Homer Crawford pulled it from the scabbard. It was of scimitar type, the weapon which had once conquered half the known world.

From within the huge circle of men, Abd-el-Kader swung his own blade in flashing arcs and called out something undoubtedly insulting, but which was lost in the babble of the multitude.

"Well, here we go," Crawford grunted. "You fellows better station yourselves around just on the off chance that those Ouled Touameur bully-boys don't like the decision."

"We'll worry about that," Abe said unhappily. "You just see you get out of this in one piece. Anything happens to you and the head office'll make me head of this team-and frankly, man I don't want the job."

Homer grinned at him, and began pushing his way through to the center.

* * * * *

The Arab cut a last switch in the air, with his whistling blade and started forward, in practiced posture. Homer awaited him, legs spread slightly, his hands extended slightly, the sword held at the ready but with point low.

Abe Baker growled, unhappily, "He said he didn't know anything about the swords, and the way he holds it bears him out. That Arab'll cut Homer to ribbons. Maybe we ought to do something about it." As usual, under stress, he'd dropped his beatnik patter.

Elmer Allen looked at him. "Such as what? There are at least three thousand of these tribesmen chaps here watching their favorite sport. What did you have in mind doing?"

Abd-el-Kader hadn't remained the victor of a score of similar duels through making such mistakes as underestimating his foe. In spite of the black stranger's seeming ignorance of his weapon, the Arab had no intention of being sucked into a trap. He advanced with care.

His sword darted forward, quickly, experimentally, and Homer Crawford barely caught its razor edge on his own.

Save for his own four companions, the crowd laughed aloud. None among them were so clumsy as this.

The Ouled Touameur chief was convinced. He stepped in fast, the blade flicked in and out in a quick feint, then flicked in again. Homer Crawford countered clumsily.

And then there was a roar as the American's blade left his hand and flew high in the air to come to the ground again a score of feet behind the desert swordsman.

For a brief moment Abd-el-Kader stepped back to observe his foe, and there was mockery in his face. "So thy manhood has been spat upon by one who fights only with his mouth! Almost, braggart, I am inclined to give you your life so that you may spend the rest of it in shame. Now die, unbeliever!"

Crawford stood hopelessly, in a semicrouch, his hands still slightly forward. The Arab came in fast, his sword at the ready for the death stroke.

Suddenly, the American moved forward and then jumped a full yard into the air, feet forward and into the belly of the advancing Arab. The heavily shod right foot struck at the point in the abdomen immediately below the sternum, the solar plexus, and the left was as low as the groin. In a motion that was almost a bounce off the other's body, Crawford came lithely back to his feet, jumped back two steps, crouched again.

But Abd-el-Kader was through, his eyes popping agony, his body writhing on the ground. The whole thing, from the time the Arab had advanced on the disarmed man for the kill, hadn't taken five seconds.

His groans were the only sounds which broke the unbelieving silence of the Chaambra tribesmen. Homer Crawford picked up the fallen leader's sword and then strolled over and retrieved that of El Aicha. Ignoring Abd-el-Kader, he crossed to where the tribal elders had assembled to watch the fight and held out the borrowed sword to its owner.

El Aicha sheathed it while looking into Homer Crawford's face. "It has still never been drawn to commit dishonor."

"My thanks," Crawford said.

Over the noise of the crowd which now was beginning to murmur its incredulity at their champion's fantastic defeat, came the voice of Abe Baker swearing in Arabic and yelling for a way to be cleared for him. He was driving one of the hovercraft.

He drew it up next to the still agonized Abd-el-Kader and got out accompanied by Bey-ag-Akhamouk. Silently and without undue roughness they picked up the fallen clan chief and put him into the back of the hover-lorry, ignoring the crowd.

Homer Crawford came up and said in English, "All right, let's get out of here. Don't hurry, but on the other hand don't let's prolong it. One of those Ouled Touameur might collect himself to the point of deciding he ought to rescue his leader."

Abe looked at him disgustedly. "Like, where'd you learn that little party trick, man?"

Crawford yawned. "I said I didn't know anything about swords. You didn't ask me about judo. I once taught judo in the Marines."

"Well, why didn't you take him sooner? He like to cut your head off with that cheese knife before you landed on him."

"I couldn't do it sooner. Not until he knocked the sword out of my hand. Until then it was a sword fight. But as soon as I had no sword then in the eyes of every Chaambra present, I had the right to use any method possible to save myself."

Bey-ag-Akhamouk looked up at the sun to check the time. "We better speed it up if we want to get this man to Columb-Béchar and then get on down over the desert to Timbuktu and that meeting."

"Let's go," Homer said. The second hovercraft joined them, driven by Elmer Allen, and they made their way through the staring, but motionless, crowds of Chaambra.

IV

Once the city of Timbuktu was more important in population, in commerce, in learning than the London, the Paris or the Rome of the time. It was the crossroads where African traffic, east and west, met African traffic, north and south; Timbuktu dominated all. In its commercial houses accumulated the wealth of Africa; in its universities and mosques the wisdom of Greece, Rome, Byzantium and the Near East-at a time when such learning was being destroyed in Dark Ages beset Europe.

Timbuktu's day lasted but two or three hundred years at most. By the middle of the Twentieth Century it had deteriorated into what looked nothing so much as a New Mexico ghost town, built largely of adobe. Its palaces and markets has melted away to caricatures of their former selves, its universities were a memory of yesteryear, its population fallen off to a few thousands. Not until the Niger Projects, the dams and irrigation projects, of the latter part of the Twentieth Century did the city begin to regain a semblance of its old importance.

Homer Crawford's team had come down over the Tanezrouft route, Reggan, Bidon Cinq and Tessalit; that of Isobel Cunningham, Jacob Armstrong and Clifford Jackson, up from Timbuktu's Niger River port of Kabara. They met in the former great market square, bordered on two sides by the one time French Administration buildings.

Isobel reacted first. "Abe!" she yelled, pointing accusingly at him.

Abe Baker pretended to cringe, then reacted. "Isobel! Somebody *told* me you were over here!"

She ran over the heavy sand, which drifted through the streets, to the hovercraft in which he had just pulled up. He popped out to meet her, grinning widely.

"Why didn't you look me up?" she said accusingly, presenting a cheek to be kissed.

"In Africa, man?" he laughed. "Kinda big, Africa. Like, I didn't know if you were in the Sahara, or maybe down in Angola, or wherever."

She frowned. "Heaven forbid."

Abe turned to the others of his team who had crowded up behind him. It had been a long time since any of them had seen other than native women.

"Isobel," he said, "I hate to do this, but let me introduce you to Homer Crawford, my immediate boss and slave driver, late of the University of Michigan where he must've found out where the body was-they gave him a doctorate. Then here's Elmer Allen, late of Jamaica-British West Indies, not Long Island-all he's got is a master's, also in sociology. And this is Kenneth Ballalou, hails from San Francisco, I don't think Kenny ever went to school, but he seems to speak every language ever." Abe turned to his final companion. "And this is our sole *real* African, Bey-ag-Akhamouk, of Tuareg blood, so beware, they don't call the Tuareg the Apaches of the Sahara for nothing."

Bey pretended to wince as he held out his hand. "Since Abe seems to be an education snob, I might as well mention the University of Minnesota and my Political Science."

Jake Armstrong and Cliff Jackson had come up behind Isobel, and were now introduced in turn. The older man said, "A Tuareg in a Reunited Nations team? Not that it makes any difference to me, but I thought there was some sort of policy."

"I was taken to the States when I was three," Bey said. "I'm an American citizen."

Isobel was chattering, in animation, with Abe Baker. It developed they'd both been reporters on the school paper at Columbia. At least, they'd both started as reporters, Isobel had wound up editor.

Since their introduction, Homer Crawford had been vaguely frowning at her. Now he said, "I've been trying to place where I'd seen you before. Now I know. Some photographs of Lena Horne, she was —"

Isobel dropped a mock curtsy. "Thank you, kind sir, you don't have to tell me about Lena Horne, she's a favorite. I have scads of tapes of her."

"Brother," Elmer Allen said dourly, "how's anybody going to top that? Homer's got the inside track now. Let's get over to this meeting. By the cars, helio-copters and hovercraft around here, you got more of a turnout than I expected, Homer."

The meeting was held in what had once been an assembly chamber of the officials of the former *Cercle de Tombouctou*, when this had all been part of French Sudan. It was the only room in the vicinity which would comfortably hold all of them.

* * * * *

Elmer Allen had been right, there was something like a hundred persons present, almost all men but with a sprinkling of women, such as Isobel. More than half were in native costume running the gamut from Nigeria to Morocco and from Mauritania to Ethiopia. They were a competent looking, confident voiced gathering.

Homer Crawford knocked with a knuckle on the table that stood at the head of the hall and called for silence. "Sorry we're late," he said, "Particularly in view of the fact that the idea of this meeting originated with my team. We had some difficulty with a nomad raider, up in Chaambra country."

Someone from halfway back in the hall said bitterly, "I suppose in typical African Development Project style, you killed the poor man."

Crawford said dryly, *"Poor man* isn't too accurate a description of the gentleman involved. However, he is at present in jail awaiting trial." He got back to the meeting. "I had originally thought of this being an informal get-together of a score or so of us, but in view of the numbers I suggest we appoint a temporary chairman."

"You're doing all right," Jake Armstrong said from the second row of chairs.

"I second that," an unknown called from further back.

Crawford shrugged. His manner had a cool competence. "All right. If there is no objection, I'll carry on until the meeting decides, if it ever does, that there is need of elected officers."

"I object." In the third row a white haired, but Prussian-erect man had come to his feet. "I wish to know the meaning of this meeting. I object to it being held at all."

Abe Baker called to him, "Dad, how can you object to it being held if you don't know what it's for?"

Homer Crawford said, "Suppose I briefly sum up our mutual situation and if there are any motions to be made-including calling the meeting quits-or decisions to come to, we can start from there."

There was a murmur of assent. The objector sat down in a huff.

Crawford looked out over them. "I don't know most of you. The word of this meeting must have spread from one group or team to another. So what I'll do is start from the beginning, saying little at first with which you aren't already familiar, but we'll lay a foundation."

He went on. "This situation which we find in Africa is only a part of a world-wide condition. Perhaps to some, particularly in the Western World as they call it, Africa isn't of primary importance. But, needless to say, it is to we here in the field. Not too many years ago, at the same period the African colonies were bursting their bonds and achieving independence, an international situation was developing that threatened future peace. The rich nations were getting richer, the poor were getting poorer, and the rate of this change was accelerating. The reasons were various. The population growth in the backward countries, unhampered by birth control and rocketing upward due to new sanitation, new health measures, and the conquest of a score of diseases that have bedeviled man down through the centuries, was fantastic. Try as they would to increase per capita income in the have-not nations, population grew faster than new industry and new agricultural methods could keep up. On top of that handicap was another; the have-not nations were so far behind economically that they couldn't get going. Why build a bicycle factory in Morocco which might be able to turn out bikes for, say, fifty dollars apiece, when you could buy them from automated factories in Europe, Japan or the United States for twenty-five dollars?"

Most of his audience were nodding agreement, some of them impatiently, as though wanting him to get on with it.

Crawford continued. "For a time aid to these backward nations was left in the hands of the individual nations-especially to the United States and Russia. However, in spite of speeches of politicians to the contrary, governments are not motivated by humanitarian purposes. The government of a country does what it does for the benefit of the ruling class of that country. That was the reason it was appointed the government. Any government that doesn't live up to this dictum soon stops being the government."

"That isn't always so," somebody called.

Homer Crawford grinned. "Bear with me a while," he said. "We can debate till the Niger freezes over-later on."

He went on. "For instance, the United States would *aid* Country X with a billion dollars at, say four per cent interest, stipulating that the money be spent in America. This is aid? It certainly is for American business. But then our friends the Russians come along and loan the same country a billion rubles at a very low interest rate and with supposedly no strings attached, to build, say, a railroad. Very fine indeed, but first of all the railroad, built Russian style and with Russian equipment, soon needs replacements, new locomotives, more rolling stock. Where must it come from? Russia, of course. Besides that, in order to build and run the railroad it became necessary to send Russian technicians to Country X and also to send students from Country X to Moscow to study Russian technology so that they could operate the railroad." Crawford's voice went wry. "Few countries, other than commie ones, much desire to have their students study in Moscow."

* * * * *

There was a slight stirring in his audience and Homer Crawford grinned slightly. "You'll pardon me if in this little summation, I step on a few ideological toes-of both East and West.

"Needless to say, under these conditions of *aid* in short order the economies of various countries fell under the domination of the two great collossi. At the same time the other have nations including Great Britain, France, Germany and the newly awakening China, began to realize that unless they got into the *aid* act that they would disappear as competitors for the tremendous markets in the newly freed former colonial lands. Also along in here it became obvious that philanthropy with a mercenary basis doesn't always work out to the benefit of the receiver and the world began to take measures to administer aid more efficiently and through world bodies rather than national ones.

"But there was still another problem, particularly here in Africa. The newly freed former colonies were wary of the nations that had formerly owned them and often for good reasons, always remembering that governments are not motivated by humanitarian reasons. England did not free India because her heart bled for the Indian people, nor did France finally free Algeria because the French conscience was stirred with thoughts of Freedom, Equality and Fraternity."

A voice broke in from halfway down the hall, a voice heavy with British accent. "I say, why did you Yanks free the Philippines?"

Homer Crawford laughed, as did several other Americans present. "That's the first time I've ever been called a Yankee," he said. "But the point is well taken. By freeing the islands we washed our hands of the responsibility of such expensive matters as their health and education, and at the same time we granted freedom we made military and economic treaties which perpetuated our fundamental control of the Philippines.

"The point is made. The distrust of the European and the white man as a whole was prevalent, especially here in Africa. However, and particularly in Africa, the citizens of the new countries were almost unbelievably uneducated, untrained, incapable of engineering their own destiny. In whole nations there was not a single lawyer or —"

"That's no handicap," somebody called.

There was laughter through the hall.

Homer Crawford laughed, too, and nodded as though in solemn agreement. "However, there were also no doctors, engineers, scientists. There were whole nations without a single college graduate."

He paused and his eyes swept the hall. "That's where we came in. Most of us here this afternoon are from the States, however, also represented to my knowledge are British West Indians, a Canadian or two, at least one Panamanian, and possibly some Cubans. Down in the southern part of the continent I know of teams working in the Portuguese areas who are Brazilian in background. All of us, of course, are Africans racially, but few if any of us know from what part of Africa his forebears came. My own grandfather was born a slave in Mississippi and didn't know his father; my grandmother was already a hopeless mixture of a score of African tribes.

"That, I assume, is the story of most if not all of us. Our ancestors were wrenched from the lands of their birth and shipped under conditions worse than cattle to the New World." He added simply, "Now we return."

There was a murmur throughout his listeners, but no one interrupted.

"When the great powers of Europe arbitrarily split up Africa in the Nineteenth Century they didn't bother with race, tribe, not even geographic boundaries. Largely they seemed to draw their boundary lines with ruler and pencil on a Mercator projection. Often, not only were native nations split in twain but even tribes and clans, and sometimes split not only one way but two or three. It was chaotic to the old tribal system. Of course, when the white man left various efforts were made from the very start to join that which had been torn apart a century earlier. Right here in this area, Senegal and what was then French Sudan merged to form the short-lived Mali Federation. Ghana and French Guinea formed a shaky alliance. More successful was the federation of Kenya, Tanganyika, Uganda and Zanzibar, which of course, has since grown.

"But there were fantastic difficulties. Many of the old tribal institutions had been torn down, but new political institutions had been introduced only in a half-baked way. African politicians, supposedly 'democratically' elected, had no intention of facing the possibility of giving up their individual powers by uniting with their neighbors. Not only had the Africans been divided tribally but now politically as well. But obviously, so long as they continued to be Balkanized the chances of rapid progress were minimized.

"Other difficulties were manifold. So far as socio-economics were concerned, African society ran the scale from bottom to top. The Bushmen of the Ermelo district of the Transvaal and the Kalahari are stone age people still-savages. Throughout the continent we find tribes at an ethnic level which American Anthropologist Lewis Henry Morgan called barbarism. In some places we find socio-economic systems based on chattle slavery, elsewhere feudalism. In comparatively few areas, Casablanca, Algiers, Dakar, Cairo and possibly the Union we find a rapidly expanding capitalism.

"Needless to say, if Africa was to progress, to increase rapidly her per capita income, to depart the ranks of the have-nots and become have nations, these obstacles had to be overcome. That is why we are here."

"Speak for yourself, Mr. Crawford," the white haired objector of ten minutes earlier, bit out.

* * * * *

Homer Crawford nodded. "You are correct, sir. I should have said that is the reason the teams of the Reunited Nations African Development Project are here. I note among us various members of this project besides those belonging to my own team, by the way. However, most of you are under other auspices. We of the Reunited Nations teams are here because as Africans racially but not nationally, we have no affiliation with clan, tribe or African nation. We are free to work for Africa's progress without prejudice. Our job is to remove obstacles wherever we find them. To break up log jams. To eliminate prejudices against the steps that must be taken if Africa is to run down the path of progress, rather than to crawl. We usually operate in teams of about half a dozen. There are hundreds of such teams in North Africa alone."

He rapped his knuckle against the small table behind which he stood. "Which brings us to the present and to the purpose of suggesting this meeting. Most of you are operating under other auspices than the Reunited Nations. Many of you duplicate some of our work. It occurred to me, and my team mates, that it might be a good idea for us to get together and see if there is ground for co-operation."

Jake Armstrong called out, "What kind of co-operation?"

Crawford shrugged. "How would I know? Largely, I don't even know who you represent, or the exact nature of the tasks you are trying to perform. I suggest that each group of us represented here, stand up and announce their position. Possibly, it will lead to something of value."

"I make that a motion," Cliff Jackson said.

"Second," Elmer Allen called out.

The majority were in favor.

Homer Crawford sat down behind the table, saying, "Who'll start off?"

Armstrong said, "Isobel, you're better looking than I am. They'd rather look at you. You present our story."

Isobel came to her feet and shot him a scornful glance. "Lazy," she said.

Jake Armstrong grinned at her. "Make it good."

Isobel took her place next to the table at which Crawford sat and faced the others.

She looked at the chairman from the side of her eyes and said, "After that allegedly *brief* summation Mr. Crawford made, I have a sneaking suspicion that we'll be here until next week unless I set a new precedent and cut the position of the Africa for Africans Association shorter."

Isobel got her laugh, including one from Homer Crawford, and went on.

"Anyway, I suppose most of you know of the AFAA and possibly many of you belong to it, or at least contribute. We've been called the African Zionist organization and perhaps that's not too far off. We are largely, but not entirely an American association. We send out our teams, such as the one my colleagues and I belong to, in order to speed up progress and, as our chairman put it, eliminate prejudices against the steps that must be taken if Africa is to run down the path of progress instead of crawl. We also advocate that Americans and other non-African-born Negroes, educated in Europe and the Americas, return to Africa to help in its struggles. We find positions for any such who are competent, preferably doctors, educators, scientists and technicians, but also competent mechanics, construction workers and so forth. We operate a school in New York where we teach native languages and lingua franca such as Swahili and Songhai, in preparation for going to Africa. We raise our money largely from voluntary contributions, and largely from American Negroes although we have also had government grants, donations from foundations, and from individuals of other racial backgrounds. I suppose that sums it up."

Isobel smiled at them, returned to her chair to applause, probably due as much to her attractive appearance as her words.

Crawford said, "When we began this meeting we had an objection that it be held at all. I wonder if we might hear from that gentleman next?"

The white haired, ramrod erect, man stood next to his chair, not bothering to come to the head of the room. "You may indeed," he snapped. "I am Bishop Manning of the United Negro Missionaries, an organization attempting to accomplish the only truly important task that cries for completion on this largely godless continent. Accomplish this, and all else will fall into place."

Homer Crawford said, "I assume you refer to the conversion of the populace."

"I do indeed. And the work others do is meaningless until that has been accomplished. We are bringing religion to Africa, but not through white missionaries who in the past lived *off* the natives, but through Negro missionaries who live *with* them. I call upon all of you to give up your present occupations and come to our assistance."

Elmer Allan's voice was sarcastic. "These people need less superstition, not more."

The bishop spun on him. "I am not speaking of superstition, young man!"

Elmer Allen said. "All religions are superstitions, except one's own."

"And yours?" the Bishop barked.

"I'm an agnostic."

The bishop snorted his disgust and made his way to the door. There he turned and had his last word. "All you do is meaningless. I pray you, again, give it up and join in the Lord's work."

Homer Crawford nodded to him. "Thank you, Bishop Manning. I'm sure we will all consider your words." When the older man was gone, he looked out over the hall again. "Well, who is next?"

* * * * *

A thus far speechless member of the audience, seated in the first row, came to his feet. His face was serious and strained, the face of a man who pushes himself beyond the point of efficiency in the vain effort to accomplish more by expenditure of added hours.

He came to the front and said, "Since I'm possibly the only one here who also has objections to the reason for calling this meeting, I might as well have my say now." He half turned to Crawford, and continued. "Mr. Chairman, my name is Ralph Sandell and I'm an officer in the Sahara Afforestation Project, which, as you know, is also under the auspices of the Reunited Nations, though not having any other connection with your own organization."

Homer Crawford nodded. "We know of your efforts, but why do you object to calling this meeting?" He seemed mystified.

"Because, like Bishop Manning, I think your efforts misdirected. I think you are expending tremendous sums of money and the work of tens of thousands of good men and women, in directions which in the long run will hardly count."

Crawford leaned back in surprise, waiting for the other's reasoning.

Ralph Sandell obliged. "As the chairman pointed out, the problem of population explosion is a desperate one. Even today, with all the efforts of the Reunited Nations and of the individual countries involved in African aid, the population of this continent is growing at a pace that will soon outstrip the arable portion of the land. Save only Antarctica, Africa has the smallest arable percentage of land of any of the continents.

"The task of the Afforestation Project is to return the Sahara to the fertile land it once was. The job is a gargantuan one, but ultimately quite possible. Here in the south we are daming the Niger, running our irrigation projects farther and farther north. From the Mauritania area on the Atlantic we are pressing inland, using water purification and solar pumps to utilize the ocean. In the mountains of Morocco, the water available is being utilized more efficiently than ever before, and the sands being pushed back. We are all familiar with Egypt's ever increasingly successful efforts to exploit the Nile. In the Sahara itself, the new solar pumps are utilizing wells to an extent never dreamed of before. The oases are increasing in a geometric progression both in number and in size." He was caught up in his own enthusiasm.

Crawford said, interestedly, "It's a fascinating project. How long do you estimate it will be before the job is done?"

"Perhaps a century. As the trees go in by the tens of millions, there will be a change in climate. Forest begets moisture which in turn allows for more forest." He turned back to the audience as a whole. "In time we will be able to farm these million upon million of acres of fertile land. First it must go into forest, then we can return to field agriculture when climate and soil have been restored. This is our prime task! This is our basic need. I call upon all of you for your support and that of your organizations if you can bring their attention to the great need. The tasks you have set yourselves are meaningless in the face of this greater one. Let us be practical."

"Crazy man," Abe Baker said aloud. "Let's be practical and cut out all this jazz." The youthful New Yorker came to his feet. "First of all you just mentioned it was going to take a century, even though it's going like a geometric progression. Geometric progressions get going kind of slow, so I imagine that your scheme for making the Sahara fertile again, won't really be under full steam until more than halfway through that century of yours, and not really ripping ahead until, maybe two thirds of the way. Meanwhile, what's going to happen?"

"I beg your pardon!" Ralph Sandell said stiffly.

"That's all right," Abe Baker grinned at him. "The way they figure, population doubles every thirty years, under the present rate of increase. They figure there'll be three billion in the world by 1990, then by 2020 there would be six billions, and in 2050, twelve billions and twenty-four by the time your century was up. Old boy, I suggest the addition of a Sahara of rich agricultural land a century from now wouldn't be of much importance."

"Ridiculous!"

"You mean me, or you?" Abe grinned. "I once read an article by Donald Kingsbury. It's reprinted these days because it finished off the subject once and for all. He showed with mathematical rigor that given the present rate of human population increase, and an absolutely unlimited technology that allowed instantaneous intergalactical transportation and the ability to convert anything and everything into food, including interstellar dust, stars, planets, everything, it would take only seven thousand years to turn the total mass of the total universe into human flesh!"

The Sahara Afforestation official gaped at him.

The room rocked with laughter.

Irritated, Sandell snapped again, "Ridiculous!"

"It sure is, man," Abe grinned. "And the point is that the job is educating the people and freeing them to the point where they can develop their potentialities. Educate the African and he will see the same need that does the intelligent European, American, or Russian for that matter, to limit our population growth." He sat down again, and there was a scattering of applause and more laughter.

Sandell, still glowering, took his seat, too.

Homer Crawford, who'd been hard put not to join in the amusement, said, "Thanks to both of you for some interesting points. Now, who's next? Who else do we have here?"

* * * * *

When no one else answered, a smallish man, dressed in the costume of the Dogon, to the south, came to his feet and to the head of the room.

In a clipped British accent, he said, "Rex Donaldson, of Nassau, the Bahamas, in the service of Her Majesty's Government and the British Commonwealth. I have no team. Although our tasks are largely similar to those of the African Development Project, we field men of the African Department usually work as individuals. My native pseudonym is usually Dolo Anah."

He looked out over the rest. "I have no objection to such meetings as this. If nothing else, it gives chaps a bit of an opportunity to air grievances. I personally have several and may as well state them now. Among other things, it becomes increasingly clear that though some of the organizations represented here are supposedly of the Reunited Nations, actually they are dominated by Yankees. The Yankees are seeping in everywhere." He looked at Isobel. "Yes, such groups as your Africa for Africans Association has high flown slogans, but wherever you go, there go Yankee ideas, Yankee products, Yankee schools."

Homer Crawford's eyebrows went up. "What is your solution? The fact is that the United States has a hundred or more times the educated Negroes than any other country."

Donaldson said, doggedly, "The British Commonwealth has done more than any other element in bringing progress to Africa. She should be given the lead in developing the continent. A good first step would be to make the pound sterling legal tender throughout the continent. And, as things are now, there are some *seven hundred* different languages, not counting dialects. I suggest that English be made the lingua franca of—"

An excitable type, who had been first to join in the laughter at Sandell, now jumped to his feet. "*Un moment, Monsieur!* The French Community long dominated a far greater portion of Africa than the British flag flew over. Not to mention that it was the most advanced portion. If any language was to become the lingua franca of all Africa, French would be more suitable. Your ultimate purpose, Mr. Donaldson, is obvious. You and your Commonwealth African Department wish to dominate for political and economic reasons!"

He turned to the others and spread his hands in a Gallic gesture. "I introduce myself, Pierre Dupaine, operative of the African Affairs sector of the French Community."

"Ha!" Donaldson snorted. "Getting the French out of Africa was like pulling teeth. It took donkey's years. And now look. This chap wants to bring them back again."

Crawford was knuckling the table. "Gentlemen, Gentlemen," he yelled. He finally had them quieted.

Wryly he said, "May I ask if we have a representative from the government of the United States?"

A lithe, inordinately well dressed young man rose from his seat in the rear of the hall. "Frederic Ostrander, C.I.A.," he said. "I might as well tell you now, Crawford, and you other American citizens here, this meeting will not meet with the approval of the State Department."

Crawford's eyes went up. "How do you know?"

The C.I.A. man said evenly, "We've already had reports that this conference was going to be held. I might as well inform you that a protest is being made to the Sahara Division of the African Development Project."

Crawford said, "I suppose that is your privilege, sir. Now, in accord with the reason for this meeting, can you tell us why your organization is present in Africa and what it hopes to achieve?"

Ostrander looked at him testily. "Why not? There has been considerable infiltration of all of these African development organizations by subversive elements...."

"Oh, Brother," Cliff Jackson said.

"...And it is not the policy of the State Department to stand idly by while the Soviet Complex attempts to draw Africa from the ranks of the free world."

Elmer Allen said disgustedly, "Just what part of Africa would you really consider part of the Free World?"

The C.I.A. man stared at him coldly. "You know what I mean," he rapped. "And I might add, we are familiar with your record, Mr. Allen."

Homer Crawford said, "You've made a charge which is undoubtedly as unpalatable to many of those present as it is to me. Can you substantiate it? In my experience in the Sahara there is little, if any, following of the Soviet Complex."

An agreeing murmur went through the room.

Ostrander bit out, "Then who is subsidizing this El Hassan?"

Rex Donaldson, the British Commonwealth man, came to his feet. "That was a matter I was going to bring up before this meeting."

Homer Crawford, fully accompanied by Abe Baker and the rest of their team, even Elmer Allen, burst into uncontrolled laughter.

V

When Homer Crawford, Abe Baker, Kenny Ballalou, Elmer Allen and Bey-ag-Akhamouk had laughed themselves out, Frederic Ostrander, the C.I.A. operative stared at them in anger. "What's so funny?" he snapped.

From his seat in the middle of the hall, Pierre Dupaine, operative for the French Community, said worriedly, *"Messieurs*, this El Hassan is not amusing. I, too, have heard of him. His followers are evidently sweeping through the Sahara. Everywhere I hear of him."

There was confirming murmur throughout the rest of the gathering.

Still chuckling, Homer Crawford said, a hand held up for quiet, "Please, everyone. Pardon the amusement of my teammates and myself. You see, there is no such person as El Hassan."

"To the contrary!" Ostrander snapped.

"No, please," Crawford said, grinning ruefully. "You see, my team *invented* him, some time ago."

Ostrander could only stare, and for once his position was backed by everyone in the hall, Crawford's team excepted.

Crawford said doggedly, "It came about like this. These people need a hero. It's in their nomad tradition. They need a leader to follow. Given a leader, as history has often demonstrated, and the nomad will perform miracles. We wished to spread the program of the African Development Project. Such items as the need to unite, to break down the old boundaries of clan and tribe and even nation, the freeing of the slave and serf, the upgrading of women's position, the dropping of the veil and haik, the need to educate the youth, the desirability of taking jobs on the projects and to take up land on the new oases. But since we usually go about disguised as Enaden itinerant smiths, a poorly thought of caste, our ideas weren't worth much. So we invented El Hassan and everything we said we ascribed to him, this mysterious hero who was going to lead all North Africa to Utopia."

Jake Armstrong stood up and said, sheepishly, "I suppose that my team unknowingly added to this. We heard about this mysterious El Hassan and he seemed largely to be going in the same direction, and for the same reason-to give the rumors we were spreading weight-we ascribed the things we said to him."

Somebody farther back in the hall laughed and said, "So did I!"

Homer Crawford extended his hands in the direction of Ostrander, palms upward. "I'm sorry, sir. But there seems to be your mysterious subversive."

Angered, Ostrander snapped, "Then you admit that it was you, yourself, who have been spreading these subversive ideas?"

"Now, wait a minute," Crawford snapped in return. "I admit only to those slogans and ideas promulgated by the African Development Project. If any so-called subversive ideas have been ascribed to El Hassan, it has not been through my team. Frankly, I rather doubt that they have. These people aren't at any ethnic period where the program of the Soviet Complex would appeal. They're largely in a ritual-taboo tribal society and no one alleging any alliance whatsoever to Marx would contend that you can go from that primitive a culture to what the Soviets call communism."

"I'll take this up with my department chief," Ostrander said angrily. "You haven't heard the last of it, Crawford." He sat down abruptly.

Crawford looked out over the room. "Anybody else we haven't heard from?"

A middle-aged, heavy-set, Western dressed man came to his feet and cleared his throat. "Dr. Warren Harding Smythe, American Medical Relief. I assume that most of you have heard of us. An organization supported partially by government grant, partially by contributions by private citizens and institutions, as is that of Miss Isobel Cunningham's Africa for Africans Association." He added grimly, "But there the resemblance ends."

He looked at Homer Crawford. "I am to be added to the number not in favor of this conference. In fact, I am opposed to the presence of most of you here in Africa."

Crawford nodded. "You certainly have a right to your opinion, doctor. Will you elucidate?"

Dr. Smythe had worked his way to the front of the room, now he looked out over the assemblage defiantly. "I am not at all sure that the task most of you work at is a desirable one. As you know, my own organization is at work bringing medical care to Africa. We build hospitals, clinics, above all medical schools. Not a single one of our hospitals but is a school at the same time."

Abe Baker growled, "Everybody knows and values your work, Doc, but what's this bit about being opposed to ours?"

Smythe looked at him distastefully. "You people are seeking to destroy the culture of these people, and, overnight thrust them into the pressures of Twentieth Century existence. As a medical doctor, I do not think them capable of assimilating such rapid change and I fear for their mental health."

There was a prolonged silence.

Crawford said finally, "What is the alternative to the problems I presented in my summation of the situation that confronts the world due to the backward conditions of such areas as Africa?"

"I don't know, it isn't my field."

There was another silence.

Elmer Allen said finally, uncomfortably, "It *is* our field, Dr. Smythe."

Smythe turned to him, his face still holding its distaste. "I understand that the greater part of you are sociologists, political scientists and such. Frankly, ladies and gentlemen, I do not think of the social sciences as exact ones."

He looked around the room and added, deliberately, "In view of the condition of the world, I do not have a great deal of respect for the product of your efforts."

There was an uncomfortable stirring throughout the audience.

Clifford Jackson said unhappily, "We do what we must do, doctor. We do what we can."

Smythe eyed him. He said, "Some years ago I was impressed by a paragraph by a British writer named Huxley. So impressed that I copied it and have carried it with me. I'll read it now."

The heavy-set doctor took out his wallet, fumbled in it for a moment and finally brought forth an aged, many times folded, piece of yellowed paper.

He cleared his throat, then read:

"To the question quis custodiet custodes? —who will mount guard over our guardians, who will engineer the engineers? —the answer is a bland denial that they need any supervision. There seems to be a touching belief among certain Ph.Ds in sociology that Ph.Ds in sociology will never be corrupted by power. Like Sir Galahad's, their strength is the strength of ten because their heart is pure-and their heart is pure because they are scientists and have taken six thousand hours of social studies. Alas, high education is not necessarily a guarantee of higher virtue, or higher political wisdom."

The doctor finished and returned to his seat, his face still uncompromising.

* * * * *

Homer Crawford chuckled ruefully. "The point is well taken, I suppose. However, so was the one expressed by Mr. Jackson. We do what we must, and what we can." His eyes went over the assembly. "Is there any other group from which we haven't heard?"

When there was silence, he added, "No group from the Soviet Complex?"

Ostrander, the C.I.A. operative, snorted. "Do you think they would admit it?"

"Or from the Arab Union?" Crawford pursued. "Whether or not the Soviet Complex has agents in this part of Africa, we know that the Arab Union, backed by Islam everywhere, has. Frankly, we of the African Development Project seldom see eye to eye with them which results in considerable discussion at Reunited Nations meetings."

There was continued silence.

Elmer Allen came to his feet and looked at Ostrander, his face surly. "I am not an advocate of what the Soviets are currently calling communism, however, I think a point should be made here."

Ostrander stared back at him unblinkingly.

Allen snorted, "I know what you're thinking. When I was a student I signed a few peace petitions, that sort of thing. How-or why they bothered-the C.I.A. got hold of that information, I don't know, but as a Jamaican I am a bit ashamed of Her Majesty's Government. But all this is beside the point."

"What is your point, Elmer?" Crawford said. "You speak, of course, as an individual not as an employee of the Reunited Nations nor even as a member of my team."

"Our team," Elmer Allen reminded him. He frowned at his chief, as though surprised at Crawford's stand. But then he looked back at the rest. "I don't like the fact that the C.I.A. is present at all. I grow increasingly weary of the righteousness of the prying for what it calls subversion. The latest definition of subversive seems to be any chap who doesn't vote either Republican or Democrat in the States, or Conservative in England."

Ostrander grunted scorn.

Allen looked at him again. "So far as this job is concerned-and by the looks of things, most of us will be kept busy at it for the rest of our lives —I am not particularly favorable to the position of either side in this never-warming cold war between you and the Soviet Complex. I have suspected for some time that neither of you actually want an ending of it. For different reasons, possibly. So far as the States are concerned, I suspect an end of your fantastic military budgets would mean a collapse of your economy. So far as the Soviets are concerned, I suspect they use the continual *threat* of attack by the West to keep up their military and police powers and suppress the freedom of their people. Wasn't it an old adage of the Romans that if you feared trouble at home, stir up war abroad? At any rate, I'd like to have it on the record that I protest the Cold War being dragged into our work in Africa-by either side."

"All right, Elmer," Crawford said, "you're on record. Is that all?"

"That's all," Elmer Allen said. He sat down abruptly.

"Any comment, Mr. Ostrander?" Crawford said.

Ostrander grunted, "Fuzzy thinking." Didn't bother with anything more.

The chairman looked out over the hall. "Any further discussion, any motions?" He smiled and added, "Anything-period?"

Finally Jake Armstrong came to his feet. He said, "I don't agree with everything Mr. Allen just said; however, there was one item where I'll follow along. The fact that most of us will be busy at this job for the rest of our lives-if we stick. With this in mind, the fact that we have lots of time, I make the following proposal. This meeting was called to see if there was any prospect of we field workers co-operating on a field worker's level, if we could in any way help each other, avoid duplication of effort, that sort of thing. I suggest now that this meeting be adjourned and that all of us think it over and discuss it with the other teams, the other field workers in our respective organizations. I propose further that another meeting be held within the year and that meanwhile Mr. Crawford be elected chairman of the group until the next gathering, and that Miss Cunningham be elected secretary. We can all correspond with Mr. Crawford, until the time of the next meeting, giving him such suggestions as might come to us. When he sees fit to call the next meeting, undoubtedly he will have some concrete proposals to put before us."

Isobel said, *sotto voce*, "Secretaries invariably do all the work, why is it that men always nominate a woman for the job?"

Jake grinned at her, "I'll never tell." He sat down.

"I'll make that a motion," Rex Donaldson clipped out.

"Second," someone else called.

Homer Crawford said, "All in favor?"

Those in favor predominated considerably.

They broke up into small groups for a time, debating it out, and then most left for various places for lunch.

Homer Crawford, separated from the other members of his team, in the animated discussions that went on about him, finally left the fascinating subject of what had happened to the Cuban group in Sudan, and who had done it, and went looking for his own lunch.

He strolled down the sand-blown street in the general direction of the smaller market, in the center of Timbuktu, passing the aged, wind corroded house which had once sheltered Major Alexander Gordon Laing, first white man to reach the forbidden city in the year 1826. Laing remained only three days before being murdered by the Tuareg who controlled the town at that time. There was a plaque on the door revealing those basic facts. Crawford had read elsewhere that the city was not captured until 1893 by a Major Joffre, later to become a Marshal of France and a prominent Allied leader in the First World War.

By chance he met Isobel in front of the large community butcher shop, still operated in the old tradition by the local Gabibi and Fulbe, formerly Songhoi serfs. He knew of a Syrian operated restaurant nearby, and since she hadn't eaten either they made their way there.

The menu was limited largely to local products. Timbuktu was still remote enough to make transportation of frozen foodstuffs exorbitant. While they looked at the bill of fare he told her a story about his first trip to the city some years ago while he was still a student.

He had visited the local American missionary and had dinner with the family in their home. They had canned plums for desert and Homer had politely commented upon their quality. The missionary had said that they should be good, he estimated the quart jar to be worth something like one hundred dollars. It seems that some kindly old lady in Iowa, figuring that missionaries in such places as Timbuktu must be in dire need of her State Fair prize winning canned plums, shipped off a box of twelve quarts to missionary headquarters in New York. At that time, France still owned French Sudan, so it was necessary for the plums to be sent to Paris, and thence, eventually to Dakar. At Dakar they were shipped through Senegal to Bamako by narrow gauge railroad which ran periodically. In Bamako they had to wait for an end to the rainy season so roads would be passable. By this time, a few of the jars had fermented and blown up, and a few others had been pilfered. When the roads were dry enough, a desert freight truck took the plums to Mopti, on the Niger River where they waited again until the river was high enough that a tug pulling barges could navigate, by slow stages, down to Kabara. By this time, one or two jars had been broken by inexpert handling and more pilfered. In Kabara they were packed onto a camel and taken to Timbuktu and delivered to the missionary. Total time elapsed since leaving Iowa? Two years. Total number of jars that got through? One.

Isobel looked at Homer Crawford when he finished the story, and laughed. "Why in the world didn't that missionary society refuse the old lady's gift?"

He laughed in return and shrugged. "They couldn't. She might get into a huff and not mention them in her will. Missionary societies can't afford to discourage gifts."

She made her selection from the menu, and told the waiter in French, and then settled back. She resumed the conversation. "The cost of maintaining a missionary in this sort of country must have been fantastic."

"Um-m-m," Crawford growled. "I sometimes wonder how many millions upon millions of dollars, pounds and francs have been plowed into this continent on such projects. This particular missionary wasn't a medical man and didn't even run a school and in the six years he was here didn't make a single convert."

Isobel said, "Which brings us to our own pet projects. Homer—I can call you Homer, I suppose, being your brand new secretary...."

He grinned at her. "I'll make that concession."

"...What's your own dream?"

He broke some bread, automatically doing it with his left hand, as prescribed in the Koran. They both noticed it, and both laughed.

"I'm conditioned," he said.

"Me, too," Isobel admitted. "It's all I can do to use a knife and fork."

He went back to her question, scowling. "My dream? I don't know. Right now I feel a little depressed about it all. When Elmer Allen spoke about spending the rest of our lives on this job, I suddenly realized that was about it. And, you know" —he looked up at her —"I don't particularly like Africa. I'm an American."

She looked at him oddly. "Then why stay here?"

"Because there's so much that needs to be done."

"Yes, you're right and what Cliff Jackson said to the doctor was correct, too. We all do what we must do and what we can do."

"Well, that brings us back to your question. What is my own dream? I'm afraid I'm too far along in life to acquire new ones, and my basic dream is an American one."

"And that is —?" Isobel prompted.

He shrugged again, slightly uncomfortable under the scrutiny of this pretty girl. "I'm a sociologist, Isobel. I suppose I seek Utopia."

She frowned at him as though disappointed. "Is Utopia possible?"

"No, but there is always the search for it. It's a goal that recedes as you approach, which is as it should be. Heaven help mankind if we ever achieve it; we'll be through because there will be no place to go, and man needs to strive."

They had finished their soup and the entree had arrived. Isobel picked at it, her ordinarily smooth forehead wrinkled. "The way I see it, Utopia is not heaven. Heaven is perfect, but Utopia is an engineering optimum, the best-possible-human-techniques. Therefore we will not have *perfect* justice in Utopia, nor will *everyone* get the exactly proper treatment. We design for optimum-not perfection. But granting this, then attainment is possible."

She took a bite of the food before going on thoughtfully. "In fact, I wonder if, during man's history, he hasn't obtained his Utopias from time to time. Have you ever heard the adage that any form of government works fine and produces a Utopia provided it is managed by wise, benevolent and competent rulers?" She laughed and said mischievously, "Both Heaven and Hell are traditionally absolute monarchies-despotisms. The form of government evidently makes no difference, it's who runs it that determines."

Crawford was shaking his head. "I've heard the adage but I don't accept it. Under certain socio-economic conditions the best of men, and the wisest, could do little if they had the wrong form of government. Suppose, for instance, you had a government which was a military-theocracy which is more or less what existed in Mexico at the time of the Cortez conquest. Can you imagine such a government working efficiently if the socio-economic system had progressed to the point where there were no longer wars and where practically everyone were atheists, or, at least, agnostics?"

She had to laugh at his ludicrous example. "That's a rather silly situation, isn't it? Such wise, benevolent men, would change the governmental system."

Crawford pushed his point. "Not necessarily. Here's a better example. Immediately following the American Revolution, some of the best, wisest and most competent men the political world has ever seen were at the head of the government of Virginia. Such men as Jefferson, Madison, Monroe, Washington. Their society was based on chattel slavery and they built a Utopia *for themselves* but certainly not for the slaves who out-numbered them. Not that they weren't kindly and good men. A man of Jefferson's caliber, I am sure, would have done anything in the world for those darkies of his-except get off their backs. Except to grant them the liberty and the right to pursue happiness that he demanded for himself. He was blinded by self interest, and the interests of his class."

"Perhaps they didn't want liberty," Isobel mused. "Slavery isn't necessarily an unhappy life."

"I never thought it was. And I'm the first to admit that at a certain stage in the evolution of society, it was absolutely necessary. If society was to progress, then there had to be a class that was freed from daily drudgery of the type forced on primitive man if he was to survive. They needed the leisure time to study, to develop, to invent. With the products of their studies, they were able to advance all society. However, so long as slavery is maintained, be it necessary or not, you have no Utopia. There is no Utopia so long as one man denies another his liberty be it under chattel slavery, feudalism, or whatever."

Isobel said dryly, "I see why you say your Utopia will never be reached, that it continually recedes."

He laughed, ruefully. "Don't misunderstand. I think that particular goal can and will be reached. My point was that by the time we reach it, there will be a new goal."

* * * * *

The girl, finished with her main dish, sat back in her chair, and looked at him from the side of her eyes, as though wondering whether or not he could take what she was about to say in the right way. She said, slowly, "You know, with possibly a few exceptions, you can't enslave a man if he doesn't want to be a slave. For instance, the white man was never able to enslave the Amerind; he died before he would become a slave. The majority of Jefferson's slaves *wanted to be slaves*. If there were those among them that had the ability to revolt against slave psychology, a Jefferson would quickly promote such. A valuable human being will be treated in a manner proportionate to his value. A wise, competent, trustworthy slave became the major domo of the master's estate-with privileges and authority actually greater than that of free employees of the master."

Crawford thought about that for a moment. "I'll take that," he said. "What's the point you're trying to make?"

"I, too, was set a-thinking by some of the things said at the meeting, Homer. In particular, what Dr. Smythe had to say. Homer, are we sure these people *want* the things we are trying to give them?"

He looked at her uncomfortably. "No they don't," he said bluntly. "Otherwise we wouldn't be here, either your AFAA or my African Development Project. We utilize persuasion, skull-duggery, and even force to subvert their institutions, to destroy their present culture. Yes. I've known this a long time."

"Then how do you justify your being here?"

He grinned sourly. "Let's put it this way. Take the new government in Egypt. They send the army into some of the small back-country towns with bayoneted rifles, and orders to use them if necessary. The villagers are forced to poison their ancient village wells-one of the highest of imaginable crimes in such country, imposed on them ruthlessly. Then they are forced to dig new ones in new places that are not intimately entangled with their own sewage drainage. Naturally they hate the government. In other towns, the army has gone in and, at gun point, forced the parents to give up their children, taken the children away in trucks and 'imprisoned' them in schools. Look, back in the States we have trouble with the Amish, who don't want their children to be taught modern ways. What sort of reaction do you think the tradition-ritual-tabu-tribesmen of the six thousand year old Egyptian culture have to having modern education imposed on their children?"

Isobel was frowning at him.

Crawford wound it up. "That's the position we're in. That's what we're doing. Giving them things they need, in spite of the fact they don't want them."

"But *why*?"

He said, "You know the answer to that as well as I do. It's like giving medical care to Typhoid Mary, in spite of the fact that she didn't want it and didn't believe such things as typhoid microbes existed. We had to protect the community against her. In the world today, such backward areas as Africa are potential volcanoes. We've got to deal with them before they erupt."

The waiter came with the bill and Homer took it.

Isobel said, "Let's go Dutch on that."

He grinned at her. "Consider it a donation to the AFAA."

Out on the street again, they walked slowly in the direction of the old administration buildings where both had left their means of transportation.

Isobel, who was frowning thoughtfully, evidently over the things that had been said, said, "Let's go this way. I'd like to see the old Great Mosque, in the Dyingerey Ber section of town. It's always fascinated me."

Crawford said, looking at her and appreciating her attractiveness, all over again, "You know Timbuktu quite well, don't you?"

"I've just finished a job down in Kabara, and it's only a few miles away."

"Just what sort of thing do you do?"

She shrugged and made a moue. "Our little team concentrates on breaking down the traditional position of women in these cultures. To get them to drop the veil, go to school. That sort of thing. It's a long story and —"

Homer Crawford suddenly and violently pushed her to the side and to the ground and at the same time dropped himself and rolled frantically to the shelter of an adobe wall which had once been part of a house but now was little more than waist high.

"Down!" he yelled at her.

She bug-eyed him as though he had gone suddenly mad.

There was a heavy, stub-nosed gun suddenly in his hand. He squirmed forward on elbows and belly, until he reached the corner.

"What's the matter?" she blurted.

He said grimly, "See those three holes in the wall above you?"

She looked up, startled.

He said, grimly, "They weren't there a moment ago."

What he was saying, dawned upon her. "But ... but I heard no shots."

He cautiously peered around the wall, and was rewarded with a puff of sand inches from his face. He pulled his head back and his lips thinned over his teeth. He said to her, "Efficiently silenced guns have been around for quite a spell. Whoever that is, is up there in the mosque. Listen, beat your way around by the back streets and see if you can find the members of my team, especially Abe Baker or Bey-ag-Akhamouk. Tell them what happened and that I think I've got the guy pinned down. That mosque is too much out in the open for him to get away without my seeing him."

"But ... but who in the world would want to shoot you, Homer?"

"Search me," he growled. "My team has never operated in this immediate area."

"But then, it must be someone who was at the meeting."

VI

"That is was," Homer said grimly. "Now, go see if you can find my lads, will you? This joker is going to fall right into our laps. It's going to be interesting to find out who hates the idea of African development so much that they're willing to commit assassination."

But it didn't work out that way.

Isobel found the other teammates one by one, and they came hurrying up from different directions to the support of their chief. They had been a team for years and operating as they did and where they did, each man survived only by selfless co-operation with all the others. In action, they operated like a single unit, their ability to co-operate almost as though they had telepathic communication.

From where he lay, Homer Crawford could see Bey-ag-Akhamouk, Tommy-Noiseless in hands, snake in from the left, running low and reaching a vantage point from which he could cover one flank of the ancient adobe mosque. Homer waved to him and Bey made motions to indicate that one of the others was coming in from the other side.

Homer waited for a few more minutes, then waved to Bey to cover him. The streets were empty at this time of midday when the Sahara sun drove the town's occupants into the coolness of dark two-foot-thick walled houses. It was as though they were operating in a ghost town. Homer came to his feet and handgun in fist made a dash for the front entrance.

Bey's light automatic *flic flic flicked* its excitement and dust and dirt enveloped the wall facing Crawford. Homer reached the doorway, stood there for a full two minutes while he caught his breath. From the side of his eye he could see Elmer Allen, his excellent teeth bared as always when the Jamaican went into action, come running up to the right in that half crouch men automatically go into in combat, instinctively presenting as small a target as possible. He was evidently heading for a side door or window.

The object now was to refrain from killing the sniper. The important thing was to be able to question him. Perhaps here was the answer to the massacre of the Cubans. Homer took another deep breath, smashed the door open with a heavy shoulder and dashed inward and immediately to one side. At the same moment, Abe Baker, Tommy-Noiseless in hand, came in from the rear door, his eyes darting around trying to pierce the gloom of the unlighted building.

Elmer Allen erupted through a window, rolled over on the floor and came to rest, his gun trained.

"Where is he?" Abe snapped.

Homer motioned with his head. "Must be up in the remains of the minaret."

Abe got to the creaking, age-old stairway first. In cleaning out a hostile building, the idea is to move fast and keep on the move. Stop, and you present a target.

But there was no one in the minaret.

"Got away," Homer growled. His face was puzzled. "I felt sure we'd have him."

Bey-ag-Akhamouk entered. He grunted his disappointment. "What happened, anyway? That girl Isobel said a sniper took some shots at you and you figure it must've been somebody at the meeting."

"Somebody at the meeting?" Abe said blankly. "What kind of jazz is that? You flipping, man?"

Homer looked at him strangely.

"Who else could it be, Abe? We've never operated this far south. None of the inhabitants in this area even know us, and it certainly couldn't have been an attempt at robbery."

"There were some cats at that meeting didn't appreciate our ideas, man, but I can't see that old preacher or Doc Smythe trying to put the slug on you."

Kenny Ballalou came in on the double, gun in hand, his face anxious.

Abe said sarcastically, "Man, we'd all be dead if we had to wait on you."

"That girl Isobel. She said somebody took a shot at the chief."

Homer explained it, sourly. A sniper had taken a few shots at him, then managed to get away.

Isobel entered, breathless, followed by Jake Armstrong.

Abe grunted, "Let's hold another convention. This is like old home town week."

Her eyes went from one of them to the other. "You're not hurt?"

"Nobody hurt, but the cat did all the shooting got away," Abe said unhappily.

Jake said, and his voice was worried, "Isobel told me what happened. It sounds insane."

They discussed it for a while and got exactly nowhere. Their conversation was interrupted by a clicking at Homer Crawford's wrist. He looked down at the tiny portable radio.

"Excuse me for a moment," he said to the others and went off a dozen steps or so to the side. They looked after him.

Elmer Allen said sourly, "Another assignment. What we need is a union."

Abe adopted the idea. "Man! Time and a half for overtime."

"With a special cost of living clause —" Kenny Ballalou added.

"And housing and dependents allotment!" Abe crowed.

They all looked at him.

Bey tried to imitate the other's beatnik patter. "Like, you got any dependents, man?"

Abe made a mark in the sand on the mosque's floor with the toe of his shoe, like a schoolboy up before the principal for an infraction of rules, and registered embarrassment. "Well, there's that cute little Tuareg girl up north."

"Ha!" Isobel said. "And all these years you've been leading me on."

Homer Crawford returned and his face was serious. "That does it," he muttered disgustedly. "The fat's in the fire."

"Like, what's up, man?"

Crawford looked at his right-hand man. "There are demonstrations in Mopti. Riots."

"Mopti?" Jake Armstrong said, surprised. "Our team was working there just a couple of months ago. I thought everything was going fine in Mopti."

"They're going fine, all right," Crawford growled. "So well, that the local populace wants to speed up even faster."

They were all looking their puzzlement at him.

"The demonstrations are in favor of El Hassan."

Their faces turned blank. Crawford's eyes swept his teammates. "Our instructions are to get down there and do what we can to restore order. Come on, let's go. I'm going to have to see if I can arrange some transportation. It'd take us two days to get there in our outfits."

Jake Armstrong said, "Wait a minute, Homer. My team was heading back for Dakar for a rest and new assignments. We'd be passing Mopti anyway. How many of you are there, five? If you don't haul too much luggage with you; we could give you a lift."

"Great," Homer told him. "We'll take you up on that. Abe, Elmer, let's get going. We'll have to repack. Bey, Kenny, see about finding some place we can leave the lorries until we come back. This job shouldn't take more than a few days at most."

"Huh," Abe said. "I hope you got plans, man. How do you go about stopping demonstrations in favor of a legend you created yourself?"

* * * * *

Mopti, also on the Niger, lies approximately three hundred kilometers to the south and slightly west of Timbuktu, as the bird flies. However, one does not travel as the bird flies in the Niger bend. Not even when one goes by aircraft. A forced landing in the endless swamps, bogs, shallow lakes and river tributaries which make up the Niger at this point, would be suicidal. The whole area is more like the Florida Everglades than a river, and a rescue team would be hard put to find your wreckage. There are no roads, no railroads. Traffic follows the well marked navigational route of the main channel.

Homer Crawford had been sitting quietly next to Cliff Jackson who was piloting. Isobel and Jake Armstrong were immediately behind them and Abe and the rest of Crawford's team took up the remainder of the aircraft's eight seats. Abe was regaling the others with his customary chaff.

Out of a clear sky, Crawford said bitterly, "Has it occurred to any of you that what we're doing here in North Africa is committing genocide?"

The others stared at him, taken aback. Isobel said, "I beg your pardon?"

"Genocide," Crawford said bitterly. "We're doing here much what the white men did when they cleared the Amerinds from the plains, the mountains and forests of North America."

Isobel, Cliff and Jake frowned their puzzlement. Abe said, "Man, you just don't make sense. And, among other things, there're more Indians in the United States than there was when Columbus landed."

Crawford shook his head. "No. They're a different people. Those cultures that inhabited the United States when the first white men came, are gone." He shook his head as though soured by his thoughts. "Take the Sioux. They had a way of life based on the buffalo. So the whites deliberately exterminated the buffalo. It made the plains Indians' culture impossible. A culture based on buffalo herds cannot exist if there are no buffalo."

"I keep telling you, man, there's more Sioux now than there were then."

Crawford still shook his head. "But they're a different people, a different race, a different culture. A mere fraction, say ten per cent, of the original Sioux, might have adapted to the new life. The others beat their heads out against the new ways. They fought-the Sitting Bull wars took place after the buffalo were already gone-they drank themselves to death on the white man's firewater, they committed suicide; in a dozen different ways they called it quits. Those that survived, the ten per cent, were the exceptions. They were able to adapt. They had a built-in genetically-conferred self discipline enough to face the new problems. Possibly eighty per cent of their children couldn't face the new problems either and they in turn went under. But by now, a hundred years later, the majority of the Sioux nation have probably adapted. But, you see, the point I'm trying to make? They're not the *real* Sioux, the original Sioux; they're a new breed. The plains living, buffalo based culture, Sioux are all dead. The white men killed them."

Jake Armstrong was scowling. "I get your point, but what has it to do with our work here in North Africa?"

"We're doing the same thing to the Tuareg, the Teda and the Chaambra, and most of the others in the area in which we operate. The type of human psychology that's based on the nomad life can't endure settled community living. Wipe out the nomad way of life and these human beings must die."

Abe said, unusually thoughtful, "I see what you mean, man. *Fish gotta swim, bird gotta fly* —and nomad gotta roam. He flips if he doesn't."

Homer Crawford pursued it. "Sure, there'll be Tuareg afterward ... but all descended from the fraction of deviant Tuareg who were so abnormal-speaking from the Tuareg viewpoint-that they liked settled community life." He rubbed a hand along his jawbone, unhappily. "Put it this way. Think of them as a tribe of genetic claustrophobes. No matter what a claustrophobe promises, he can't work in a mine. He has no choice but to break his promise and escape ... or kill himself trying."

Isobel was staring at him. "What you say, is disturbing, Homer. I didn't come to Africa to destroy a people."

He looked back at her, oddly. "None of us did."

Cliff said from behind the aircraft's controls, "If you believe what you're saying, how do you justify being here yourself?"

"I don't know," Crawford said unhappily. "I don't know what started me on this kick, but I seem to have been doing more inner searching this past week or so than I have in the past couple of decades. And I don't seem to come up with much in the way of answers."

"Well, man," Abe said. "If you find any, let us know."

Jake said, his voice warm, "Look Homer, don't beat yourself about this. What you say figures, but you've got to take it from this angle. The plains Indians had to go. The world is developing too fast for a few thousand people to tie up millions of acres of some of the most fertile farm land anywhere, because they needed it for their game-the buffalo-to run on."

"Um-m-m," Homer said, his voice lacking conviction.

"Maybe it's unfortunate the *way* it was done. The story of the American's dealing with the Amerind isn't a pretty one, and usually comfortably ignored when we pat ourselves on the back these days and tell ourselves what a noble, honest, generous and peace loving people we are. But it did have to be done, and the job we're doing in North Africa has to be done, too."

Crawford said softly, "And sometimes it isn't very pretty either."

* * * * *

Mopti as a town had grown. Once a small river port city of about five thousand population, it had been a river and caravan crossroads somewhat similar to Timbuktu, and noted in particular for its spice market and its Great Mosque, probably the largest building of worship ever made of mud. Plastered newly at least twice a year with fresh adobe, at a distance of only a few hundred feet the Great Mosque, in the middle of the day and in the glare of the Sudanese sun, looks as though made of gold. From the air it is more attractive than the grandest Gothic cathedrals of Europe.

Isobel pointed. "There, the Great Mosque."

Elmer Allen said, "Yes, and there. See those mobs?" He looked at Homer Crawford and said sourly, "Let's try and remember who it was who first thought of the El Hassan idea. Then we can blame it on him."

Kenny Ballalou grumbled, "We all thought about it. Remember, we pulled into Tessalit and found that prehistoric refrigerator that worked on kerosene and there were a couple of dozen quarts of Norwegian beer, of all things, in it."

"And we bought them all," Abe recalled happily. "Man, we hung one on."

Homer Crawford said to Cliff, "The Mopti airport is about twelve miles over to the east of the town."

"Yeah, I know. Been here before," Cliff said. He called back to Ballalou, "And then what happened?"

"We took the beer out into the desert and sat on a big dune. You can just begin to see the Southern Cross from there. Hangs right on the horizon. Beautiful."

Bey said, "I've never heard Kenny wax poetic before. I don't know which sounds more lyrical, though, that cold beer or the Southern Cross."

Kenny said, "Anyway, that's when El Hassan was dreamed up. We kicked the idea around until the beer was all gone. And when we awoke in the morning, complete with hangover, we had the gimmick which we hung all our propaganda on."

"El Hassan is turning out to be a hangover all right," Elmer Allen grunted, choosing to misinterpret his teammate's words. He peered down below. "And there the poor blokes are, rioting in favor of the product of those beer bottles."

"It was crazy beer, man," Abe protested. "Real crazy."

Homer Crawford said, "I wish headquarters had more information to give us on this. All they said was there were demonstrations in favor of El Hassan and they were afraid if things went too far that some of the hard work that's been done here the past ten years might dissolve in the excitement; Dogon, Mosse, Tellum, Sonrai start fighting among each other."

Jake Armstrong said, "That's not my big worry. I'm afraid some ambitious lad will come along and supply what these people evidently want."

"How's that?" Cliff said.

"They want a leader. Someone to come out of the wilderness and lead them to the promised land." The older man grumbled sourly. "All your life you figure you're in favor of democracy.

You devote your career to expanding it. Then you come to a place like North Africa. You're just kidding yourself. Democracy is meaningless here. They haven't got to the point where they can conceive of it."

"And —" Elmer Allen prodded.

Jake Armstrong shrugged. "When it comes to governments and social institutions people usually come up with what they want, sooner or later. If those mobs down there want a leader, they'll probably wind up with one." He grunted deprecation. "And then probably we'll be able to say, Heaven help them."

Isobel puckered her lips. "A leader isn't necessarily a misleader, Jake."

"Perhaps not necessarily," he said. "However, it's an indication of how far back these people are, how much work we've still got to do, when that's what they're seeking."

"Well, I'm landing," Cliff said. "The airport looks free of any kind of manifestations."

"That's a good word," Abe said. "Manifestations. Like, I'll have to remember that one. Man's been to school and all that jazz."

Cliff grinned at him. "Where'd you like to get socked, beatnik?"

"About two feet above my head," Abe said earnestly.

* * * * *

The aircraft had hardly come to a halt before Homer Crawford clipped out, "All right, boys, time's a wasting. Bey, you and Kenny get over to those administration buildings and scare us up some transportation. Use no more pressure than you have to. Abe, you and Elmer start getting our equipment out of the luggage —"

Jake Armstrong said suddenly, "Look here, Homer, do you need any help?"

Crawford looked at him questioningly.

Jake said, "Isobel, Cliff, what do you think?"

Isobel said quickly, "I'm game. I don't know what they'll say back at AFAA headquarters, though. Our co-operating with a Sahara Development Project team."

Cliff scowled. "I don't know. Frankly, I took this job purely for the dough, and as outlined it didn't include getting roughed up in some riot that doesn't actually concern the job."

"Oh, come along, Cliff," Isobel urged. "It'll give you some experience you don't know when you'll be able to use."

He shrugged his acceptance, grudgingly.

Jake Armstrong looked back at Homer Crawford. "If you need us, we're available."

"Thanks," Crawford said briefly, and turned off the unhappy stare he'd been giving Cliff. "We can use all the manpower we can get. You people ever worked with mobs before?"

Bey and Kenny climbed from the plane and made their way at a trot toward the airport's administration buildings. Abe and Elmer climbed out, too, and opened the baggage compartment in the rear of the aircraft.

"Well, no," Jake Armstrong said.

"It's quite a technique. Mostly you have to play it by ear, because nothing is so changeable as the temper of a mob. Always keep in mind that to begin with, at least, only a small fraction of the crowd is really involved in what's going on. Possibly only one out of ten is interested in the issue. The rest start off, at least, as idle observers, watching the fun. That's one of the first things you've got to control. Don't let the innocent bystanders become excited and get into the spirit of it all. Once they do, then you've got a mess on your hands."

Isobel, Jake and Cliff listened to him in fascination.

Cliff said uncomfortably, "Well, what do we do to get the whole thing back to tranquillity? What I mean is, how do we end these demonstrations?"

"We bore them to tears," Homer growled.

They looked at him blankly.

"We assume leadership of the whole thing and put up speakers."

Jake protested, "You sound as though you're sustaining not placating it."

"We put up speakers and they speak and speak, and speak. It's almost like a fillibuster. You don't say anything particularly interesting, and certainly nothing exciting. You agree with the basic feeling of the demonstrating mob, certainly you say nothing to antagonize them. In this case we speak in favor of El Hassan and his great, and noble, and inspiring, and so on and so forth, teachings. We speak in not too loud a voice, so that those in the rear have a hard time hearing, if they can hear at all."

Cliff said worriedly, "Suppose some of the hotheads get tired of this and try to take over?"

Homer said evenly, "We have a couple of bully boys in the crowd to take care of them."

Jake twisted his mouth, in objection. "Might that not strike the spark that would start up violence?"

Homer Crawford grinned and began climbing out of the plane. "Not with the weapons we use."

"Weapons!" Isobel snapped. "Do you intend to use weapons on those poor people? Why, it was you yourself, you and your team, who started this whole El Hassan movement. I'm shocked. I've heard about your reputation, you and the Sahara Development Project teams. Your ruthlessness —"

Crawford chuckled ruefully and held up a hand to stem the tide. "Hold it, hold it," he said. "These are special weapons, and, after all, we've got to keep those crowds together long enough to bore them to the point where they go home."

Abe came up with an armful of what looked something like tent-poles. "The quarterstaffs, eh, Homer?"

"Um-m-m," Crawford said. "Under the circumstances."

"Quarterstaffs?" Cliff Jackson ejaculated.

Abe grinned at him. "Man, just call them pilgrim's staffs. The least obnoxious looking weapon in the world." He looked at Cliff and Jake. "You two cats been checked out on quarterstaffs?"

Jake said, "The more I talk to you people, the less I seem to understand what's going on. Aren't quarterstaffs what, well, Robin Hood and his Merry Men used to fight with?"

"That's right," Homer said. He took one from Abe and grasping it expertly with two hands whirled it about, getting its balance. Then suddenly, he drooped, leaning on it as a staff. His face expressed weariness. His youth and virility seemed to drop away and suddenly he was an aged religious pilgrim as seen throughout the Moslem world.

"I'll be damned," Cliff blurted. "Oop, sorry Isobel."

"I'll be damned, too," Isobel said. "What in the world can you do with that, Homer? I was thinking in terms of you mowing those people down with machine guns or something."

Crawford stood erect again laughingly, and demonstrated. "It's probably the most efficient handweapon ever devised. The weapon of the British yeoman. With one of these you can disarm a swordsman in a matter of seconds. A good man with a quarterstaff can unhorse a knight in armor and batter him to death, in a minute or so. The only other handweapon capable of countering it is another quarterstaff. Watch this, with the favorable two-hand leverage the ends of the staff can be made to move at invisibly high speeds."

Bey and Kenny drove up in an aged wheeled truck and Abe and Elmer began loading equipment.

Crawford looked at Bey who said apologetically, "I had to liberate it. Didn't have time for all the dickering the guy wanted to go through."

Crawford grunted and looked at Isobel. "Those European clothes won't do. We've got some spare things along. You can improvise. Men and women's clothes don't differ that much around here."

"I'll make out all right," Isobel said. "I can change in the plane."

"Hey, Isobel," Abe called out. "Why not dress up like one of these Dogon babes?"

"Some chance," Isobel hissed menacingly at him. "A strip tease you want, yet. You'll see me in a haik and like it, wise guy."

"Shucks," Abe grinned.

Crawford looked critically at the clothing of Jake and Cliff. "I suppose you'll do in western stuff," he said. "After all, this El Hassan is supposed to be the voice of the future. A lot of his potential followers will already be wearing shirts and pants. Don't look *too* civilized, though."

When Isobel returned, Crawford briefed his seven followers. They were to operate in teams of two. One of his men, complete with quarterstaff would accompany each of the others. Abe with Jake, Bey with Cliff, and he'd be with Isobel. Elmer and Kenny would be the other twosome, and, both armed with quarterstaffs would be troubleshooters.

"We're playing it off the cuff," he said. "Do what comes naturally to get this thing under control. If you run into each other, co-operate, of course. If there's trouble, use your wrist radios." He looked at Abe and Bey. "I know you two are packing guns underneath those *gandouras*. I hope you know enough not to use them."

Abe and Bey looked innocent.

Homer turned and led the way into the truck. "O.K., let's get going."

VII

Driving into town over the dusty, pocked road, Homer gave the newcomers to his group more background on the care and control of the genus *mob*. He was obviously speaking through considerable experience.

"Using these quarterstaffs brings to mind some of the other supposedly innoxious devices used by police authorities in controlling unruly demonstrations," he said. "Some of them are beauties. For instance, I was in Tangier when the Moroccans put on their revolution against the French and for the return of the Sultan. The rumor went through town that the mob was going to storm the French Consulate the next day. During the night, the French brought in elements of the Foreign Legion and entrenched the consulate grounds. But their commander had another problem. Journalists were all over town and so were tourists. Tangier was still supposedly an international zone and the French were in no position to slaughter the citizens. So they brought in some special equipment. One item was a vehicle that looked quite a bit like a gasoline truck, but was filled with water and armored against thrown cobblestones and such. On the roof of the cabin was what looked something like a fifty caliber but which was actually a hose which shot water at terrific pressure. When the mob came, the French unlimbered this vehicle and all the journalists could say was that the mob was dispersed by squirting water on it, which doesn't sound too bad after all."

Isobel said, "Well, certainly that's preferable to firing on them."

Homer looked at her oddly. "Possibly. However, I was standing next to the Moorish boy who was cut entirely in half by the pressure spray of water."

The expression on the girl's face sickened.

Homer said, "They had another interesting device for dispersing mobs. It was a noise bomb. The French set off several."

"A noise bomb?" Cliff said. "I don't get it."

"They make a tremendous noise, but do nothing else. However, members of the mob who aren't really too interested in the whole thing-just sort of along for the fun-figure that things are getting earnest and that the troops are shelling them. So they remember some business they had elsewhere and take off."

Isobel said suddenly, "You like this sort of work, don't you?"

Elmer Allen grunted bitterly.

"No," Homer Crawford said flatly. "I don't. But I like the goal."

"And the end justifies the means?"

Homer Crawford said slowly, "I've never answered that to my own satisfaction. But I'll say this. I've never met a person, no matter how idealistic, no matter how much he played lip service to the contention that the ends do not justify the means, who did not himself use the means he found available to reach the ends he believed correct. It seems to be a matter of each man feeling the teaching applies to everyone else, but that he is free to utilize any means to achieve his own noble ends."

"Man, all that jazz is too much for me," Abe said.

They were entering the outskirts of Mopti. Small groups of obviously excited Africans of various tribal groups, were heading for the center of town.

"Abe, Jake," Crawford said. "We'll drop you here. Mingle around. We'll hold the big meeting in front of the Great Mosque in an hour or so."

"Crazy," Abe said, dropping off the back of the truck which Kenny Ballalou, who was driving, brought almost to a complete stop. The older Jake followed him.

The rest went on a quarter of a mile and dropped Bey and Cliff.

Homer said to Kenny, "Park the truck somewhere near the spice market. Preferably inside some building, if you can. For all we know, they're already turning over vehicles and burning them."

Crawford and Isobel dropped off near the pottery market, on the banks of the Niger. The milling throngs here were largely women. Elements of half a dozen tribes and races were represented.

Homer Crawford stood a moment. He ran a hand back over his short hair and looked at her. "I don't know," he muttered. "Now I'm sorry we brought you along." He leaned on his staff and looked at her worriedly. "You're not very ... ah, husky, are you?"

She laughed at him. "Get about your business, sir knight. I spent nearly two weeks living with these people once. I know dozens of them by name. Watch this cat operate, as Abe would say."

She darted to one of the over-turned pirogues which had been dragged up on the bank from the river, and climbed atop it. She held her hands high and began a stream of what was gibberish to Crawford who didn't understand Wolof, the Senegalese lingua franca. Some elements of the crowd began drifting in her direction. She spoke for a few moments, the only words the surprised Homer Crawford could make out were *El Hassan*. And she used them often.

She switched suddenly to Arabic, and he could follow her now. The drift of her talk was that word had come through that El Hassan was to make a great announcement in the near future and that meanwhile all his people were to await his word. But that there was to be a great meeting before the Mosque within the hour.

She switched again to Songhoi and repeated substantially what she'd said before. By now she had every woman hanging on her words.

A man on the outskirts of the gathering called out in high irritation, "But what of the storming of the administration buildings? Our leaders have proclaimed the storming of the reactionaries!"

Crawford, leaning heavily on the pilgrim staff, drifted over to the other. "Quiet, O young one," he said. "I wish to listen to the words of the girl who tells of the teachings of the great El Hassan."

The other turned angrily on him. "Be silent thyself, old man!" He raised a hand as though to cuff the American.

Homer Crawford neatly rapped him on the right shin bone with his quarterstaff to the other's intense agony. The women who witnessed the brief spat dissolved in laughter at the plight of the younger man. Homer Crawford drifted away again before the heckler recovered.

He let Isobel handle the bulk of the reverse-rabble rousing. His bit was to come later, and as yet he didn't want to reveal himself to the throngs.

* * * * *

They went from one gathering place of women to another. To the spice market, to the fish and meat market, to the bathing and laundering locations along the river. And everywhere they found animated groups of women, Isobel went into her speech.

At one point, while Homer stood idly in the crowd, feeling its temper and the extent to which the girl was dominating them, he felt someone press next to him.

A voice said, "What is the plan of operation, Yank?"

Homer Crawford's eyebrows went up and he shot a quick glance at the other. It was Rex Donaldson of the Commonwealth African Department. The operative who worked as the witchman, Dolo Anah. Crawford was glad to see him. This was Donaldson's area of operations, the man must have got here almost as soon as Crawford's team, when he had heard of the trouble.

Crawford said in English, "They've been gathering for an outbreak of violence, evidently directed at the Reunited Nations projects administration buildings. I've seen a few banners calling for El Hassan to come to power, Africa for the Africans, that sort of thing."

The small Bahamian snorted. "You chaps certainly started something with this El Hassan farce. What are your immediate plans? How can I co-operate with you?"

A teenage boy who had been heckling Isobel, stooped now to pick up some dried cow dung. Almost absently, Crawford put his staff between the other's legs and tripped him up, when the lad sprawled on his face the American rapped him smartly on the head.

Crawford said, "Thanks a lot, we can use you, especially since you speak Dogon, I don't think any of my group does. We're going to hold a big meeting in front of the square and give them a long monotonous talk, saying little but sounding as though we're promising a great deal. When we've taken most of the steam out of them, we'll locate the ringleaders and have a big indoor meeting. My boys will be spotted throughout the gang. They'll nominate me to be spokesman, and nominate each other to be my committee and we'll be sent to find El Hassan and urge him to take power. That should keep them quiet for a while. At least long enough for headquarters in Dakar to decide what to do."

"Good Heavens," Donaldson said in admiration. "You Yanks are certainly good at this sort of thing."

"Takes practice," Homer Crawford said. "If you want to help, ferret out the groups who speak Dogon and give them the word."

Out of a sidestreet came running Abe Baker at the head of possibly two or three hundred arm waving, shouting, stick brandishing Africans. A few of them had banners which were being waved in such confusion that nobody could read the words inscribed. Most of them seemed to be younger men, even teen-agers.

"Good Heavens," Donaldson said again.

At first snap opinion, Crawford thought his assistant was being pursued and started forward to the hopeless rescue, but then he realized that Abe was heading the mob. Waving his staff, the New Yorker was shouting slogans, most of which had something to do with "El Hassan" but otherwise were difficult to make out.

The small mob charged out of the street and through the square, still shouting. Abe began to drop back into the ranks, and then to the edge of the charging, gesticulating crowd. Already, though, some of them seemed to be slowing up, even stopping and drifting away, puzzlement or frustration on their faces.

Those who were still at excitement's peak, charged up another street at the other side of the square.

In a few moments, Abe Baker came up to them, breathing hard and wiping sweat from his forehead. He grinned wryly. "Man, those cats are way out. This is really Endsville." He looked up at where Isobel was haranguing her own crowd, which hadn't been fazed by the men who'd charged through the square going nowhere. "Look at old Isobel up there. Man, this whole town's like a combination of Hyde Park and Union Square. You oughta hear old Jake making with a speech."

"What just happened?" Homer asked, motioning with his head to where the last elements of the mob Abe'd been leading were disappearing down a dead-end street.

"Ah, nothing," Abe said, still watching Isobel and grinning at her. "Those cats were the nucleus of a bunch wanted to start some action. Burn a few cars, raid the library, that sort of jazz. So I took over for a while, led them up one street and down the other. I feel like I just been star at a track meet."

"Good Heavens," Donaldson said still again.

"They're all scattered around now," Abe explained to him. "Either that or their tongues are hanging out to the point they'll have to take five to have a beer. They're finished for a while."

Isobel finished her little talk and joined them. "What gives now?" she asked.

Rex Donaldson said, "I'd like to stay around and watch you chaps operate. It's fascinating. However, I'd better get over to the park. That's probably where the greater number of the Dogon will be." He grumbled sourly, "I'll roast those blokes with a half dozen bits of magic and send them all back to Sangha. It'll be donkey's years before they ever show face around here again." He left them.

Homer Crawford looked after him. "Good man," he said.

Abe had about caught his breath. "What gives now, man?" he said. "I ought to get back to Jake. He's all alone up near the mosque."

"It's about time all of us got over there," Crawford said. He looked at Isobel as they walked. "How does it feel being a sort of reverse agent provocateur?"

Her forehead was wrinkled, characteristically. "I suppose it has to be done, but frankly, I'm not too sure just what we are doing. Here we go about pushing these supposed teachings of El Hassan and when we're taken up by the people and they actually attempt to accomplish what we taught them, we draw in on the reins."

"Man, you're right," Abe said unhappily. He looked at his chief. "What'd you say, Homer?"

"Of course she's right," Crawford growled. "It's just premature, is all. There's no program, no plan of action. If there was one, this thing here in Mopti might be the spark that united all North Africa. As it is, we have to put the damper on it until there is a definite program." He added sourly, "I'm just wondering if the Reunited Nations is the organization that can come up with one. And, if it isn't, where is there one?"

The mosque loomed up before them. The square before it was jam packed with milling Africans.

"Great guns," Isobel snorted, "there're more people here than the whole population of Mopti. Where'd they all come from?"

"They've been filtering in from the country," Crawford said.

"Well, we'll filter 'em back," Abe promised.

* * * * *

They spotted a ruckus and could see Elmer Allen in the middle of it, his quarterstaff flailing.

"On the double," Homer bit out, and he and Abe broke into a trot for the point of conflict. The idea was to get this sort of thing over as quickly as possible before it had a chance to spread.

They arrived too late. Elmer was leaning on his staff, as though needing it for support, and explaining mildly to two men who evidently were friends of a third who was stretched out on the ground, dead to the world and with a nasty lump on his shaven head.

Homer came up and said to Elmer, in Songhai, "What has transpired, O Holy One?" He made a sign of obeisance to the Jamaican.

The two Africans were taken aback by the term of address. They were unprepared to continue further debate, not to speak of physical action, against a holy man.

Elmer said with dignity, "He spoke against El Hassan, our great leader."

For a moment the two Africans seemed to be willing to deny that, but Abe Baker took up the cue and turned to the crowd that was beginning to gather. He held his hands out, palms upward questioningly, "And why should these young men beset a Holy One whose only crime is to love El Hassan?"

The crowd began to murmur and the two hurriedly picked up their fallen companion and took off with him.

Homer said in English, "What really happened?"

"Oh, this chap was one of the hot heads," Elmer explained. "Wanted some immediate action. I gave it to him."

Abe chuckled, "Holy One, yet."

Spotted through the square, holding forth to various gatherings of the mob were Jake Armstrong, Kenny Ballalou and Cliff Jackson. Even as Homer Crawford sized up the situation and the temper of the throngs of tribesmen, Bey entered the square from the far side at the head of two or three thousand more, most of whom were already beginning to look bored to death from talk, talk, talk.

Isobel came up and looked questioningly at Homer Crawford.

He said, "Abe, get the truck and drive it up before the entrance to the mosque. We'll speak from that. Isobel can open the hoe down, get the crowd over and then introduce me."

Abe left and Crawford said to Isobel, "Introduce me as Omar ben Crawf, the great friend and assistant of El Hassan. Build it up."

"Right," she said.

Crawford said, "Elmer first round up the boys and get them spotted through the audience. You're the cheerleaders and also the sergeants at arms, of course. Nail the hecklers quickly, before they can get organized among themselves. In short, the standard deal." He thought a moment. "And see about getting a hall where we can hold a meeting of the ringleaders, those are the ones we're going to have to cool out."

"Wizard," Elmer said and was gone on his mission.

Isobel and Homer stood for a moment, waiting for Abe and the truck.

She said, "You seem to have this all down pat."

"It's routine," he said absently. "The brain of a mob is no larger than that of its minimum member. Any disciplined group, almost no matter how small can model it to order."

"Just in case we don't have the opportunity to get together again, what happens at the hall meeting of ringleaders? What do Jake, Cliff and I do?"

"What comes naturally," Homer said. "We'll elect each other to the most important positions. But everybody else that seems to have anything at all on the ball will be elected to some committee or other. Give them jobs compiling reports to El Hassan or something. Keep them busy. Give Reunited Nations headquarters in Dakar time to come up with something."

She said worriedly, "Suppose some of these ringleaders are capable, aggressive types and won't stand for us getting all the important positions?"

Crawford grunted. "We're *more* aggressive and more capable. Let my team handle that. One of the boys will jump up and accuse the guy of being a spy and an enemy of El Hassan, and one of the other boys will bear him out, and a couple of others will hustle him out of the hall." Homer yawned. "It's all routine, Isobel."

Abe was driving up the truck.

Crawford said, "O.K., let's go, gal."

"Roger," she said, climbing first into the back of the vehicle and then up onto the roof of the cab.

Isobel held her hands high above her head and in the cab Abe bore down on the horn for a long moment.

Isobel shrilled, "Hear what the messenger from El Hassan has come to tell us! Hear the friend and devoted follower of El Hassan!"

At the same time, Jake, Kenny, and Cliff discontinued their own harangues and themselves headed for the new speaker.

* * * * *

They stayed for three days and had it well wrapped up in that time. The tribesmen, bored when the excitement fell away and it became obvious that there were to be no further riots, and certainly no violence, drifted back to their villages. The city dwellers returned to the routine of daily existence. And the police, who had mysteriously disappeared from the streets at the height of the demonstrations, now magically reappeared and began asserting their authority somewhat truculently.

At the hall meetings, mighty slogans were drafted and endless committees formed. The more articulate, the more educated and able of the demonstrators were marked out for future reference, but for the moment given meaningless tasks to keep them busy and out of trouble.

On the fourth day, Homer Crawford received orders to proceed to Dakar, leaving the rest of the team behind to keep an eye on the situation.

Abe groaned, "There's luck for you. Dakar, nearest thing to a good old sin city in a thousand miles. And who gets to go? Old sour puss, here. Got no more interest in the hot spots —"

Homer said, "You can come along, Abe."

Kenny Ballalou said, "Orders were only you, Homer."

Crawford growled, "Yes, but I have a suspicion I'm being called on the carpet for one of our recent escapades and I want backing if I need it." He added, "Besides, nothing is going to happen here."

"Crazy man," Abe said appreciatively.

Jake said, "We three were planning to head for Dakar today ourselves. Isobel, in particular, is exhausted and needs a prolonged rest before going out among the natives any more. You might as well continue to let us supply your transportation."

"Fine," Homer told him. "Come on Abe, let's get our things together."

"What do we do while you chaps are gone?" Elmer Allen said sourly. "I wouldn't mind a period in a city myself."

"Read a book, man," Abe told him. "Improve your mind."

"I've read a book," Elmer said glumly. "Any other ideas?"

* * * * *

Dakar is a big, bustling, prosperous and modern city shockingly set down in the middle of the poverty that is Africa. It should be, by its appearance, on the French Riviera, on the California coast, or possibly that of Florida, but it isn't. It's in Senegal, in the area once known as French West Africa.

Their aircraft swept in and landed at the busy airport.

They were assigned an African Development Project air-cushion car and drove into the city proper.

Dakar boasts some of the few skyscrapers in all Africa. The Reunited Nations occupied one of these in its entirety. Dakar was the center of activities for the whole Western Sahara and down into the Sudan. Across the street from its offices, a street still named Rue des Résistance in spite of the fact that the French were long gone, was the Hotel Juan-les-Pins.

Crawford and Abe Baker had radioed ahead and accommodations were ready for them. Their western clothing and other gear had been brought up from storage in the cellar.

At the desk, the clerk didn't blink at the Tuareg costume the two still wore. This was commonplace. He probably wouldn't have blinked had Isobel arrived in the costume of the Dogon. "Your suite is ready, Dr. Crawford," he said.

The manager came up and shook hands with an old customer and Homer Crawford introduced him to Isobel, Jake and Cliff, requesting he do his best for them. He and Abe then made their excuses and headed for the paradise of hot water, towels, western drink and the other amenities of civilization.

On the way up in the elevator, Abe said happily, "Man, I can just *taste* that bath I'm going to take. Crazy!"

"Personally," Crawford said, trying to reflect some of the other's typically lighthearted enthusiasm, "I have in mind a few belts out of a bottle of stone-age cognac, then a steak yea big and a flock of French fries, followed by vanilla ice cream."

Abe's eyes went round. "Man, you mean we can't get a good dish of cous cous in this town?"

"Cous cous," Crawford said in agony.

Abe made his voice so soulful. "With a good dollop of rancid camel butter right on top."

Homer laughed as they reached their floor and started for the suite. "You make it sound so good, I almost believe you." Inside he said, "Dibbers on the first bath. How about phoning down for a bottle of Napoleon and some soda and ice? When it comes, just mix me one and bring it in, that hand you see emerging from the soap bubbles in that tub, will be mine."

"I hear and obey, O Bwana!" Abe said in a servile tone.

By the time they'd cleaned up and had eaten an enormous western style meal in the dining room of the Juan-les-Pins, it was well past the hour when they could have made contact with their Reunited Nations superiors. They had a couple of cognacs in the bar, then, whistling happily, Abe Baker went out on the town.

Homer Crawford looked up Isobel, Jake and Cliff who had, sure enough, found accommodations in the same hotel.

Isobel stepped back in mock surprise when she saw Crawford in western garb. "Heavens to Betsy," she said. "The man is absolutely extinguished in a double-breasted charcoal gray."

He tried a scowl and couldn't manage it. "The word is *distinguished*, not extinguished," he said. He looked down at the suit, critically. "You know, I feel uncomfortable. I wonder if I'll be able to sit down in a chair instead of squatting." He looked at her own evening frock. "Wow," he said.

Cliff Jackson said menacingly, "None of that stuff, Crawford. Isobel has already been asked for, let's have no wolfing around."

Isobel said tartly, "Asked for but she didn't answer the summons." She took Homer by the arm. "And I just adore extinguish-oops, I mean distinguished looking men."

They trooped laughingly into the hotel cocktail lounge.

The time passed pleasantly. Jake and Cliff were good men in a field close to Homer Crawford's heart. Isobel was possibly the most attractive woman he'd ever met. They discussed in detail each other's work and all had stories of wonder to describe.

Crawford wondered vaguely if there was ever going to be a time, in this life of his, for a woman and all that one usually connects with womanhood. What was it Elmer Allen had said at the Timbuktu meeting? "*... most of us will be kept busy the rest of our lives at this.*"

In his present state of mind, it didn't seem too desirable a prospect. But there was no way out for such as Homer Crawford. What had Cliff Jackson said at the same meeting? "*We do what we must do.*" Which, come to think of it, didn't jibe too well with Cliff's claim at Mopti to be in it solely for the job. Probably the man disguised his basic idealism under a cloak of cynicism; if so, he wouldn't be the first.

They said their goodnights early. All of them were used to Sahara hours. Up at dawn, to bed shortly after sunset; the desert has little fuel to waste on illumination.

In the suite again, Homer Crawford noted that Abe hadn't returned as yet. He snorted deprecation. The younger man would probably be out until dawn. Dakar had much to offer in the way of civilization's fleshpots.

He took up the bottle of cognac and poured himself a healthy shot, wishing that he'd remembered to pick up a paperback at the hotel's newsstand before coming to bed.

He swirled the expensive brandy in the glass and brought it to his nose to savor the bouquet.

But fifteen-year-old brandy from the cognac district of France should not boast a bouquet involving elements of bitter almonds. With an automatic startled gesture, Crawford jerked his face away from the glass.

He scowled down at it for a long moment, then took up the bottle and sniffed it. He wondered how a would-be murderer went about getting hold of cyanide in Dakar.

Homer Crawford phoned the desk and got the manager. Somebody had been in the suite during his absence. Was there any way of checking?

He didn't expect satisfaction and didn't receive any. The manager, after finding that nothing seemed to be missing, seemed to think that perhaps Dr. Crawford had made a mistake. Homer didn't bother to tell him about the poisoned brandy. He hung up, took the bottle into the bathroom and poured it away.

In the way of precautions, he checked the windows to see if there were any possibilities of entrance by an intruder, locked the door securely, put his handgun beneath his pillow and fell off to sleep. When and if Abe returned, he could bang on the door.

* * * * *

In the morning, clad in American business suits and frankly feeling a trifle uncomfortable in them, Homer Crawford and Abraham Baker presented themselves at the offices of the African Development Project, Sahara Division, of the Reunited Nations. Uncharacteristically, there was no waiting in anterooms, no dealing with subordinates. Dr. Crawford and his lieutenant were ushered directly to the office of Sven Zetterberg.

Upon their entrance the Swede came to his feet, shook hands abruptly with both of them and sat down again. He scowled at Abe and said to Homer in excellent English, "It was requested that your team remain in Mopti." Then he added, "Sit down, gentlemen."

They took chairs. Crawford said mildly, "Mr. Baker is my right-hand man. I assume he'd take over the team if anything happened to me." He added dryly, "Besides, there were a few things he felt he had to do about town."

Abe cleared his throat but remained silent.

Zetterberg continued to frown but evidently for a different reason now. He said, "There have been more complaints about your ... ah ... cavalier tactics."

Homer looked at him but said nothing.

Zetterberg said in irritation, "It becomes necessary to warn you almost every time you come in contact with this office, Dr. Crawford."

Homer said evenly, "My team and I work in the field Dr. Zetterberg. We have to think on our feet and usually come to decisions in split seconds. Sometimes our lives are at stake. We do what we think best under the conditions. At any time your office feels my efforts are misdirected, my resignation is available."

The Swede cleared his throat. "The Arab Union has made a full complaint in the Reunited Nations of a group of our men massacring thirty-five of their troopers."

Homer said, "They were well into the Ahaggar with a convoy of modern weapons, obviously meant for adherents of theirs. Given the opportunity, the Arab Union would take over North Africa."

"This is no reason to butcher thirty-five men."

"We were fired upon first," Crawford said.

"That is not the way they tell it. They claim you ambushed them."

Abe put in innocently, "How would the Arab Union know? We didn't leave any survivors."

Zetterberg glared at him. "It is not easy, Mr. Baker, for we who do the paper work involved in this operation, to account for the activities of you hair-trigger men in the field."

"We appreciate your difficulties," Homer said evenly. "But we can only continue to do what we think best on being confronted with an emergency."

The Swede drummed his fingers on the desk top. "Perhaps I should remind you that the policy of this project is to encourage amalgamation of the peoples of the area. Possibly, the Arab Union will prove to be the best force to accomplish such a union."

Abe grunted.

Homer Crawford was shaking his head. "You don't believe that Dr. Zetterberg, and I doubt if there are many non-Moslems who do. Mohammed sprung out of the deserts and his religion is one based on the surroundings, both physical and socio-economic."

Zetterberg grumbled, argumentatively, though his voice lacked conviction, "So did its two sister religions, Judaism and Christianity."

Crawford waggled a finger negatively. "Both of them adapted to changing times, with considerable success. Islam has remained the same and in all the world there is not one example of a highly developed socio-economic system in a Moslem country. The reason is that in your country, and mine, and in the other advanced countries of the West, we pay lip service to our religions, but we don't let them interfere with our day by day life. But the Moslem, like the rapidly disappearing ultra-orthodox Jews, lives his religion every day and by the rules set down by the Prophet fifteen centuries ago. Everything a Moslem does from the moment he gets up in the morning is all mapped out in the Koran. What fingers of the hand to eat with, what hand to break bread with-and so on and so forth. It can get ludicrous. You should see the bathroom of a wealthy Moslem in some modern city such as Tangier. Mohammed never dreamed of such institutions as toilet paper. His followers still obey the rules he set down as an alternative."

"What's your point?"

"That North Africa cannot be united under the banner of Islam if she is going to progress rapidly. If it ever unites, it will be in spite of local religions-Islam and pagan as well; they hold up the wheels of progress."

Zetterberg stared at him. The truth of the matter was that he agreed with the American and they both knew it.

He said, "This matter of physically assaulting and then arresting the chieftain" —he looked down at a paper on his desk —"of the Ouled Touameur clan of the Chaambra confederation, Abd-el-Kader. From your report, the man was evidently attempting to unify the tribes."

Crawford was shaking his head impatiently. "No. He didn't have the ...dream. He was a raider, a racketeer, not a leader of purposeful men. Perhaps it's true that these people need a hero to act as a symbol for them, but he can't be such as Abd-el-Kader."

"I suppose you're right," the Swede said grudgingly. "See here, have you heard reports of a group of Cubans, in the Anglo-Egyptian Sudan to help with the new sugar refining there, being attacked?"

The eyes of both Crawford and Baker narrowed. There'd been talk about this at Timbuktu. "Only a few rumors," Crawford said.

The Swede drummed his desk with his nervous fingers. "The rumors are correct. The whole group was either killed or wounded." He said suddenly, "You had nothing to do with this, I suppose?"

Crawford held his palms up, in surprise, "My team has never been within a thousand miles of Khartoum."

Zetterberg said, "See here, we suspect the Cubans might have supported Soviet Complex viewpoints."

Crawford shrugged, "I know nothing about them at all."

Zetterberg said, "Do you think this might be the work of El Hassan and his followers?"

Abe started to chuckle something, but Homer shook his head slightly in warning and said, "I don't know."

"How did that affair in Mopti turn out, these riots in favor of El Hassan?"

Homer Crawford shrugged. "Routine. Must have been as many as ten thousand of them at one point. We used standard tactics in gaining control and then dispersing them. I'll have a complete written report to you before the day is out."

Zetterberg said, "You've heard about this El Hassan before?"

"Quite a bit."

"From the rumors that have come into this office, he backs neither East nor West in international politics. He also seems to agree with your summation of the Islamic problem. He teaches separation of Church and State."

"They're the same thing in Moslem countries," Abe muttered.

Zetterberg tossed his bombshell out of a clear sky. "Dr. Crawford," he snapped, "in spite of the warnings we've had to issue to you repeatedly, you are admittedly our best man in the field. We're giving you a new assignment. Find this El Hassan and bring him here!"

Zetterberg leaned forward, an expression of somewhat anxious sincerity in his whole demeanor.

VIII

Abe Baker choked, and then suddenly laughed.

Sven Zetterberg stared at him. "What's so funny?"

"Well, nothing," Abe admitted. He looked to Homer Crawford.

Crawford said to the Swede carefully, "Why?"

Zetterberg said impatiently, "Isn't it obvious, after the conversation we've had here? Possibly this El Hassan is the man we're looking for. Perhaps this is the force that will bind North Africa together. Thus far, all we've heard about him has been rumor. We don't seem to be able to find anyone who has seen him, nor is the exact strength of his following known. We'd like to confer with him, before he gets any larger."

Crawford said carefully, "It's hard to track down a rumor."

"That's why we give the assignment to our best team in the field," the Swede told him. "You've got a roving commission. Find El Hassan and bring him here to Dakar."

Abe grinned and said, "Suppose he doesn't want to come?"

"Use any methods you find necessary. If you need more manpower, let us know. But we must talk to El Hassan."

Homer said, still watching his words, "Why the urgency?"

The Reunited Nations official looked at him for a long moment, as though debating whether to let him in on higher policy. "Because, frankly, Dr. Crawford, the elements which first went together to produce the African Development Project, are, shall we say, becoming somewhat unstuck."

"The glue was never too strong," Abe muttered.

Zetterberg nodded. "The attempt to find competent, intelligent men to work for the project, who were at the same time altruistic and unaffected by personal or national interests, has always been a difficult one. If you don't mind my saying so, we Scandinavians, particularly those not affiliated with NATO come closest to filling the bill. We have no designs on Africa. It is unfortunate that we have practically no Negro citizens who could do field work."

"Are you suggesting other countries have designs on Africa?" Homer said.

For the first time the Swede laughed. A short, choppy laugh. "Are you suggesting they haven't? What was that convoy of the Arab Union bringing into the Sahara? Guns, with which to forward their cause of taking over all North Africa. What were those Cubans doing in Sudan, that someone else felt it necessary to assassinate them? What is the program of the Soviet Complex as it applies to this area, and how does it differ from that of the United States? And how do the ultimate programs of the British Commonwealth and the French Community differ from each other and from both the United States and Russia?"

"That's why we have a Reunited Nations," Crawford said calmly.

"Theoretically, yes. But it is coming apart at the seams. I sometimes wonder if an organization composed of a membership each with its own selfish needs can ever really unite in an altruistic task. Remember the early days when the Congo was first given her freedom? Supposedly the United Nations went in to help. Actually, each element in the United Nations had its own irons in the fire, and usually their desires differed."

The Swede shrugged hugely. "I don't know, but I am about convinced, and so are a good many other officers of this project, that unless we soon find a competent leader to act as a symbol around which all North Africans can unite, find such a man and back him, that all our work will crumble in this area under pressure from outside. That's why we want El Hassan."

Homer Crawford came to his feet, his face in a scowl. "I'll let you know by tomorrow, if I can take the assignment," he said.

"Why tomorrow?" the Swede demanded.

"There are some ramifications I have to consider."

"Very well," the Swede said stiffly. He came to his own feet and shook hands with them again. "Oh, there's just one other thing. This spontaneous meeting you held in Timbuktu with elements from various other organizations. How did it come out?"

Crawford was wary. "Very little result, actually."

Zetterberg chuckled. "As I expected. However, we would appreciate it, doctor, if you and your team would refrain from such activities in the future. You are, after all, hired by the Reunited Nations and owe it all your time and allegiance. We have no desire to see you fritter away this time with religious fanatics and other crackpot groups."

"I see," Crawford said.

The other laughed cheerfully. "I'm sure you do, Dr. Crawford. A word to the wise."

* * * * *

They remained silent on the way back to the hotel.

In the lobby they ran into Isobel Cunningham.

Homer Crawford looked at her thoughtfully. He said, "We've got some thinking to do and some ideas to bat back and forth. I value your opinion and experience, Isobel, could you come up to the suite and sit in?"

She tilted her head, looked at him from the side of her eyes. "Something big has happened, hasn't it?"

"I suppose so. I don't know. We've got to make some decisions."

"Come on Isobel," Abe said. "You can give us the feminine viewpoint and all that jazz."

They started for the elevator and Isobel said to Abe, "If you'd just be consistent with that pseudo-beatnik chatter of yours, I wouldn't mind. But half the time you talk like an English lit major when you forget to put on your act."

"Man," Abe said to her, "maybe I was wrong inviting you to sit in on this bull session. I can see you're in a bad mood."

In the living room of the suite, Isobel took an easy-chair and Abe threw himself full length on his back on a couch. Homer Crawford paced the floor.

"Well?" Isobel said.

Crawford said abruptly, "Somebody tried to poison me last night. Got into this room somehow and put cyanide in a bottle of cognac Abe and I were drinking out of earlier in the evening."

Isobel stared at him. Her eyes went from him to Abe and back. "But ... but, why?"

Crawford ran his hand back over his wiry hair in puzzlement. "I ... I don't know. That's what's driving me batty. I can't figure out why anybody would want to kill me."

"I can," Abe said bluntly. "And that interview we just had with Sven Zetterberg just bears me out."

"Zetterberg," Isobel said, surprised. "Is he in Africa?"

Crawford nodded to her question but his eyes were on Abe.

Abe put his hands behind his head and said to the ceiling, "Zetterberg just gave Homer's team the assignment of bringing in El Hassan."

"El Hassan? But you boys told us all in Timbuktu that there was no El Hassan. You invented him and then the rest of us, more or less spontaneously, though unknowingly, took up the falsification and spread your work."

"That's right," Crawford said, still looking at Abe.

"But didn't you tell Sven Zetterberg?" Isobel demanded. "He's too big a man to play jokes upon."

"No, I didn't and I'm not sure I know why."

"I know why," Abe said. He sat up suddenly and swung his feet around and to the floor.

The other two watched him, both frowning.

Abe said slowly, "Homer, you *are* El Hassan."

His chief scowled at him. "What is that supposed to mean?"

The younger man gestured impatiently. "Figure it out. Somebody else already has, the some-body who took a shot at you from that mosque. Look, put it all together and it makes sense.

"These North Africans aren't going to make it, not in the short period of time that we want them to, unless a leader appears on the scene. These people are just beginning to emerge from tribal society. In the tribes, people live by rituals and taboos, by traditions. But at the next step in the evolution of society they follow a Hero-and the traditions are thrown overboard. It's one step up the ladder of cultural evolution. Just for the record, the Heroes almost invariably get clobbered in the end, since a Hero must be perfect. Once he is found wanting in any respect, he's a false prophet, a cheat, and a new, perfect and faultless Hero must be found.

"O.K. At this stage we need a Hero to unite North Africa, but this time we need a real super-Hero. In this modern age, the old style one won't do. We need one with education, and altruism, one with the dream, as you call it. We need a man who has no affiliations, no preferences for Tuareg, Teda, Chaambra, Dogon, Moor or whatever. He's got to be truly neutral. O.K., you're it. You're an American Negro, educated, competent, widely experienced. You're a natural for the job. You speak Arabic, French, Tamabeq, Songhai and even Swahili."

Abe stopped momentarily and twisted his face in a grimace. "But there's one other thing that's possibly the most important of all. Homer, you're a born leader."

"Who *me?*" Crawford snorted. "I hate to be put in a position where I have to lead men, make decisions, that sort of thing.

"That's beside the point. There in Timbuktu you had them in the palm of your hand. All except one or two, like Doc Smythe and that missionary. And I have an idea even they'd come around. Everybody there felt it. They were in favor of anything you suggested. Isobel?"

She nodded, very seriously. "Yes. You have a personality that goes over, Homer. I think it would be a rare person who could conceive of you cheating, or misleading. You're so obviously sincere, competent and intelligent that it, well, *projects* itself. I noticed it even more in Mopti than Timbuktu. You had that city in your palm in a matter of a few hours."

Homer Crawford shifted his shoulders, uncomfortably.

Abe said, "You might dislike the job, but it's a job that needs doing."

Crawford ran his hand around the back of his neck, uncomfortably. "You think such a project would get the support of the various teams and organizations working North Africa, eh?"

"Practically a hundred per cent. And even if some organizations or even countries, with their own row to hoe, tried to buck you, their individual members and teams would come over. Why? Because it makes sense."

Homer Crawford said worriedly, "Actually, I've realized this, partially subconsciously, for some time. But I didn't put myself in the role. I ...I wish there really was an El Hassan. I'd throw my efforts behind him."

"There will be an El Hassan," Abe said definitely. "And you can be him."

Crawford stared at Abe, undecided.

Isobel said, suddenly, "I think Abe's right, Homer."

* * * * *

Abe seemed to switch the tempo of his talk. He said, "There's just one thing, Homer. It's a long range question, but it's an important one."

"Yes?"

"What're your politics?"

"My politics? I haven't any politics here in North Africa."

"I mean back home. I've never discussed politics with you, Homer, partly because I haven't wanted to reveal my own. But now the question comes up. What is your position, ultimately, speaking on a world-wide basis?"

Homer looked at him quizzically, trying to get at what was behind the other's words. "I don't belong to any political party," he said slowly.

Abe said evenly, "I do, Homer. I'm a Party member."

Crawford was beginning to get it. "If you mean do I ultimately support the program of the Soviet Complex, the answer is definitely no. Whether or not it's desirable for Russia or for China, is up to the Russians and Chinese to decide. But I don't believe it's desirable for such advanced countries as the United States and most of Western Europe. We've got large problems that need answering, but the commies don't supply the answers so far as I'm concerned."

"I see," Abe said. He was far, far different than the laughing, beatnik jabbering, youngster he had always seemed. "That's not so good."

"Why not?" Homer demanded. His eyes went to where Isobel sat, her face strained at all this, but he could read nothing in her expression, and she said nothing.

Abe said, "Because, admittedly, North Africa isn't ready for a communist program as yet. It's in too primitive a condition. However, it's progressing fast, fantastically fast, and the coming of El Hassan is going to speed things up still more."

Abe said deliberately, "Possibly twenty years from now the area *will* be ready for a communist program. And at that time we don't want somebody with El Hassan's power and prestige against us. We take the long view, Homer, and it dictates that El Hassan has to be secretly on the Party's side."

Homer was nodding. "I see. So that's why you shot at me in Timbuktu."

Abe's eyes went wary. He said, "I didn't know you knew."

Crawford nodded. "It just came to me. It had to be you. Supposedly, you broke into the mosque from the back at the same moment I came in the front. Actually, you were already inside." Homer grunted. "Besides, it would have been awfully difficult for anyone else to have doped that bottle of cognac on me. What I couldn't understand, and still can't, was motive. We've been in the clutch together more than once, Abe."

"That's right, Homer, but there are some things so important that friendship goes by the board. I could see as far back as that meeting something that hadn't occurred to either you or the others. You were a born El Hassan. I figured it was necessary to get you out of the way and put one of our own-perhaps me, even-in your place. No ill feelings, Homer. In fact, now I've just given you your chance. You could come in with us —"

Even as he was speaking, his eyes moved in a way Homer Crawford recognized. He'd seen Abe Baker in action often enough. A gun flicked out of an under-the-arm holster, but Crawford moved in anticipation. The flat of his hand darted forward, chopped and the hand weapon was on the floor.

As Isobel screamed, Abe countered the attack. He reached forward in a jujitsu maneuver, grabbed a coat sleeve and a handful of suit coat. He twisted quickly, threw the other man over one hip and to the floor.

But Homer Crawford was already expertly rolling with the fall, rolling out to get a fresh start.

Abe Baker knew that in the long go, in spite of his somewhat greater heft, he wouldn't be able to take his former chief in the other man's own field. Now he threw himself on the other, on the floor. Legs and arms tangled in half realized, quickly defeated holds and maneuvers.

Abe called, "Quick, Isobel, the gun. Get the gun and cover him."

She shook her head, desperately. "Oh no. No!"

Abe bit out, his teeth grinding under the punishment he was taking, "That's an order, *Comrade Cunningham*! Get the gun!"

"No. No, I can't!" She turned and fled the room.

Abe muttered an obscenity, bridged and crabbed out of the desperate position he was in. And now his fingers were but a few inches from the weapon. He stretched.

Homer Crawford, heavy veins in his own forehead from his exertions, panted, "Abe, I can't let you get that gun. Call it quits."

"Can't, Homer," Abe gritted. His fingers were a few fractions of an inch from the weapon.

Crawford panted, "Abe, there's just one thing I can do. A karate blow. *I* can chop your windpipe with the side of my hand. Abe, if I do, only immediate surgery could save your —"

Abe's fingers closed about the gun and Crawford, calling on his last resources, lashed out. He could feel the cartilage collapse, a sound of air, for a moment, almost like a shriek filled the room.

The gun was meaningless now. Homer Crawford, his face agonized, was on his knees beside the other who was threshing on the floor. "Abe," he groaned. "You made me."

Abe Baker's face was quickly going ashen in his impossible quest for oxygen. For a last second there was a gleam in his eyes and his lips moved. Crawford bent down. He wasn't sure, but he thought that somehow the other found enough air to get out a last, "Crazy man."

When it was over, Homer Crawford stood again, and looked down at the body, his face expressionless.

From behind him a voice said, "So I got here too late."

Crawford turned. It was Elmer Allen, gun in hand.

Homer Crawford said dully, "What are you doing here?"

Elmer looked at the body, then back at his chief. "Bey figured out what must have happened at the mosque there in Timbuktu. We didn't know what might be motivating Abe, but we got here as quick as we could."

"He was a commie," Crawford said dully. "Evidently, the Party decided I stood in its way. Where are the others?"

"Scouring the town to find you."

Crawford said wearily, "Find the others and bring them here. We've got to get rid of poor Abe, there, and then I've got something to tell you."

"Very well, chief," Elmer said, holstering his gun. "Oh, just one thing before I go. You know that chap Rex Donaldson? Well, we had some discussion after you left. This'll probably surprise you Homer, but-hold onto your hat, as you Americans say-Donaldson thinks you ought to *become* El Hassan. And Bey, Kenny and I agree."

Crawford said, "We'll talk about it later, Elmer."

* * * * *

He knocked at her door and a moment later she came. She saw who it was, opened for him and returned to the room beyond. She had obviously been crying.

Homer Crawford said, but with no reproach in his voice, "You should have helped me, to be consistent."

"I knew you'd win."

"Nevertheless, once you'd switched sides, you should have attempted to help me. If you had, maybe Abe would still be alive."

She took a quick agonized breath, and sat down in one of the two chairs, her hands clasped tightly in her lap. She said, "I ...I've known Abe since my early teens."

He said nothing.

"In college, he was the cell leader. He enlisted me into the Party."

Crawford still didn't speak.

She said defiantly, "He was an idealist, Homer."

"I know that," Crawford said. "And along with it, he's saved my life, on at least three different occasions in the past few years. He was a good man."

It was her turn to hold silence.

Homer hit the palm of his left hand with the fist of his right. "That's what so many don't realize. They think this is all a kind of cowboys and Indians affair. The good guys and the bad guys fighting it out. And, of course, all the good guys are on our side and their side is composed of bad guys. They don't realize that many, even most, of the enemy are fighting for an ideal, too-and are willing to die for it, or do things sometimes even harder than dying."

He paced the floor for an agonized moment, before adding. "The fact that the ideal is a false one-or so, at least, is my opinion-is beside the point."

He suddenly dropped it and switched subjects. "This isn't as much a surprise to me as you possibly think, Isobel. There was only one way that episode in Timbuktu could have taken place. Abe was waiting for me to pass that mosque. But I had to pass. I had to be *fingered* as the old gangster expression had it. And you led me into the ambush."

He looked down at her. "But what changed his mind? Why did he offer, tonight, to let me take over the El Hassan leadership?"

Isobel said, her voice low. "In Timbuktu, when Abe saw the way things were going, he realized you'd have to be liquidated, otherwise El Hassan would be a leader the Party couldn't control. He tried to eliminate you, and then tried again with the cognac. Last night, however, he checked with local party leaders and they decided that he'd acted too precipitately. They suggested you be given the opportunity to line up with the Party."

"And if I didn't?" Homer said.

"Then you were to be liquidated."

"So the finger is still on me, eh?"

"Yes, you'll have to be careful."

He looked full into her face. "How do you stand now?"

She returned his frank look. "I'm the first follower to dedicate her services to El Hassan."

"So you want to come along?"

"Yes," she said simply.

"And you remember what Abe said? That in the end the Hero invariably gets clobbered? Sooner or later, North Africa will outgrow the need for a Hero to follow and then ... then El Hassan and his closest followers have a good chance of winding up before a firing squad."

"Yes, I know that."

Homer Crawford ran his hand back over his short hair, wearily. "O.K., Isobel. Your first instructions are to contact those two friends of yours, Jake Armstrong and Cliff Jackson. Try to convert them."

"What are you going to be doing ... El Hassan?"

"I'm going over to the Reunited Nations to resign from the African Development Project. I have a sneaking suspicion that in the future they will not always be seeing eye to eye with El Hassan. Nor will the other organizations currently helping to advance Africa-whilst still at the same time keeping their own irons in the fire. Possibly the commies won't be the only ones in favor of liquidating El Hassan's assets."

Border, Breed nor Birth

I

El Hassan, would-be tyrant of all North Africa, was on the run.

His followers at this point numbered six, one of whom was a wisp of a twenty-four year old girl. Arrayed against him and his dream, he knew, was the combined power of the world in the form of the Reunited Nations, and, in addition, such individual powers as the United States of the Americas, the Soviet Complex, Common Europe, the French Community, the British Commonwealth and the Arab Union, working both together and unilaterally.

Immediate survival depended upon getting into the Great Erg of the Sahara where even the greatest powers the world had ever developed would have their work cut out locating El Hassan and his people.

* * * * *

Bey-ag-Akhamouk who was riding next to Elmer Allen in the lead air cushion hover-lorry, held a hand high. Both of the solar powered desert vehicles ground to a halt.

Homer Crawford vaulted out of the seat of the second lorry before it had settled to the sand. "What's up, Bey?" he called.

Bey pointed to the south and west. They were in the vicinity of Tessalit, in what was once known as French Sudan, and immediately to the south of Algeria. They were deliberately avoiding what little existed in this area in the way of trails, the Tanezrouft route which crossed the Sahara from Colomb-Béchar to Gao, on the Niger, was some fifty miles to the west.

Homer Crawford stared up into the sky in the direction Bey pointed and his face went wan.

The others were piling out of the vehicles.

"What is it?" Isobel Cunningham said, squinting and trying to catch what the others had already spotted.

"Aircraft," Bey growled. "A rocket-plane."

"Which means the military in this part of the world," Homer said.

The rest of them looked to him for instructions, but Bey suddenly took over. He said to Homer, "You better get on over beneath that outcropping of rock. The rest of us will handle this."

Homer looked at him.

Bey said, flatly, "If one of the rest of us gets it, or even if all of us do, the El Hassan movement goes on. But if something happens to you, the movement dies. We've already taken our stand and too much is at stake to risk your life."

Homer Crawford opened his mouth to protest, then closed it. He reached inside the solar-powered lorry and fetched forth a Tommy-Noiseless and started for the rock outcropping at a trot. Having made his decision, he wasn't going to cramp Bey-ag-Akhamouk's style with needless palaver.

Isobel Cunningham, Cliff Jackson, Elmer Allen and Kenny Ballalou gathered around the tall, American educated Tuareg.

"What's the plan?" Elmer said. Either he or Kenny Ballalou could have taken over as competently, but they were as capable of taking orders as giving them, a desirable trait in fighting men.

Bey was still staring at the oncoming speck. He growled, "We can't even hope he hasn't seen the pillars of sand and dust these vehicles throw up. He's spotted us all right. And we've got to figure he's looking for us, even though we can hope he's not."

The side of his mouth began to tic, characteristically. "He'll make three passes. The first one high, as an initial check. The second time he'll come in low just to make sure. The third pass and he'll clobber us."

The aircraft was coming on, high but nearer now.

"So," Elmer said reasonably, "we either get him the second pass he makes, or we've had it." The young Jamaican's lips were thinned back over his excellent teeth, as always when he went into combat.

"That's it," Bey agreed. "Kenny, you and Cliff get the flac rifle, and have it handy in the back of the second truck. Be sure he doesn't see it on this first pass. Elmer, get on the radio and check anything he sends."

Kenny Ballalou and the hulking Cliff Jackson ran to carry out orders.

Isobel said, "Got an extra gun for me?"

Bey scowled at her. "You better get over there with Homer where it's safer."

She said evenly, "I've always considered myself a pacifist, but when somebody starts shooting at me, I forget about it and am inclined to shoot back."

"I haven't got time to argue with you," Bey said. "There aren't any extra guns except handguns and they'd be useless." As he spoke, he pulled his own Tommy-Noiseless from its scabbard on the front door of the air cushion lorry, and checked its clip of two hundred .10 caliber ultra-high velocity rounds. He flicked the selector to the explosive side of the clip.

* * * * *

The plane was roaring in on what would be its first pass, if Bey had guessed correctly. If he had guessed incorrectly, this might be the end. A charge of napalm would fry everything for a quarter of a mile around, or the craft might even be equipped with a mini-fission bomb. In this area a minor nuclear explosion would probably go undetected.

Bey yelled, "Don't anybody even try to fire at him at this range. He'll be back. It takes half the sky to turn around in with that crate, but he'll be back, lower next time."

Cliff Jackson said cheerlessly, "Maybe he's just looking for us. He won't necessarily take a crack at us."

Bey grunted. "Elmer?"

"Nothing on the radio," Elmer said. "If he was just scouting us out, he'd report to his base. But if his orders are to clobber us, then he wouldn't put it on the air."

The plane was turning in the sky, coming back.

Cliff argued, "Well, we can't fire unless we know if he's just hunting us out, or trying to do us in."

Elmer said patiently, "For just finding us, that first pass would be all he needed. He could radio back that he'd found us. But if he comes in again, he's looking for trouble."

"Here he comes!" Bey yelled. "Kenny-Cliff ... the rifle!"

Isobel suddenly dashed out into the sands a dozen yards or so from the vehicles and began running around and around in a circle as though demented.

Bey stared at her. "Get back here," he roared. "Under one of the trucks!"

She ignored him.

The rocket-plane was coming in, low and obviously as slow as the pilot could retard its speed.

The flac rifle began jumping and tracers reached out from it-inaccurately. The Tommy-Noiseless automatics in the hands of Bey and Elmer Allen gave their silenced *flic flic flic* sounds, equally ineffective.

On the ultra-stubby wings of the fast moving aircraft, a row of brilliant cherries flickered and a row of explosive shells plowed across the desert, digging twin ditches, miraculously going between the air cushion lorries but missing both. It was upon them, over and gone, before the men on the ground could turn to fire after.

Elmer Allen muttered an obscenity under his breath.

Cliff Jackson looked around in desperation. "What can we do now? He won't come close enough for us to even fire at him, next time."

Bey said nothing. Isobel had collapsed into the sand. Elmer Allen looked over at her. "Nice try, Isobel," he said. "I think he came in lower and slower than he would have otherwise-trying to see what the devil it was you were doing."

She shrugged, hopelessly.

"Hey!" Kenny Ballalou pointed.

The rocketcraft was wobbling, shuddering, in the sky. Suddenly it burst into a black cloud of fire and smoke and explosion.

At the same moment, Homer Crawford got up from the sand dune behind which he'd stationed himself and plowed awkwardly through the sand toward them.

Bey glared at him.

Homer shrugged and said, "I checked the way he came in the first time and figured he'd repeat the run. Then I got behind that dune there and faced in the other direction and started firing where I *thought* he'd be, a few seconds before he came over. He evidently ran right into it."

Bey said indignantly, "Look, wise guy, you're no longer the leader of a five-man Reunited Nations African Development Project team. Then, you were expendable. Now, you're El Hassan. You give the orders. Other people are expendable."

Homer Crawford grinned at him, somewhat ruefully and held up his hands as though in supplication. "Listen to the man, is that any way to talk to El Hassan?"

Elmer Allen said worriedly, "He's right, though, Homer. You shouldn't take chances."

Homer Crawford went serious. "Actually, none of us should, if we can avoid it. In a way, El Hassan isn't one person. It's this team here, and Jake Armstrong, who by this time I hope is on his way to the States."

Bey was shaking his head in stubborn determination. "No," he said. "I'm not sure that you comprehend this yourself, Homer, but you're Number One. You're the symbol, the hero these people are going to follow if we put this thing over. They couldn't understand a sextet leadership. They want a leader, someone to dominate and tell them what to do. A team you need, admittedly, but not so much as the team needs you. Remember Alexander? He had a team starting off with Aristotle for a brain-trust, and Parmenion, one of the greatest generals of all time for his right-hand man. Then he had a group of field men such as Ptolemy, Antipater, Antigonus and Seleucus-not to be rivaled until Napoleon built his team, two thousand years later. And what happened to this super-team when Alexander died?"

Homer looked at him thoughtfully.

Bey wound it up doggedly. "You're our Alexander. Our Caesar. Our Napoleon. So don't go getting yourself killed, damn it. Excuse me, Isobel."

Isobel grinned her pixielike grin. "I agree," she said. "Dammit."

Homer said, "I'm not sure I go all along with you or not. We'll think about it." His voice took a sharper note. "Let's go over and see if there's enough left in that wreckage to give us an idea of who the pilot represented. I can't believe it was a Reunited Nations man, and I'd like to know who, of our potential enemies, dislikes the idea of El Hassan so much that they figure we should all be bumped off before we even get under way."

* * * * *

It had begun-if there is ever a beginning-in Dakar. In the offices of Sven Zetterberg the Swedish head of the Sahara Division of the African Development Project of the Reunited Nations.

Homer Crawford, head of a five-man trouble-shooting team, had reported for orders. In one hand he held them, when he was ushered into the other's presence.

Zetterberg shook hands abruptly, said, "Sit down, Dr. Crawford."

Homer Crawford looked at the secretary who had ushered him in.

Zetterberg said, scowling, "What's the matter?"

"I think I have something to be discussed privately."

The secretary shrugged and turned and left.

Zetterberg, still scowling, resumed his own place behind the desk and said, "Claud Hansen is a trusted Reunited Nations man. What could possibly be so secret...?"

Homer indicated the orders he held. "This assignment. It takes some consideration."

Sven Zetterberg was not a patient man. He said, in irritation, "It should be perfectly clear. This El Hassan we've been hearing so much about. This mystery man come out of the desert attempting to unify all North America. We want to talk to him."

"Why?" Crawford said.

"Confound it," Zetterberg snapped. "I thought we'd gone into this yesterday. In spite of the complaints that come into this office in regard to your cavalier tactics in carrying out your assignments, you and your team are our most competent operatives. So we've given you the assignment of finding El Hassan."

"I mean, why do you want to talk to him?"

The Swede glared at him for a moment, as though the American was being deliberately dense. "Dr. Crawford," he said, "when the African Development Project was first begun we had high hopes. Seemingly all Reunited Nations members were being motivated by high humanitarian reasons. Our task was to bring all Africa to a level of progress comparable to the advanced nations. It was more than a duty, it was a crying need, a demand. Africa is and has been throughout history a *have-not* continent. While Europe, the Americas, Australia and now even Asia, industrialized and largely conquered man's old socio-economic problems, Africa lagged behind. The reasons were manifold, colonialism, lingering tribal society ...various others. Now that very lagging has become a potential explosive situation. With the coming of antibiotics and other break-throughs in medicine, the African population is growing with an all but geometric progression. So fast is it growing, that what advances were being made did less than keep up the level of per capita gross product. It was bad enough to have a per capita gross product averaging less than a hundred dollars a year, but it actually sank below that point."

Homer Crawford was nodding.

Zetterberg continued the basic lecture with which he knew the other was already completely familiar. "So the Reunited Nations took on the task of advancing as rapidly as possible the African economy and all the things that must be done before an economy *can* be advanced. It was self-preservation, I suppose. *Have-not* nations, not to speak of *have-not* races and *have-not* continents, have a tendency eventually to explode upon their wealthier neighbors."

The Swede pressed his lips together before continuing. "Unfortunately, the Reunited Nations as the United Nations and the League of Nations before it, is composed of members each with its own irons in the fire. Each with its own plans and schemes." His voice was bitter now. "The Arab Union with its desire to unite all Islam into one. The Soviet Complex with its ultimate dream of a soviet world. The capitalistic economies of the British Commonwealth, Common Europe, and your United States of the Americas, with their hunger for, positive need for, sources of raw materials and markets for their manufactured products. All, though playing lip service to the African Development Project, have still their own ambitions."

Sven Zetterberg waggled a finger at Homer Crawford. "I do not charge that your United States is attempting to take over Africa, or even any section of it, in the old colonialistic sense. Even England and France have discovered that it is much simpler to dominate economically than to go through all the expense and effort of governing another people. That is the basic reason they gave up their empires. No, your United States would love to so dominate Africa that her products, her entrepreneurs, would flood the continent to the virtual exclusion of such economic competitors as Common Europe. The Commonwealth feels the same, so does the French Community. The Soviets and Arabs have different motivations, but they, too, wish to take over. The result...." The Swede tossed up his hands in a gesture more Gallic than Scandinavian.

* * * * *

"What has all this got to do with El Hassan?" Homer Crawford asked softly.

The Swede leaned forward. "If we more devoted adherents of the Reunited Nations are ever to see our hopes come true, Africa must be united and made strong. And this must be done through the efforts of *Africans* not Russians, British, French, Arabs ... nor even Scandinavians. Socio-economic changes should not, possibly cannot, be inflicted upon a people from without. Look at the mess the Russians made in such countries as Hungary, or the Americans in such as South Korea."

"The people themselves must have the dream," Crawford said softly.

"I beg your pardon?"

"Nothing. Go on."

Zetterberg said, "On the surface, great progress seems to be continuing. Afforestation of the Sahara, the solar pumps creating new oases, the water purification plants on the Atlantic and Mediterranean, pushing back the desert, the oil fields, the mines, the roads, the damming of the Niger. But already cracks can be seen. A week or so ago, a team of Cubans, supposedly, at least, in the Sudan to improve sugar refining methods, were machine-gunned to death. By whom? By the Sudanese? Unlikely. No, this Cuban massacre was one of many recent signs of conflict between the great powers in their efforts to dominate. Our problem, of course, deals only with North Africa, but I have heard rumors in Geneva that much the same situation is developing in the south as well."

"At any rate, Dr. Crawford, when the rumors of El Hassan began to come into this office they brought with them a breath of hope. From all we have heard, he teaches our basic program — a breaking down of old tribal society, education, economic progress, Pan-African unity. Dr. Crawford, no one with whom this office is connected seems ever to have seen this El Hassan but we are most anxious to talk to him. Perhaps this is the man behind whom we can throw our support. Your task is to find him."

Homer Crawford raked the fingers of his right hand back over his short wiry hair, and grimaced. He said, "It won't be necessary."

"I beg your pardon, Doctor?"

Crawford said, "It won't be necessary to go looking for El Hassan."

The Swede scowled his irritation at the other. "See here...."

Crawford said, "I'm El Hassan."

Sven Zetterberg stared at him, uncomprehending.

Homer Crawford said, "I suppose it's your turn to listen and for me to do the talking." He shifted in his chair, uncomfortably. "Dr. Zetterberg, even before the Reunited Nations evolved the idea of the African Development Project, it became obvious that the field work was going to have to be in the hands of Negroes. The reason is doublefold. First, the African doesn't trust the white man, for good reason. Second, the white man is a citizen of his own country, first of all, and finds it difficult not to have motives connected with his own race and nation. But the African Negro, too, has his tribal and sometimes national affiliations and cannot be trusted not to be prejudiced in their favor. The answer? The educated American Negro, such as myself."

"I haven't the slightest idea from whence came my ancestors, from what part of Africa, what tribe, what nation. But I am a Negro and ... well, have the dream of bettering my race. I have no irons in the fire, beyond altruistic ones. Of course, when I say American Negroes I don't exclude Canadian ones, or those of Latin America or the Caribbean. It is simply that there are greater numbers of educated American Negroes than you find elsewhere."

Zetterberg said impatiently, "Please, Dr. Crawford. Come to the point. That ridiculous statement you made about El Hassan."

"Of course, I am merely giving background. Most of we field workers, not only the African Development teams, but such organizations as the Africa for Africans Association and the representatives of the African Department of the British Commonwealth, and of the French Community's African Affairs sector, are composed of Negroes."

Zetterberg was nodding. "All right, I know."

Homer Crawford said, "The teams of all these organizations do their best to spur African progress, in our case, in North Africa, especially the area between the Niger and the Mediterranean. Often we disguise ourselves as natives since in that manner we are more quickly trusted. We wear the clothes, speak the local language or lingua franca."

The American hesitated a moment, then plunged in. "Dr. Zetterberg, the African is still a primitive but newly beginning to move out of a tradition-ritual-taboo tribal society. He seeks a hero to follow, a man of towering prestige who knows the answers to all questions. We may not *like* this fact, we with our traditions of democracy, but it is so. The African is simply not yet at that stage of society where political democracy is applicable."

"My team does most of its work posing as Enaden-low caste itinerant smiths of the Sahara. As such we can go any place and are everywhere accepted, a necessary sector of the Saharan economy. As such, we continually spread the ...ah, propaganda of the Reunited Nations-the need for education, the need for taking jobs on the new projects, the need for casting aside old institutions and embracing the new. Early in the game we found our words had little weight coming from simple Enaden smiths so we ...well, *invented* this mysterious El Hassan, and everything we said we attributed to him."

"News spreads fast in the desert, astonishingly fast. El Hassan started with us but soon other teams, hearing about him and realizing that his message was the same as that they were trying to propagate, did the same thing. That is, attributed the messages they had to spread to El Hassan. It was amusing when a group of us got together last week in Timbuktu, to find that we'd all taken to kowtowing to this mythical desert hero who planned to unite all North Africa."

The Swede was staring at him unbelievingly. "But, a bit earlier you said you were El Hassan."

Homer Crawford looked into his chief's face and nodded seriously. "I've been conferring with various other field workers, both Reunited Nations and otherwise. The situation calls for a real El Hassan. If we don't provide him, someone else will. I propose to take over the position."

Sven Zetterberg's face was suddenly cold. "And why, Dr. Crawford, do you think you are more qualified than others?"

The American Negro could hardly fail to note the other's disapproval. He said evenly, but definitely, "Through experience. Through education. Through ...through having the dream, Dr. Zetterberg."

"The Reunited Nations cannot support such a project, Dr. Crawford. I absolutely forbid you to consider it."

"Forbid me?"

* * * * *

It was as though a strange something entered the atmosphere of the room, almost as though a new *presence* was there. And almost, it seemed to Sven Zetterberg, that the already tall, solidly built man across from him grew physically as his voice seemed to swell, to reach out, to dominate. There was a new, and all but unbelievable Homer Crawford here.

The Swedish official regathered his forces. This was ridiculous. He said again, "I forbid you to...." the sentence dribbled away under the cold disdain in the air now.

Homer Crawford said flatly, "You don't seem to understand, Zetterberg. The Reunited Nations has no control over El Hassan. Homer Crawford, as of this meeting, has resigned his post with the African Development Project. And El Hassan has begun his task of uniting all North Africa."

Sven Zetterberg, shaken by this new and unsuspected force the other seemed to be able to bring to his command, fought back. "It will be simple to discredit you, to let it be known that you are no more than an ambitious American out to seize power illegally."

Crawford's scorn held an element of amusement. "Try it. I suspect your attempts to discredit El Hassan will prove unsuccessful. He has already been rumored to be everything from an Ethiopian to the Second Coming of the Messiah. Your attempt to brand him an American adventurer will be swallowed up in the flood of other rumor."

The Swede was still shaken by the strange manner in which his once subordinate had suddenly dominated him. Sven Zetterberg was not a man to be dominated, to be made unsure.

Time folded back on itself and for a moment he was again a lad and on vacation with his father in Bavaria. They were having lunch in the famed Hofbraühaus, largest of the Munich beercellars, and even a ten-year-old could sense an anticipation in the air, particularly among the large number of brownshirted men who had gathered to one side of the ground level of the beer hall. His father was telling Sven of the history of the medieval building when a silence fell. Into the beer hall had come a pasty faced, trenchcoat garbed little man, his face set in stern lines but insufficiently to offset the ludicrous mustache. He was accompanied by an elderly soldier in the uniform of a Field Marshal, by a large tub of a man whose face beamed-but evilly-and by a pinch faced cripple. All were men of command, all except the pasty faced one, to whom they seemingly and surprisingly, deferred. And then he stood on a heavy chair and spoke. And then his *power* reached out and grasped all within reach of his shrill voice. Grasped them and compelled them and they became a shouting, red faced, arm brandishing mob, demanding to be led to glory. And Sven's father had bustled the shocked boy from the building.

It came back to him now, clearly and forcefully, and he realized that whatever it was with which the Beast of Berchtesgaden had enchanted his people, that power was on call in Homer Crawford. Whether he used it for good or evil, that enchanting power was on call. And again Sven Zetterberg was shaken.

Homer Crawford was on his feet, preparatory to leaving.

The Swede simply *had* to reassert himself. "Dr. Crawford, the Reunited Nations is not without resources. You'll be arrested before you leave Dakar."

An element of the tenseness left the air when Crawford smiled and said, "Doctor, for several years now I have been playing hide and seek in the Sahara, doing your work. You mentioned earlier that my team is the most experienced and capable. Just whom are you going to send to pick me up? Members of some of the other teams? Old friends and comrades in arms. Many of whom owe their lives to my team when all bets were down. Please do send them, Doctor, I am going to need recruits."

He swung and left the office and even as he went could hear the angry Reunited Nations chief blasting into an interoffice communicator. He decided he'd better see if there wasn't a back door or window through which to leave the building. He'd have to phone Bey, Isobel and the others and get together for a meeting to plan developments. El Hassan was getting off to a fast start, already he was on the lam.

* * * * *

Homer Crawford played it safe. From the nearest public phone he called Isobel Cunningham at the Hotel Juan-le-Pin. No matter how fast Sven Zetterberg swung into action, it would take his operatives some time to connect Isobel with Homer and his team. As an employee of the Africa for Africans Association, she would ordinarily come in little contact with the Reunited Nations teams.

He said, "Isobel? Homer here. Can you talk?"

She said, "Cliff and Jake are here."

He said, "Have you sounded them out? How do they feel about the El Hassan project?"

"They're in. At least, Jake is. We're still arguing with Cliff."

"O.K. Now listen, carefully. Zetterberg turned thumbs down on the whole deal, for various reasons we can discuss later. In fact, he's incensed and threatened to take steps to keep us from leaving Dakar."

Isobel was alerted but she snorted deprecation. "What do you want?"

"They're probably already looking for me, and in a matter of minutes will probably try to pick up Bey-ag-Akhamouk, Elmer Allen and Kenny Ballalou, the other members of my team. Get in touch with them immediately and tell them to get into native costume and into hiding. You and Jake-and Cliff-do the same."

"Right. Where do we meet and when?"

"In the *souk*, in the food market. There's a native restaurant there, run by a former Vietnamese. We'll meet there at approximately noon."

"Right. Anything else?"

Homer said, "Tell Bey to bring along an extra 9mm Recoilless for me."

"Yes, El Hassan," she said, her voice expressionless. She didn't waste time. Homer Crawford heard the phone click as she hung up.

He was in a branch building of the post and telegraph network on the Rue des Resistance. Before leaving it, he looked out a window. Half a block away was the office of the Sahara Division of the African Development Project. Even as he watched, a dozen men hurried out the front door, fanned out in all directions.

Homer grinned sourly. Old Sven was moving fast.

He shot a quick glance around the lobby of the building. He had to get going. Zetterberg had started with a dozen men to trail down El Hassan. He'd probably have a hundred involved before the hour was out.

A corridor turned off to the right. Homer hurried down it. At each door he looked inside. To whoever occupied the room he murmured a few words of apology in Wolof, the Sengalese lingua franca. The fourth office was empty.

Homer stood there before it for a long, agonizing moment, waiting for the right person to pass. Finally, the man he needed came along. About six feet tall, about a hundred and eighty; dressed in the local native dress and on the ragged side.

Homer said to him authoritatively, in the Wolof tongue, "You there, come in here!" He opened the door, and pointed into the office.

The other, taken aback, demurred.

Homer's face and tone went still more commanding. "Step in here, before I call the police."

It was all a mistake, of course. The Senegalese made the gesture equivalent to the European's shrug, and entered the office.

Homer came in behind him, closed the door. He wasted no time in preliminaries. Before the native turned, the American's hand lashed out in a karate blow which stunned the other. Homer Crawford caught him, even as he fell, and lowered him gently to the floor.

"Sorry, old boy," he muttered, "but this is probably the most profitable thing that's happened to you this year."

He stripped off the other's clothes, as rapidly as he could make his hands fly. The other was still out and probably would be for another ten minutes, Crawford estimated. He stripped off his own clothes and donned the native's.

Last of all, he took his wallet from his pocket, divided the money it contained and stuffed a considerable wad of it into the European clothing he was abandoning.

"Don't spend all of that in one place," he growled softly.

Homer dragged the other to a side of the room so that the body could not be spotted from the entrance. Then he crossed to the door, opened it and stepped into the corridor beyond.

There was no need for sulking. He walked out the front door and headed away from the dock and administration buildings area and toward the native section, passing the Reunited Nations building on the way.

Dakar teems with multitudes of a dozen tribes come in from the jungles and the bush, the desert and the swamp areas of the sources of the Niger, to look for work on the new projects, to visit relatives, to market for the products of civilization-or to gawk. Homer Crawford disappeared into them. One among many.

Toward noon, he entered the cleared area which was the restaurant he had named to Isobel and squatted before the pots to the far end of the Vietnamese owned eatery, examining them with care. He chose a large chunk of barbequed goat and was served it with a half pound piece of unsalted Senegalese bread, torn from a monstrous loaf, and a twisted piece of newspaper into which had been measured an ounce or so of coarse salt. He took his meal and went to as secluded a corner as he could find.

Homer Crawford chuckled inwardly. That morning he had breakfasted in the most swank hotel in West Africa. He wished there was some manner in which he could have invited Sven Zetterberg to dine here with him. Or, come to think of it, a group of the students he had once taught sociology at the University of Michigan. Or, possibly, prexy Wallington, under whom he had worked while taking his doctor's degree.

Yes, it would have been interesting to have had a luncheon companion.

A native woman, on the stoutish side but with her hair done up in one of the fabulously ornate hair styles specialized in by the Senegalese, and wearing a flowing, shapeless dress of the garish textiles run off purposely for this market in Japan and Manchester, waddled up to take a place nearby. She bore a huge skewer of barbequed beef chunks, and a hunk of bread not unlike Homer's own.

She grumbled uncomfortably, her back to the American, as she settled into a position on the floor. And she mumbled as she began chewing at the meat.

No table manners, Homer Crawford grinned inwardly. He wondered how long it would take for the others to get here. He wasn't worried about Isobel, Cliff Jackson and Jake Armstrong. It would take time before Zetterberg's Reunited Nations cloak and dagger boys got around to them, but he wasn't sure that she'd be able to locate his own team in time. That bit he'd given the Swede official about his being so bully-bully with the other Reunited Nations teams was in the way of being an exaggeration, with the idea of throwing the other off. Actually, working in the field on definite assignments, it was seldom you ran into other African Development Project men. But perhaps it would tie Zetterberg up, wondering just who he could trust to send looking for El Hassan.

He finished off his barbequed goat and the bread and wiped his hands on his clothes. Nobody here yet. To have an excuse for staying, he would have to buy a bottle of Gazelle beer, the cheap Senegalese brew which came in quart bottles and was warm and on the gassy side.

It was then that the woman in front of him, without turning, said softly, "El Hassan?"

II

Homer Crawford stared at her, unbelievingly. The woman couldn't possibly be an emissary from Isobel or from one of his own companions. This situation demanded the utmost secrecy, they hadn't had time to screen any outsiders as to trustworthiness.

She turned. It was Isobel. She chuckled softly, "You should see your face."

His eyes went to her figure.

"Done with mirrors," Isobel said. "Or, at least, with pillows."

Homer didn't waste time. "Where are the others? They should be here by now."

"We figured that the fewer of us seen on the streets, the better. So they're waiting for you. Since I was the most easily disguised, the least suspicious looking, I was elected to come get you."

"Waiting where?"

She licked the side of her mouth, a disconcerting characteristic of hers, and looked at him archly. "Those pals of yours have quite a bit on the ball on their own. They decided that there was a fairly good chance that Sven Zetterberg wasn't exactly going to fall into your arms, so they took preliminary measures. Kenny Ballalou rented a small house, here in the native quarter. We've all rendezvoused there. See, you aren't the only one on the ball."

Homer frowned at her, for the moment being in no mood for humor. "What was the idea of sitting here for the past five minutes without even speaking? You must have recognized me, knowing what to look for."

She nodded. "I...I wasn't sure, Homer, but I had the darnedest feeling I was being followed."

His glance was sharp now. First at her, then a quick darting around the vicinity. "Woman's intuition," he snapped, "or something substantial?"

She frowned at him. "I'm not a ninny, Homer."

His voice softened and he said quickly, "Don't misunderstand, Isobel. I know that."

She forgot about her objection to his tone. "Even intuition doesn't come out of a clear sky. Something sparks it. Subconscious psi, possibly, but a spark."

"However?" he prodded.

"I took all precautions. I can't seem to put my finger on anything."

"O.K.," he said decisively. "Let's go then." He came to his feet and reached a hand down for her.

"Heavens to Betsy," she said, "don't do that."

"What?"

"Help a woman in public. You'll look suspicious." She came to her own feet, without aid.

Damn, he thought. She was right. The last thing he wanted was to draw attention to a man who acted peculiarly.

* * * * *

They made their way out of the food market and into the *souk* proper, Homer walking three or four paces ahead of her, Isobel demurely behind, her eyes on the ground. They passed the native stands and tiny shops, and the even smaller venders and hucksters with their products of the mass production industries of East and West, side by side with the native handicrafts ranging from carved wooden statues, jewelry, *gris gris* charms and kambu fetishes, to ceramics whose designs went back to an age before the Portuguese first cruised off this coast. And everywhere was color; there are no people on earth more color conscious than the Senegalese.

Isobel guided him, her voice quiet and still maintaining its uncharacteristic demure quality.

He would never have recognized Isobel, Homer Crawford told himself. Isobel Cunningham, late of Columbia University where she'd taken her Master's in anthropology. Isobel Cunningham, whom he had told on their first meeting that she looked like the former singing star, Lena Horne. Isobel Cunningham, slight of build, pixie of face, crisply modern American with her tongue and wit. Was he in love with her? He didn't know. El Hassan had no time, at present, for those things love implied.

She said, "Here," and led the way down a brick paved passage to a small house, almost a hut, that lay beyond.

Homer Crawford looked about him critically before entering. He said, "I suppose this has been scouted out adequately. Where's the back entrance?" He scowled. "Haven't the boys posted a sentry?"

A voice next to his ear said pleasantly, "Stick 'em up, stranger. Where'd you get that zoot suit?"

He jerked his head about. There was a very small opening in the wooden wall next to him. It was Kenny Ballalou's voice.

"Zoot suit, yet!" Homer snorted. "I haven't heard that term since I was in rompers."

"You in rompers I'd like to see," Kenny snorted in his turn. "Come on in, everybody's here."

The aged, unpainted, warped, wooden house consisted of two rooms, the one three times as large as the second. The furniture was minimal, but there was sitting room on chair, stool and bed for the seven of them.

"Hail, O El Hassan!" Elmer Allen called sourly, as Homer entered.

"And the hail with you," Homer called back, then, "Oops, sorry, Isobel."

Isobel put her hands on her hips, greatly widened by the stuffing she'd placed beneath her skirts. "Look," she said. "Thus far, the El Hassan organization, which claims rule of all North Africa, consists of six men and one dame ... ah, that is, one lady. Just so the lady won't continually feel that she's being a drag on the conversation, you are hereby allowed in moments of stress such shocking profanity as an occasional damn or hell. But only if said lady is also allowed such expletives during periods of similar stress."

Everyone laughed, and found chairs.

"I'm in love with Isobel Cunningham," Bey announced definitely.

"Second the motion," Elmer said.

The rest of them called, "Aye."

"O.K.," Homer Crawford said glumly, "I can see that this is going to be one tight knit organization. Six men in love with the one dame ... ah, that is, lady. Kind of a reverse harem deal. Oh, this is going to lead to great co-operation."

* * * * *

They laughed again and then Jake said, "Well, what's the story, Homer? How does the El Hassan project sound to Zetterberg and the Reunited Nations?"

Cliff Jackson laughed bitterly. "Why do you think we're in hiding?" Only he and Jake Armstrong wore western clothing. Kenny Ballalou, Bey-ag-Akhamouk and Elmer Allen were in native dress, similar to that of Homer Crawford. Elmer Allen even bore a pilgrim's staff.

Crawford, glad that the edge of tenseness had been taken off the group by the banter with Isobel, turned serious now.

He said, "This is where we each take our stand. You can turn back at this point, any one of you, and things will undoubtedly go on as before. You'll keep your jobs, have no marks against you. Beyond this point, and there's no turning back. I want you all to think it over, before coming to any snap decisions."

Elmer Allen said, his face wearing its usual all but sullen expression. "How about you?"

Homer said evenly, "I've already taken my stand."

Kenny Ballalou yawned and said, "I've been in this team for three or four years, I'm too lazy to switch now Besides, I've always wanted to be a corrupt politician. Can I be treasurer in this El Hassan regime?"

"No," Homer said. "Bey?"

Bey-ag-Akhamouk said, "I've always wanted to be a general. I'll come in under those circumstances."

Homer said, his voice still even. "That's out. From this point in, you're a Field Marshal and Minister of Defense."

"Shucks," Bey said. "I'd always wanted to be a general."

Homer Crawford said dryly, "Doesn't anybody take this seriously? It's probably going to mean all your necks before it's through, you know."

Elmer Allen said dourly, "I take it seriously. I spent the idealistic years, the school years, working for peace, democracy, a better world. Now, here I am, helping to attempt to establish a tyranny over half the continent of my racial background. But I'm in."

"Right," Homer said, the side of his mouth twitching. "You can be our Minister of Propaganda."

"Minister of Propaganda!" Elmer wailed. "You mean like Goebbels? Me!"

Homer laughed. "O.K., we'll call it Minister of Information, or Press Secretary to El Hassan. It all means the same thing." He looked at Jacob Armstrong and said, "How old are you, Jake?"

"That's none of your business," the white-haired Jake said aggressively. "I'm in. El Hassan is the only answer. North Africa has got to be united, both for internal and external purposes. If you … if we … don't do the job first, somebody else will, and off hand, I can't think of anybody else I trust. I'm in."

Homer Crawford looked at him for a long moment. "Yes," he said finally. "Of course you are. Jake, you've just been made our combined Foreign Minister and Plenipotentiary Extraordinary to the Reunited Nations. You'll leave immediately, first for Geneva, to present our demands to the Reunited Nations, then to New York."

"What do I do in New York?" Jake Armstrong said blankly, trying to assimilate the curves that were being thrown to him.

"You raise money and support from starry eyed Negro groups and individuals. You line up such organizations as the Africa for Africans Association behind El Hassan. You give speeches, and ruin your liver eating at banquets every night in the week. You send out releases to the press. You get all the publicity for the El Hassan movement you can. You send official protests to the governments of every country in the world, every time they do something that doesn't fit in with our needs. You locate recruits and send them here to Africa to take over some of the load. I don't have to tell you what to do. You can think on your feet as well as I can. Do what is necessary. You're our Foreign Minister. Don't let us see your face again until El Hassan is in control of North Africa."

Jake Armstrong blinked. "How will I prove I'm your representative? I'll need more than just a note *To Whom It May Concern*."

Homer Crawford thought about that.

* * * * *

Bey said, "One of our first jobs is going to have to be to capture a town where they have a broadcast station, say Zinder or In Salah. When we do, we'll announce that you're Foreign Minister."

Crawford nodded. "That's obviously the ticket. By that time you should be in New York, with an office opened."

Jake rubbed a black hand over his cheek as though checking his morning shave. "It's going to take some money to get started. Once started I can depend on contributions, perhaps, but at first...."

Homer interrupted with, "Cliff, you're Minister of the Treasury. Raise some money."

"Eh?" Cliff Jackson said blankly. The king-size, easy-going Californian looked more like the early Joe Louis than ever.

Everybody laughed. Elmer Allen came forth with his wallet and began pulling out such notes as it contained. "I don't know what we'd be doing with this in the desert," he said.

Isobel said, "I have almost three thousand dollars in a checking account in New York. Let's see if I have my checkbook here."

The others were going through their pockets. As bank notes in British pounds, American dollars, French francs and Common Europe marks emerged they were tossed to the center of the small table which wobbled on three legs in the middle of the room.

Elmer Allen said, "I have an account with the Bank of Jamaica in Kingston. About four hundred pounds, I think. I'll have it transferred."

Cliff took up the money and began counting it, making notations on a notebook pad as he went.

Bey said, "We're only going to be able to give Jake part of this."

"How's that?" Elmer growled. "What use have we for money in the Sahara? Jake's got to put up a decent front in Geneva and New York."

Bey said doggedly, "As Defense Minister, I'm opposed to El Hassan's followers *ever* taking anything without generous payment. We'll need food and various services. From the beginning, we're going to have to pay our way. We can't afford to let rumors start going around that we're nothing but a bunch of brigands."

"Bey's right," Homer nodded. "The El Hassan movement is going to have to maintain itself on the highest ethical level. We're going to take over where the French Camel Corps left off and police North Africa. There can't be a man from Somaliland to Mauretania who can say that one of El Hassan's followers liberated him from as much as a date."

Kenny Ballalou said, "You can always requisition whatever you need and give them a receipt, and then we'll pay off when we come to power."

"That's out!" Bey snapped. "Most of these people can't read. And even those that do don't trust what they read. A piece of paper, in their eyes, is no return for some goats, or flour, camels, horses, or whatever else it might be we need. No, we're going to have to pay our way."

Crawford raked a hand back through his wiry hair. "Bey's right, Kenny. It's going to be a rough go, especially at first."

Kenny snorted. "What do you mean, *at first?* What's going to happen, *at second* to make it any easier? Where're we going to get all this money we'll need to pay for even what we ourselves use, not to speak of the thousands of men we're going to have to have if El Hassan is ever to come to power?"

Bey's eyebrows went up in shocked innocence. "Kenny, dear boy, don't misunderstand. We don't requisition anything from individuals, or clans, or small settlements. But if we take over a town such as Gao, or Niamey, or Colomb-Béchar, or wherever, there is nothing to say that a legal government such as that of El Hassan, can't requisition the contents of the local banks."

Homer Crawford said with dignity, "The term, my dear Minister of Defense, currently is to *nationalize* the bank. Whether or not we wish to have the banks remain nationalized, after we take over, we can figure out later. But in the early stages, I'm afraid we're going to have to nationalize just about every bank we come in contact with."

Cliff Jackson said cautiously, "I haven't said whether or not I'll come in yet, but just as a point, I might mention issuing your own legal tender. As soon as you liberate a printing press somewhere, of course."

Everyone was charmed at the idea.

Isobel said, "You can see Cliff was *meant* to be Minister of Treasury. He's got *wholesale* larceny in his soul, none of this picayunish stuff such as robbing nomads of their sheep."

Elmer Allen was shaking his head sadly. "This whole conversation started with Bey protesting that we couldn't allow ourselves to be thought of as brigands. Now listen to you all."

Kenny Ballalou said with considerable dignity, "See here, friend. Don't you know the difference between brigandage and international finance?"

"No," Elmer said flatly.

"Hm-m-m," Kenny said.

"Let's get on with this," Homer said. "The forming of El Hassan's basic government is beginning to take on aspects of a minstrel show. Then we've all declared ourselves in … except Cliff."

All eyes turned to the bulky Californian.

He sat scowling.

Homer said, easily, "You're not being urged, Cliff. You can turn back at this point."

Elmer Allen growled, "You came to Africa to help your race develop its continent. To conquer such problems as sufficient food, clothing and shelter for all. To bring education and decent medical care to a people who have had possibly the lowest living standards anywhere. Can you see any way of achieving this beyond the El Hassan movement?"

Cliff looked at him, still scowling stubbornly. "That's not why I came to Africa."

Their eyes were all on him, but they remained silent.

He said, defensively, "I'm no do-gooder. I took a job with the Africa for Africans Association because it was the best job I could find."

Isobel broke the silence by saying softly, "I doubt it, Cliff."

The big man stood up from where he'd been seated on the bed. "O.K., O.K. Possibly there were other angles. I wanted to travel. Wanted to see Africa. Besides, it was good background for some future job. I figured it wouldn't hurt me any, in later years, applying for some future job. Maybe with some Negro concern in the States. I'd be able to say I'd put in a few years in Africa. Something like a Jew in New York who was a veteran of the Israel-Arab wars, before the debacle."

They still looked at him, none of them accusingly.

He was irritated as he paced. "Don't you see? Everybody doesn't have this *dream* that Homer's always talking about. That doesn't mean I'm abnormal. I just don't have the interest you do. All I want is a good job, some money in the bank, security back in the States. I'm not interested in dashing all over the globe, getting shot at, dying for some ideal."

Homer said gently, "It's up to you, Cliff. Nobody's twisting your arm."

There was sweat on the big man's forehead. "All I came to Africa for was the job, the money I got out of it," he repeated, insisting.

* * * * *

To Homer Crawford suddenly came the realization that the other needed an out, an excuse. An explanation to himself for doing something he wanted to do but wouldn't admit because it went against the opportunistic code he told himself he followed.

Homer said, "All right. How much are you making as a field worker for the Africa for Africans Association?"

Cliff looked at him, uncomprehending. "Eight thousand dollars, plus expenses."

"O.K., we'll double that. Sixteen thousand to begin with, as El Hassan's Minister of Treasury and whatever other duties we can think of to hang on you."

There was a long moment of silence, unbroken by any of the others. Finally in a gesture of desperation, Cliff Jackson waved at the money and checks sitting on the center table. "Sixteen thousand a year! The whole organization doesn't have enough to pay me six months' salary."

Homer said mildly, "That's why your pay was doubled. You have to take risks to make money in this world, Cliff. If El Hassan does come to power, undoubtedly you'll get other raises-along with greater responsibility."

He looked into Cliff Jackson's face, and although his words had dealt with money, a man's dream looked out from his eyes. And the force of personality that could emanate from Homer Crawford, possibly unbeknownst to himself, flooded over the huge Californian. The others in the room could feel it. Elmer Allen cleared his throat; Isobel held her elbows to her sides, in a feminine protest against naked male psychic strength.

Kenny Ballalou said without inflection, "Put up or shut up, Cliff old pal."

Cliff Jackson sank back onto the spot on the bed he'd occupied before. "I'm in," he muttered, so softly as hardly to be heard.

"None of you are in," a voice from the doorway said.

The figure that stood there held a thin, but heavy calibered automatic in his hand.

* * * * *

He was a dapper man, neat, trim, smart. His clothes were those of Greater Washington, rather than Dakar and West Africa. His facial expression seemed overly alert, overly bright, and his features were more Caucasian than Negroid.

He said, "I believe you all know me. Fredric Ostrander."

"Of the Central Intelligence Agency," Homer Crawford said dryly. He as well as Bey, Elmer and Kenny had risen to their feet when the newcomer entered from the smaller of the hut's two rooms. "What's the gun for, Ostrander?"

"You're under arrest," the C.I.A. man said evenly.

Elmer Allen snorted. "Under whose authority are you working? As a Jamaican, I'm a citizen of the West Indies and a subject of Her Majesty."

"We'll figure that out later," Ostrander rapped. "I'm sure the appropriate Commonwealth authorities will co-operate with the State Department and the Reunited Nations in this matter." The gun unwaveringly went from one of them to the other, retraced itself.

Bey looked at Homer Crawford.

Crawford shook his head gently.

He said to the newcomer, "The question still stands, Ostrander. Under whose authority are you operating? I don't think you have jurisdiction over us. We're in Africa, not in the United States of the Americas."

Ostrander said tightly, "Right now I'm operating under the authority of this weapon in my hand. Dr. Crawford. Do you realize that all of you Americans here are risking your citizenship?"

Kenny Ballalou said, "Oh? Tell us more, Mr. State Department man."

"You're serving in the armed forces of a foreign power."

Even the dour Elmer Allen laughed at that one.

Crawford said, "The fact of the matter is, we *are* the foreign power."

"You're not amusing, Dr. Crawford," Ostrander said. "I've kept up with this situation since you had that conference in Timbuktu. The State Department has no intention of allowing some opportunist, backed by known communists and fellow travelers, to seize power in this portion of the world. In a matter of months the Soviets would be in here."

Isobel said evenly, "I was formerly a member of the Party. I no longer am. I am an active opponent of the Soviet Complex at the moment, especially in regard to its activity in Africa."

Ostrander snorted his disbelief.

Elmer Allen said, "You chaps never forget, do you?" He looked at the others and explained. "Back during college days, I signed a few peace petitions, that sort of thing. Ever since, every time I come in contact with these people, you'd think I was Lenin or Trotsky."

Homer Crawford said, "My opinion is, Ostrander, that you've had to move too quickly to check back with your superiors. Has the State Department actually instructed you to arrest me and my companions here on foreign soil, without a warrant?"

Ostrander clipped, "That's my responsibility. I'm taking you all in. We'll solve such problems as jurisdiction and warrants when I get you to the Reunited Nations headquarters."

"Ah?" Homer Crawford said. "And then what happens to us?"

Ostrander jiggled the gun, impatiently. "Sven Zetterberg is of the opinion that you should immediately be flown out of Africa and the case brought before the High Council of the African Development Project. What measures will be taken beyond that point I have no way of knowing."

Bey took a step to the left, Kenny Ballalou one to the right. Homer Crawford remained immediately before the C.I.A. operative, his hands slightly out from his sides, palms slightly forward.

Ostrander snapped, "I'm prepared to fire, you men. I don't underestimate the importance of this situation. If your crazy scheme makes any progress at all, it might well result in the death of thousands. I know your background, Crawford. You once taught judo in the Marines. I'm not unfamiliar with the art myself."

Isobel had a hand to her mouth, her eyes were wide. "Boys, don't ..." she began.

Elmer Allen had been leaning on his pilgrim's staff, as though weary with this whole matter. He said to Ostrander, interestedly, "So you've been checked out on judo? Know anything about the use of the quarterstaff?"

Ostrander kept his gun traversing between the four of them. "Eh?" he said.

Elmer Allen shifted his grip on his staff infinitesimally. Of a sudden, the end of the staff, now gripped with both hands near the center, moved at invisibly high speed. There was a crack of the wrist bone, and the gun went flying. The other end of the staff flicked out and rapped the C.I.A. operative smartly on the head.

Fredric Ostrander crumbled to the floor.

* * * * *

"Confound it, Elmer," Crawford said. "What'd you have to go and do that for? I wanted to talk to him some more and send a message back to Zetterberg. Sooner or later we've got to make our peace with the Reunited Nations."

Elmer said embarrassedly, "Sorry, it just happened. I was merely going to knock the gun out of his hand, but then I couldn't help myself. I was tired of hearing that holier-than-thou voice of his."

Kenny Ballalou looked down at the fallen man gloomily. "He'll be out for an hour. You're lucky you didn't crack his skull."

"Holy Mackerel," Cliff Jackson said. "I'm going to have to learn to operate one of those things."

Elmer Allen handed him the supposed pilgrim's staff. "Best hand-to-hand combat weapon ever invented," he said. "The British yeoman's quarterstaff. Of course, this is a modernized version. Made of epoxy resin glass-fiber material, treated to look like wood. That stuff can turn a high-velocity bullet, let alone a sword, and it can be bent in a ninety degree arc without the slightest effect, although it'd take a power-driven testing machine to do it."

"All right, all right," Homer said. "We haven't got time for lessons in the use of the quarterstaff. Let's put some thought to this situation. If Ostrander here was able to find us, somebody else would, too."

Isobel licked the side of her mouth. "He was probably following me. Remember, I told you Homer?"

Kenny said, "If he had anyone with him, he'd have brought them along to cover him. You've got to give him credit for bravery, taking on the whole bunch of us by himself."

"Um-m-m," Homer said. "I wish he was with us instead of against us."

Jake Armstrong said, "Well, this solves one problem."

They looked at him.

He said, "Just as sure as sure, he's got a car parked somewhere. A car with some sort of United States or Reunited Nations emblem on it."

"So what?" Kenny said.

"So you've got to get out of town before the search for you *really* gets under way. With such a car, you can get past any roadblock that might already be up between here and the Yoff airport."

Elmer Allen had sunk to his knees and was searching the fallen C.I.A. man. He came up with car keys and a wallet.

Homer said to Jake Armstrong, "Why the Yoff airport?"

"Our plane is there," Jake told him. "The one assigned Isobel, Cliff and me by the AFAA. You're going to have to make time. Get somewhere out in the ah, boondocks, where you can begin operations."

Bey said thoughtfully, "He's right, Homer. Anybody against us, like our friend here" — he nodded at Ostrander —"is going to try to get us quick, before we can get the El Hassan movement under way. We've got to get out of Dakar and into some area where they'll have their work cut out trying to locate us."

Homer Crawford accepted their council. "O.K., let's get going. Jake, you'll stay in Dakar, and at first play innocent. As soon as possible, take plane for Geneva. As soon as you're there, send out press releases to all the news associations and the larger papers. Announce yourself as Foreign Minister of El Hassan and demand that he be recognized as the legal head of state of all North Africa."

"Wow," Cliff Jackson said.

"Then play it by ear," Homer finished.

He turned to the others. "Bey, where'd you leave our two hover-lorries when you came here to Dakar?"

"Stashed away in the ruins of a former mansion in Timbuktu. Hired two Songhai to watch them."

"O.K. Cliff, you're the only one in European dress. Take this wallet of Ostrander's. You'll drive the car. If we run into any roadblocks between here and the Yoff airport, slow down a little and hold the wallet out to show your supposed identification. They won't take the time to check the photo. Bluff your way past, don't completely stop the car."

"What happens if they do stop us?" Cliff said worriedly.

Kenny Ballalou said, "That'll be just too bad for them."

Bey stooped and scooped up the fallen automatic of Fredric Ostrander and tucked it into the voluminous folds of his native robe. "Here we go again," he said.

III

The man whose undercover name was Anton, landed at Gibraltar in a BEA roco-jet, passed quickly through customs and immigration with his Commonwealth passport and made his way into town. He checked with a Bobby and found that he had a two-hour wait until the Mons Capa ferry left for Tangier, and spent the time wandering up and down Main Street, staring into the Indian shops with their tax-free cameras from Common Europe, textiles from England, optical equipment from Japan, and cheap souvenirs from everywhere. Gibraltar, the tourist's shopping paradise.

The trip between Gibraltar and Tangier takes approximately two hours. If you've never made it before, you stand on deck and watch Spain recede behind you, and Africa loom closer. This was where Hercules supposedly threw up his Pillars, Gibraltar being the one on the European shore. Those who have made the trip again and again, sit down in the bar and enjoy the tax-free prices. The man named Anton stood on the deck. He was African by birth, but he'd never been to Morocco before.

When he landed, he made the initial error of expecting the local citizenry to speak Arabic. They didn't. Rif, a Berber tongue, was the first language. The man called Anton had to speak French to make known his needs. He took a Chico cab up from the port to the El Minza hotel, immediately off the Plaza de France, the main square of the European section.

At the hotel entrance were two jet-black doormen attired in a pseudo-Moroccan costume of red fez, voluminous pants and yellow barusha slippers. They made no note of his complexion, there is no color bar in the Islamic world.

He had reservations at the desk. He left his passport there to go through the standard routine, including being checked by the police, had his bag sent up to his room and, a few minutes later, hands nonchalantly in pockets, strolled along the Rue de Liberté toward the casbah area of the medina. Up from the native section of town streamed hordes of costumed Rifs, Arabs, Berbers of a dozen tribes, even an occasional Blue Man. At least half the women still wore the haik and veil, half the men the burnoose. Africa changes slowly, the man called Anton admitted to himself all over again-so slowly.

Down from the European section, which could have been a Californian city, filtered every nation of the West, from every section of Common Europe, the Americas, the Soviet Complex. If any city in the world is a melting pot, it is Tangier, where Africa meets Europe and where East meets West.

He passed through the teaming Grand Zocco market, and through the gates of the old city. He took Rue Singhalese, the only street in the medina wide enough to accommodate a vehicle and went almost as far as the Zocco Chico, once considered the most notorious square in the world.

For a moment the man called Anton stood before one of the Indian shops and stared at the window's contents. Carved ivory statuettes from the Far East, cameras from Japan, ebony figurines, chess sets of water jade, gimcracks from everywhere.

A Hindu stood in the doorway and rubbed his hands in a gesture so stereotyped as to be ludicrous. "Sir, would you like to enter my shop? I have amazing bargains."

The man they called Anton entered.

He looked about the shop, otherwise empty of customers. Vaguely, he wondered if the other ever sold anything, and, if so, to whom.

He said, "I was looking for an ivory elephant, from the East."

The Indian's eyebrows rose. "A white elephant?"

"A red elephant," the man called Anton said.

"In here," the Hindu said evenly, and led the way to the rear.

The rooms beyond were comfortable but not ostentatious. They passed through a livingroom-study to an office beyond. The door was open and the Indian merely gestured in the way of introduction, and then left.

Kirill Menzhinsky, agent superior of the *Chrezvychainaya Komissiya* for North Africa, looked up from his desk, smiled his pleasure, came to his feet and held out his hand.

"Anton!" he said. "I've been expecting you."

The man they called Anton smiled honestly and shook. "Kirill," he said. "It's been a long time."

The other motioned to a comfortable armchair, resumed his own seat. "It's been a long time all right-almost five years. As I recall, I was slung over your shoulder, and you were wading through those confounded swamps. The..."

"The Everglades."

"Yes." The heavy-set Russian espionage chief chuckled. "You are much stronger than you look, Anton. As I recall, I ordered you to abandon me."

The wiry Negro grunted deprecation. "You were delirious from your wound."

The Russian came to his feet, turned his back and went to a small improvised bar. He said, his voice low, "No, Anton, I wasn't delirious. Perhaps a bit afraid, but then the baying of dogs is disconcerting."

The man they called Anton said, "It is all over now."

The Russian returned and said, "A drink, Anton? As I recall you were never the man to refuse a drink. Scotch, bourbon, vodka?"

The other shrugged. "I believe in drinking the local product. What is the beverage of Tangier?"

Kirill Menzhinsky took up a full bottle the contents of which had a greenish, somewhat *oily* tinge. "Absinthe," he said. "Guaranteed to turn your brains to mush if you take it long enough. What was the name of that French painter...?"

"Toulouse Lautrec," Anton supplied. "I thought the stuff was illegal these days." He watched the other add water to the potent liqueur.

The Russian chuckled. "Nothing is illegal in Tangier, my dear Anton, except the Party." He laughed at his own joke and handed the other his glass. He poured himself a jolt of vodka and returned to his chair. "To the world revolution, Anton."

The Negro saluted with his drink. "The revolution!"

They drank.

The Russian put down his glass and sighed. "I wish we were some place in our own lands, Anton. Dinner, many drinks, perhaps some girls, eh?"

Anton shrugged. "Another time, Kirill."

"Yes. As it is, we should not be seen together. Nor, for that matter should you even return here. The imperialists are not stupid. Very possibly, American and Common Europe espionage agents know of this headquarters. Not to speak of the Arab Union. I shall try to give you the whole story and your assignment in this next half hour. Then you should depart immediately."

* * * * *

The man they called Anton sipped his drink and relaxed in his chair. He looked at his superior without comment.

The Russian took another jolt of his water-clear drink. "Have you ever heard of El Hassan?"

The Negro thought a moment before saying, "Vaguely. Evidently an Arab, or possibly a Tuareg. North African nationalist. No, that wouldn't be the word, since he is international. At any rate, he seems to be drawing a following in the Sahara and as far south as the Sudan. Backs modernization and wants unity of all North Africa. Is he connected with the Party?"

The espionage chief was shaking his head. "That is the answer I expected you to give, and is approximately what anyone else would have said. Actually, there is no such person as El Hassan."

Anton frowned. "I'm afraid you're wrong there, Kirill. I've heard about him in half a dozen places. Very mysterious figure. Nobody seems to have seen him, but word of his program is passed around from Ethiopia to Mauretania."

The Russian was shaking his head negatively. "That I know. It's a rather strange story and one rather hard to believe if it wasn't for the fact that one of my operatives was in on the, ah, *manufacturing* of this Saharan leader."

"Manufacturing?"

"I'll give you the details later. Were you acquainted with Abraham Baker, the American comrade?"

"Were? I *am* acquainted with him. Abe is a friend as well as a comrade."

The Russian shook his head again. "Baker is dead, Anton. As you possibly know, his assignment for the past few years has been with a Reunited Nations African Development Project team, working in the Sahara region. We planted him there expecting the time to arrive when his services would be of considerable value. He worked with a five-man team headed by a Dr. Homer Crawford and largely the team's task was to eliminate bottlenecks that developed as the various modernization projects spread over the desert."

"But what's this got to do with *manufacturing* El Hassan?"

"I'm coming to that. Crawford's team, including Comrade Baker, usually disguised themselves as Enaden smiths. As such, their opinions carried little weight so in order to spread Reunited Nations propaganda, they hit upon the idea of imputing everything they said to this great hero of the desert, El Hassan."

"I see," the man called Anton said.

"Others, without knowing the origin of our El Hassan, took up the idea and spread it. These nomads are at an ethnic level where they want a hero to follow, a leader. So in order to give prestige to their teachings the various organizations trying to advance North Africa followed in Crawford's footsteps and attributed their teachings to this mysterious El Hassan."

"And it snowballed."

"Correct! But the point is that after a time Crawford came around to the belief that there should be a real El Hassan. That the primary task at this point is to unite the area, to break down the old tribal society and introduce the populace to the new world."

"He's probably right," the man called Anton growled. He finished his drink, got up from his chair and on his own went over and mixed another. "More vodka?" he asked.

"Please." The Russian held up his glass and went on talking. "Yes, undoubtedly that is what is needed at this point. As it is, things are trending toward a collapse. The imperialists, especially the Americans, of course, wish to dominate the area for their capitalistic purposes. The Arab Union wishes to take over *in toto* and make it part of their Islamic world. We, of course, cannot afford to let either succeed."

The Negro resumed his chair, sipped at his drink and listened, nodding from time to time.

Kirill Menzhinsky said, "As you know, Marx and Engels when founding scientific socialism had no expectation that their followers would first come to power in such backward countries as the Russia of 1917 or the China of 1949. In fact, the establishment of true socialism presupposes a highly developed industrial economy. It is simply impossible without such an economy. When Lenin came to power in 1917, as a result of the chaotic conditions that prevailed upon the military collapse of Imperial Russia, he had no expectation of going it alone, as the British would say. He expected immediate revolutions in such countries as Germany and France and supposed that these more advanced countries would then come to the assistance of the Soviet Union and all would advance together to true socialism."

* * * * *

"It didn't work out that way," the man called Anton said dryly.

"No, it didn't. And Lenin didn't live to see the steps that Stalin would take in order to build the necessary industrial base in Russia." Kirill Menzhinsky looked about the room, almost as though checking to see if anyone else was listening. "Some of our more unorthodox theoreticians are inclined to think that had Lenin survived the assassin's bullet, that Comrade Stalin would have found it necessary to, ah, liquidate him."

The Russian cleared his throat. "Be that as it may, basic changes were made in Marxist teachings to fit into Stalin's and later Khrushchev's new concepts of the worker's State. And the Soviet Union muddled through, as the British have it. Today, the Soviet Complex is as powerful as the imperialist powers."

The espionage leader knocked back his vodka with a practiced stiff wristed motion. "Which brings us to the present and to North Africa." He leaned forward in emphasis. "Comrade, if the past half century and more has taught us anything, it is that you cannot establish socialism in a really backward country. In short, communism is impossible in North Africa at this point in her social evolution. Impossible. You cannot go directly from tribal society to communism. At this historic point, there is no place for the party's program in North Africa."

The man called Anton scowled.

The Russian waggled his hand negatively. "Yes, yes. I know. Ultimately, the whole world must become Soviet. Only that way will we achieve our eventual goal. But that is the long view. Realistically, we must face it, as the Yankees say. This area is not at present soil for our seed."

"Things move fast these days," the Negro growled. "Industrialization, education, can be a geometric progression."

His superior nodded emphatically. "Of course, and as little as ten or fifteen years from now, given progress at the present rate, perhaps there will be opportunity for our movement. But now? No."

The other said, "What has all this to do with El Hassan, or Crawford, or whatever the man's name is?"

"Yes," the Russian said. "Homer Crawford has evidently decided to become El Hassan."

"Ahhh."

"Yes. At this point, in short, he is traveling in our direction. He is doing what we realize must be done."

"Then we will support him?"

"Now we come to the point, Anton. Homer Crawford is not sympathetic to the Party. To the contrary. Our suspicion, although we have no proof, is that he killed Comrade Abe Baker, when Baker approached him on his stand in regard to the Party's long view."

"I see," the man called Anton said.

The Russian nodded. "We must keep in some sort of touch with him-some sort of control. If this El Hassan realizes his scheme and unites all North Africa, sooner or later we will have to deal with him. If he is antagonistic, we will have to find means to liquidate him."

"And my assignment...?"

"He will be gathering followers at this point. Many followers, most of whom will be unknown to him. You will become one of them. Raise yourself to as high a rank as you find possible in his group. Become a close friend, if that can be done...."

"He killed Abe Baker, eh?"

The Russian frowned. "This is an assignment, Comrade Anton. There is no room for personal feelings. You are a good field man. Among the best. You are being given this task because the Party feels you are the man for it. Possibly it is an assignment that will take years in the fulfilling."

The Negro said nothing.

"Are there any questions?"

"Do we have any other operatives working on this?"

The frown became a scowl. "An Isobel Cunningham worked with Comrade Baker, but it has been suspected that she has been drifting away from the party these past few years. Her present status is unknown, but she is believed to be with Homer Crawford and his followers. Possibly she has defected. If so, you will take whatever measures seem necessary. You will be working almost completely on your own, Comrade. You must think on your feet, as the Yankees say."

The man called Anton thought a moment. He said, "You'd better give me as thorough a run down as possible on this Homer Crawford and his immediate followers."

* * * * *

Menzhinsky settled back in his chair and took up a sheaf of papers from the desk. "We have fairly complete dossiers. I'll give you the highlights, then you can take these with you to your hotel to study at leisure."

He took up the first sheet. "Homer Crawford. Born in Detroit of working-class parents. In his late teens interrupted his education to come to Africa where he joined elements of the F.L.N. in Morocco and took part in several forays into Algeria. Evidently was wounded and invalided back to the States where he resumed his education. When he came of military age, he joined the Marine Corps and spent the usual, ah, hitch I believe they call it. Following that, he resumed his education, finally taking a doctor's degree in sociology. He then taught for a time until the Reunited Nations began its African program. He accepted a position, and soon distinguished himself."

The Russian took up another paper. "According to Comrade Baker's reports, Crawford is an outstanding personality, dominating others, even in spite of himself. He would make a top party man. Idealistic, strong, clever, ruthless when ruthlessness is called for."

Menzhinsky paused for a moment, finding words hard to come by from an ultra-materialist. His tone went wry. "Comrade Baker also reported a somewhat mystical quality in our friend Crawford. An ability in times of emotional crisis to break down men's mental barriers against him. A *force* that..."

The other raised his eyebrows.

His superior chuckled, ruefully. "Comrade Baker was evidently much swayed by the man's personality. However, Anton, I might point out that similar reports have come down to us of such a dominating personality in Lenin, and, to a lesser degree, in Stalin." He twisted his mouth. "History leads us to believe that such personalities as Jesus and Mohammed seemed to have some power beyond that of we more mundane types."

"And the others?" Anton said.

The Russian took up still another paper. "Elmer Allen. Born of small farmer background on the outskirts of Kingston, on the island of Jamaica. Managed to work his way through the University of Kingston where he took a master's degree in sociology. At one time he was thought to be Party material and was active in several organizations that held social connotations, pacifist groups and so forth. However, he was never induced to join the Party. Upon graduation, he immediately took employment with the Reunited Nations and was assigned to Homer Crawford's team. He is evidently in accord with Crawford's aims as El Hassan."

The espionage chief took up another sheet. "Bey-ag-Akhamouk..."

The other scowled. "That can't be an American name."

"No. He is the only real African associated with Crawford at this point. He was evidently born a Taureg and taken to the States at an early age, three or four, by a missionary. At any rate, he was educated at the University of Minnesota where he studied political science. We have no record of where he stands politically, but Comrade Baker rated him as an outstanding intuitive soldier. A veritable genius in combat. He would seem to have had military experience somewhere, but we have no record of it. Our Bey-ag-Akhamouk seems somewhat of a mystery man."

The Russian sorted out another sheet. "Kenneth Ballalou, born in Louisiana, educated in Chicago. Another young man but evidently as capable as the others. He seems to be quite a linguist. So far as we know, he holds no political stand whatsoever."

Menzhinsky pursed his lips before saying, "The Isobel Cunningham I mentioned worked with the Africa for Africans Association with two colleagues, a Jacob Armstrong and Clifford Jackson. It is possible that these two, as well as Isobel Cunningham, have joined El Hassan. If so, we will have to check further upon them, although I understand Armstrong is rather elderly and hardly effective under the circumstances."

The man called Anton said evenly, "And this former comrade, Isobel Cunningham, has evidently joined with Crawford even though he ...was the cause of Abe Baker's death?"

"Evidently."

The Negro's eyes narrowed.

The other said, "And evidently she is a most intelligent and attractive young lady. We had rather high hopes for her formerly."

The Negro party member came to his feet and gathered up the sheaf of papers from the desk. "All right," he said. "Is there anything else?"

The espionage chief shook his head. "You do not need a step by step blueprint, Anton, that is why you have been chosen for this assignment. You are strongly based in Party doctrine. You know what is needed, we can trust you to carry on the Party's aims." After a pause, the Russian added, "Without being diverted by personal feelings."

Anton looked him in the face. "Of course," he said.

* * * * *

Fredric Ostrander was on the carpet.

His chief said, "You seem to have conducted yourself rather precipitately, Fred."

Ostrander shrugged in irritation. "I didn't have time to consult anyone. By pure luck, I spotted the Cunningham girl and since I knew she had affiliated herself with Crawford, I followed her."

The chief said dryly, "And tried to arrest the seven of them, all by yourself."

"I couldn't see anything else to do."

The C.I.A. official said, "In the first place, we have no legal jurisdiction here and you could have caused an international stink. The Russkies would just love to bring something like this onto the Reunited Nations floor. In the second place, you failed. How in the world did you expect to take on that number of men, especially Crawford and his team?"

Ostrander flushed his irritation. "Next time ..." he began.

His chief waved a hand negatively. "Let's hope there isn't going to be next time, of this type." He took up a paper from his desk. "Here's your new job, Fred. You're to locate this El Hassan and keep in continual contact with him. If he meets with any sort of success at all, and frankly our agency doubts that he will, you will attempt to bring home to Crawford and his followers the fact that they are Americans, and orientate them in the direction of the West. Above all, you are to keep in touch with us and keep us informed on all developments. Especially notify us if there is any sign that our El Hassan is in communication with the Russkies or any other foreign element."

"Right," Ostrander said.

His chief looked at him. "We're giving you this job, Fred, because you're more up on it than anyone else. You're in at the beginning, so to speak. Now, do you want me to assign you a couple of assistants?"

"White men?" Ostrander said.

His higher-up scowled. "You know you're the only Negro in our agency, Fred."

Fredric Ostrander, his voice still even, said, "That's too bad, because anyone you assigned me who wasn't a Negro would be a hindrance rather than an assistant."

The other drummed his fingers on the table in irritation. He said suddenly, "Fred, do you think I ought to do a report to Greater Washington suggesting they take more Negro operatives into the agency?"

Ostrander said dryly, "You'd better if this department is going to get much work done in Africa." He stood up. "I suppose that the sooner I get onto the job, the better. Do you have any idea at all where Crawford and his gang headed after they left me unconscious in that filthy hut?"

"No, we haven't the slightest idea of where they might be, other than that they left your car abandoned at the Yoff airport."

"Oh, great," Fredric Ostrander complained. "They've gone into hiding in an area somewhat twice the size of the original fifty United States."

"Good luck," his chief said.

* * * * *

Rex Donaldson, formerly of Nassau in the British Bahamas, formerly of the College of Anthropology, Oxford, now field man for the African Department of the British Commonwealth working at expediting native development, was taking time out for needed and unwonted relaxation. In fact, he stretched out on his back in the most comfortable bed, in the most comfortable hotel, in the Niger town of Mopti. His hands were behind his head, and his scowling eyes were on the ceiling.

He was a small, bent man, inordinately black even for the Sudan and the loincloth costume he wore was ludicrous in the Westernized comfort of the hotel room. He was attired for the bush and knew that it was sheer laziness now that kept him from taking off for the Dogon country of the Canton de Sangha where he was currently working to bring down tribal prejudices against the coming of the schools. He had his work cut out for him in the Dogon, the old men, the tribal elders they called Hogons, instinctively knew that the coming of education meant subversion of their institutions and the eventual loss of Hogon power.

His portable communicator, sitting on the bedside table, buzzed and the little man grumbled a profanity and swung his crooked legs around to the floor. His eyebrows went up when he realized it was a priority call which probably meant from London.

He flicked the reception switch and a girl's face faded onto the screen. She said, "A moment, Mr. Donaldson, Sir Winton wants you."

"Right," Rex Donaldson said. Sir Winton, yet. Head of the African Department. Other than photographs, Donaldson had never seen his ultimate superior, not to mention speaking to him personally.

The girl's face faded out and that of Sir Winton Brett-Homes faded in. The heavy-set, heavy-faced Englishman looked down, obviously checking something on his desk. He looked up again, said, "Rex Donaldson?"

"Yes, sir."

"I won't waste time on preliminaries, Donaldson. We've been discussing, here, some of the disconcerting rumors coming out of your section. Are you acquainted with this figure, El Hassan?"

The black man's eyes widened. He said, cautiously, "I have heard a good many stories and rumors."

"Yes, of course. They have been filtering into this office for more than a year. But thus far little that could be considered concrete has developed."

Rex Donaldson held his peace, waited for the other to go on.

Sir Winton said impatiently, "Actually, we are still dealing with rumors, but they are beginning to shape up. Evidently, this El Hassan has finally begun to move."

"Ahhh," the wiry little field man breathed.

The florid faced Englishman said, "As we understand it, he wishes to cut across tribal, national and geographic divisions in all North Africa, wishes to unite the whole area from Sudan to the Mediterranean."

"Yes," Donaldson nodded. "That seems to be his program."

Sir Winton said, "It has been decided that the interests of Her Majesty's government and that of the Commonwealth hardly coincide with such an attempt at this time. It would lead to chaos."

"Ahhh," Donaldson said.

Sir Winton wound it up, all but beaming. "Your instructions, then, are to seek out this El Hassan and combat his efforts with whatever means you find necessary. We consider you one of our most competent operatives, Donaldson."

Rex Donaldson said slowly, "You mean that he is to be stopped at all cost?"

The other cleared his throat. "You are given carte blanche, Donaldson. You and our other operatives in the Sahara and Sudan. Stop El Hassan."

Rex Donaldson said flatly, "You have just received my resignation, Sir Winton."

"What ... what!"

"You heard me," Donaldson said.

"But ... but what are you going to do?" The heavy face of the African Department head was going a reddish-purple, which rather fascinated Donaldson but he had no time to further contemplate the phenomenon.

"I'm going to round up a few of my colleagues, of similar mind to my own, and then I'm going to join El Hassan," the little man snapped. "Good-bye, Sir Winton."

He clicked the set off and then looked down at it. His dour face broke into a rare grin. "Now there's an ambition I've had for donkey's years," he said aloud. "To hang up on a really big mucky-muck."

IV

Following the attack of the unidentified rocketcraft, El Hassan's party was twice again nearly flushed by reconnoitering planes of unknown origin. They weren't making the time they wanted.

Beneath a projecting rock face over a gravel bottomed wadi, the two hover-lorries were hidden, whilst a slow-moving helio-jet made sweeping, high-altitude circlings above them.

The six stared glumly upward.

Cliff Jackson who was on the radio called out, "I just picked him up. He's called in to Fort Lamy reporting no luck. His fuel's running short and he'll be knocking off soon."

Homer Crawford rapped, "What language?"

"French," Cliff said, "but it's not his. I mean he's not French, just using the language."

Bey's face was as glum as any and there was a tic at the side of his mouth. He said now, "We've got to come up with something. Sooner or later one of them will spot us and this next time we won't have any fantastic breaks like Homer being able to knock him off with a Tommy-Noiseless. He'll drop a couple of neopalms and burn up a square mile of desert including El Hassan and his whole crew."

Homer looked at him. "Any ideas, Bey?"

"No," the other growled.

Homer Crawford said, "Any of the rest of you?"

Isobel was frowning, bringing something back. "Why don't we travel at night?"

"And rest during the day?" Homer said.

Kenny said, "Parking where? We just made it to this wadi. If we're caught out in the dunes somewhere when one of those planes shows up, we've had it. You couldn't hide a jackrabbit out there."

But Bey and Homer Crawford were still looking at Isobel.

She said, "I remember a story the Tuaregs used to tell about a raid some of them made back during the French occupation. They stole four hundred camels near Timbuktu one night and headed north. The French weren't worried. The next morning, they simply sent out a couple of aircraft to spot the Tuareg raiders and the camels. Like Kenny said, you couldn't hide a jackrabbit in dune country. But there was nothing to be seen. The French couldn't believe it, but they still weren't really worried. After all a camel herd can travel only thirty or so miles a day. So the next day the planes went out again, circling, circling, but they still didn't spot the thieves and their loot, nor the next day. Well, to shorten it, the Tuareg got their four hundred camels all the way up to Spanish Rio de Oro where they sold them."

She had their staring attention. "How?" Elmer blurted.

"It was simple. They traveled all night and then, at dawn, buried the camels and themselves in the sand and stayed there all day."

Homer said, "I'm sold. Boys, I hope you're in physical trim because there's going to be quite a bit of digging for the next few days."

Cliff groaned. "Some Minister of the Treasury," he complained. "They give him a shovel instead of a bankbook."

Everyone laughed.

Bey said, "Well, I suppose we stay here until nightfall."

"Right," Homer said. "Whose turn is it to pull cook duty?"

Isobel said menacingly, "I don't know whose turn it is, but I know I'm going to do the cooking. After that slumgullion Kenny whipped up yesterday, I'm a perpetual volunteer for the job of chef-strictly in self-defense."

"That was a cruel cut," Kenny protested, "however, I hereby relinquish all my rights to cooking for this expedition."

"And me!"

"And me!"

"O.K.," Homer said, "so Isobel is Minister of the Royal Kitchen." He looked at Elmer Allen. "Which reminds me. You're our junior theoretician. Are we a monarchy?"

Elmer Allen scowled sourly and sat down, his back to the wadi wall. "I wouldn't think so."

Isobel went off to make coffee in the portable galley in the rear of the second hovercraft. The others brought forth tobacco and squatted or sat near the dour Jamaican. Years in the desert had taught them the nomad's ability to relax completely given opportunity.

"So if it's not a monarchy, what'll we call El Hassan?" Kenny demanded.

Elmer said slowly, thoughtfully, "We'll call him simply *El Hassan*. Monarchies are of the past, and El Hassan is the voice of the future, something new. We won't admit he's just a latter-day tyrant, an opportunist seizing power because it's there crying to be seized. Actually,

El Hassan is in the tradition of Genghis Khan, Tamerlane, or, more recently, Napoleon. But he's a modern version, and we're not going to hang the old labels on him."

Isobel had brought the coffee. "I think you're right," she said.

"Sold," Homer agreed. "So we aren't a monarchy. We're a tyranny." His face had begun by expressing amusement, but that fell off. He added, "As a young sociologist, I never expected to wind up a literal tyrant."

Elmer Allen said, "Wait a minute. See if I can remember this. Comes from Byron." He closed his eyes and recited:

"The tyrant of the Chersonese

Was freedom's best and bravest friend.

That tyrant was Miltiades,

Oh that the present hour would lend

Another despot of the kind.

Such bonds as his were sure to bind."

Isobel, pouring coffee, laughed and said, "Why Elmer, who'd ever dream you read verse, not to speak of memorizing it, you old sourpuss."

Elmer Allen's complexion was too dark to register a flush.

Homer Crawford said, "Yeah, Miltiades. Seized power, whipped the Athenians into shape to the point where they were able to take the Persians at Marathon, which should have been impossible." He looked around at the others, winding up with Elmer. "What happened to Miltiades after Marathon and after the emergency was over?"

Elmer looked down into his coffee. "I don't remember," he lied.

* * * * *

There was a clicking from the first hover-lorry, and Cliff Jackson put down his coffee, groaned his resentment at fate, and made his way to the vehicle and the radio there.

Bey motioned with his head. "That's handy, our still being able to tune in on the broadcasts the African Development Project makes to its teams."

Kenny said, "Not that what they've been saying is much in the way of flattery."

Bey said, "They seem to think we're somewhere in the vicinity of Bidon Cinq."

"That's what worries me," Homer growled. He raked his right hand back through his short hair. "If they think we're in Southern Algeria, what are these planes doing around here? We're hundreds of miles from Bidon Cinq."

Bey shot him an oblique glance. "That's easy. That plane that tried to clobber us, and these others that have been trying to search us out, aren't really Reunited Nations craft. They're someone else."

They all looked at him. "Who?" Isobel said.

"How should I know? It could be almost anybody with an iron in the North African fire. The Soviet Complex? Very likely. The British Commonwealth or the French Community? Why not? There're elements in both that haven't really accepted giving up the old colonies and would like to regain them in one way or the other. The Arab Union? Why comment? Common Europe? Oh, Common Europe would love to have a free hand exploiting North Africa."

"You haven't mentioned the United States of the Americas," Elmer said dryly. "I hope you haven't any prejudices in favor of the land of your adoption, Mr. Minister of War."

Bey shrugged. "I just hadn't got around to her. Admittedly with the continued growth of the Soviet Complex and Common Europe, the States have slipped from the supreme position they occupied immediately following the Second War. The more power-happy elements are conscious of the ultimate value of control of Africa and doubly conscious of the danger of it falling into the hands of someone else. Oh, never fear, those planes that have been pestering us might belong to anybody at all."

Cliff Jackson hurried back from his radio, his face anxious. "Listen," he said. "That was a high priority flash, to all Reunited Nations teams. The Arab Union has just taken Tamanrasset. They pushed two columns out of Libya, evidently one from Ghat and one from further north near Ghademès."

Homer Crawford was on his feet, alert. "Well ... why?"

Cliff had what amounted to accusation on his face. "Evidently, the El Hassan rumors are spreading like wildfire. There've been more riots in Mopti, and the Reunited Nations buildings in Adrar have been stormed by mobs demonstrating for him. The Arab Union is moving in on the excuse of protecting the country against El Hassan."

Kenny Ballalou groaned, "They'll have half their Arab Legion in here before the week's out."

Cliff finished with, "The Reunited Nations is throwing a wingding. Everybody running around accusing and threatening, and, as per usual, getting nowhere."

Homer Crawford's face was working in thought. He shook his head at Kenny. "I think you're wrong. They won't send the whole Arab Legion in. They'll be afraid to. They'll want to see first what everybody else does. They know they can't stand up to a slugging match with any of the really big powers. They'll stick it out for a while and watch developments. We have, perhaps, two weeks in which to operate."

"Operate?" Cliff demanded. "What do you mean, operate?"

Homer's eyes snapped to him. "I mean to recapture Tamanrasset from the Arab Union, seize the radio and television station there, and proclaim El Hassan's regime."

The big Californian's eyes bugged at him. "You mean the six of us? There'll be ten thousand of them."

"No," Homer said decisively. "Nothing like that number. Possibly a thousand, if that many. Logistics simply doesn't allow a greater number, not on such short notice. They've put a thousand or so of their crack troops into the town. No more."

Cliff wailed, "What's the difference between a thousand and twenty thousand, so far as five men and a girl are concerned?"

The rest were saying nothing, but following the debate.

Crawford explained, not to just Cliff but to all of them. "Actually, the Arab Union is doing part of our job for us. They've openly declared that El Hassan is attempting to take over North Africa, that he's raising the tribes. Well, good. We didn't have the facilities to make the announcement ourselves. But now the whole world knows it."

* * * * *

"That's right," Elmer said, his face characteristically sullen. "Every news agency in the world is playing up the El Hassan story. In a matter of days, the most remote nomad encampment in the Sahara will know of it, one way or the other."

Homer Crawford was pacing, socking his right fist into the palm of the left. "They've given us a rallying *raison d'etre*. These people might be largely Moslem, especially in the north, but they have no love for the Arab Union. For too long the slave raiders came down from the northeast. Given time, Islam might have moved in on the whole of North Africa. But not this way, not in military columns."

He swung to Bey. "You worked over in the Teda country, before joining my team, and speak the Sudanic dialects. Head for there, Bey. Proclaim El Hassan. Organize a column. We'll rendezvous at Tamanrasset in exactly two weeks."

Bey growled, "How am I supposed to get to Faya?"

"You'll have to work that out yourself. Tonight we'll drop you near In Guezzam, they have one of the big solar pump, afforestation developments there. You should be able to, ah, requisition a truck, or possibly even a 'copter or aircraft. You're on your own, Bey."

"Right."

Homer spun to Kenny Ballalou. "You're the only one of us who gets along in the dialect of Hassania. Get over to Nemadi country and raise a column. There are no better scouts in the world. Two weeks from today at Tamanrasset."

"Got it. Drop me off tonight with Bey, we'll work together until we liberate some transport."

Bey said, "It might be worth while scouting in In Guezzam for a day or two. We might pick up a couple of El Hassan followers to help us along the way."

"Use your judgment. Elmer!"

Elmer groaned sourly, "I knew my time'd come."

"Up into Chaambra country for you. Take the second lorry. You've got a distance to go. Try to recruit former members of the French Camel Corps. Promise just about anything, but only remember that one day we'll have to keep the promises. El Hassan can't get the label of phony hung on him."

"Chaambra country," Elmer said. "Oh great. Arabs. I can just see what luck I'm going to have rousing up Arabs to fight other Arabs, and me with a complexion black as..."

Homer snapped at him, "They won't be following you, they'll be following El Hassan ... or at least the El Hassan dream. Play up the fact that the Arab Union is largely not of Africa but of the Middle East. That they're invading the country to swipe the goats and violate the women. Dig up all the old North African prejudices against the Syrians and Egyptians, and the Saudi-Arabian slave traders. You'll make out."

Cliff said, nervously, "How about me, Homer?"

Homer looked at him. Cliff Jackson, in spite of his fabulous build, hadn't a fighting man's background.

Homer grinned and said, "You'll work with me. We're going into Tuareg country. Whenever occasion calls for it, whip off that shirt and go strolling around with that overgrown chest of yours stuck out. The Tuareg consider themselves the best physical specimens in the Sahara, which they are. They admire masculine physique. You'll wow them."

Cliff grumbled, "Sounds like vaudeville."

Isobel said softly, "And me, El Hassan? What do I do?"

Homer turned to her. "You're also part of headquarters staff. The Tuareg women aren't dominated by their men. They still have a strong element of descent in the matrilinear line and women aren't second-class citizens. You'll work on pressuring them. Do you speak Tamaheq?"

"Of course."

Homer Crawford looked up into the sky, swept it. The day was rapidly coming to an end and nowhere does day become night so quickly as in the ergs of the Sahara.

"Let's get underway," Crawford said. "Time's a wastin'."

* * * * *

The range of the Ahaggar Tuareg was once known, under French administration, as the Annexe du Hoggar, and was the most difficult area ever subdued by French arms-if it was ever subdued. At the battle of Tit on May 7, 1902 the Camel Corps, under Cottenest, broke the combined military power of the Tuareg confederations, but this meant no more than that the tribes and clans carried on nomadic warfare in smaller units.

The Ahaggar covers roughly an area the size of Pennsylvania, New York, Virginia and Maryland combined, and supports a population of possibly twelve thousand, which includes about forty-five hundred Tuareg, four thousand Negro serf-slaves, and some thirty-five hundred scorned sedentary Haratin workers. The balance of the population consists of a handful of Enaden smiths and a small number of Arab shopkeepers in the largest of the sedentary centers. Europeans and other whites are all but unknown.

It is the end of the world.

Contrary to Hollywood-inspired belief, the Sahara does not consist principally of sand dunes, although these, too, are present, and all but impassable even to camels. Traffic, through the millennia, has held to the endless stretches of gravelly plains and the rock ribbed plateaus which cover most of the desert. The great sandy wastes or ergs cover roughly a fifth of the entire Sahara, and possibly two thirds of this area consists of the rolling sandy plains dotted occasionally with dunes. The remaining third, or about one fifteenth of the total Sahara, is characterized by the dune formations of popular imagination.

It was through this latter area that Homer Crawford, now with but one hover-lorry, and accompanied by Isobel Cunningham and Clifford Jackson, was heading.

For although the spectacular major dune formations of the Great Erg have defied wheeled vehicles since the era of the Carthaginian chariots, and even the desert born camel limits his daily travel in them to but a few miles, the modern hovercraft, atop its air cushion jets, finds them of only passing difficulty to traverse. And the hovercraft leaves no trail.

Cliff Jackson scowled out at the identical scenery. Identical for more than two hundred miles. For twice that distance, they had seen no other life. No animal, no bird, not a sprig of cactus. This was the Great Erg.

He muttered, "This country is so dry even the morning dew is dehydrated."

Isobel laughed-she, too, had never experienced this country before. "Why, Cliff, you made a funny!"

They were sitting three across in the front seat, with Homer Crawford at the wheel, and now all three were dressed in the costume of the Kel Rela tribe of the Ahaggar Tuareg confederation. In the back of the lorry were the jerry-cans of water and the supplies that meant the difference between life and mummification from sun and heat.

Cliff turned suddenly to the driver. "Why here?" he said bitterly. "Why pick this for a base of operations? Why not Mopti? Ten thousand Sudanese demonstrated for El Hassan there less than two weeks ago. You'd have them in the palm of your hand."

Homer didn't look up from his work at wheel, lift and acceleration levers. To achieve maximum speed over the dunes, you worked constantly at directing motion not only horizontally but vertically.

He said, "And the twenty and one enemies of the El Hassan movement would have had us in their palms. Our followers in Mopti can take care of themselves. If this movement is ever going to be worth anything, the local characters are going to have to get into the act. The current big thing is not to allow El Hassan and his immediate troupe to be eliminated before full activities can get under way. For the present, we're hiding out until we can gather forces enough to free Tamanrasset."

"Hiding out is right," Cliff snorted. "I have a sneaking suspicion that not only will they never find us, but we'll never find them again."

Homer laughed. "As a matter of fact, we're not so far right now from Silet where there's a certain amount of water-if you dig for it-and a certain amount of the yellowish grass and woody shrubs that the bedouin depend on. With luck, we'll find the Amenokal of the Tuareg there."

"Amenokal?"

"Paramount chief of the Ahaggar Tuaregs."

* * * * *

The dunes began to fall away and with the butt of his left hand Crawford struck the acceleration lever. He could make more time now when less of his attention was drawn to the ups and downs of erg travel.

Patches of thorny bush began to appear, and after a time a small herd of gazelle were flushed and high tailed their way over the horizon.

Isobel said, "Who is this Amenokal you mentioned?"

"These are the real Tuareg, the comparatively untouched. They've got three tribes, the Kel Rela, the Tégéhé Mellet and the Taitoq, each headed by a warrior clan which gives its name to the tribe as a whole. The chief of the Kel Rela clan is also chief of the Kel Rela tribe and automatically paramount chief, or Amenokal, of the whole confederation. His name is Melchizedek."

"Do you think you can win him over?" Isobel said.

"He's a smart old boy. I had some dealings with him over a year ago. Gave him a TV set in the way of a present, hoping he'd tune in on some of our Reunited Nations propaganda. He's probably the most conservative of the Tuareg leaders."

Her eyebrows went up. "And you expect to bring him around to the most liberal scheme to hit North Africa since Hannibal?"

He looked at her from the side of his eyes and grinned. "Remember Roosevelt, the American president?"

"Hardly."

"Well, you've read about him. He came into office at a time when the country was going to economic pot by the minute. Some of the measures he and his so-called brain trust took were immediately hailed by his enemies as socialistic. In answer, Roosevelt told them that in times of social stress the true conservative is a liberal, since to preserve, you have to reform. If Roosevelt hadn't done the things he did, back in the 1930s, you probably would have seen some *real* changes in the American socio-economic system. Roosevelt didn't undermine the social system of the time, he preserved it."

"Then, according to you, Roosevelt was a conservative," she said mockingly.

Crawford laughed. "I'll go even further," he said. "When social changes are pending and for whatever reason are not brought about, then reaction is the inevitable alternative. At such a time then–when sweeping socio-economic change is called for–any reform measures proposed are concealed measures of reaction, since they tend to maintain the *status quo.*"

"Holy Mackerel," Cliff protested. "Accept that and Roosevelt was not only not a liberal, but a reactionary. Stop tearing down my childhood heroes."

Isobel said, "Let's get back to this Amenokal guy. You think he's smart enough to see his only chance is in going along with..."

Homer Crawford pointed ahead and a little to the right. "We'll soon find out. This is a favorite encampment of his. With luck, he'll be there. If we can win him over, we've come a long way."

"And if we can't?" Isobel said, her eyebrows raised again.

"Then it's unfortunate that there are only three of us," Homer said simply, without looking at her.

There were possibly no more than a hundred Tuareg in all in the nomad encampment of goat leather tents when the solar powered hovercraft drew up.

When the air cushion vehicle stopped before the largest tent, Crawford said beneath his breath, "The Amenokal is here, all right. Cliff, watch your teguelmoust. If any of these people see more than your eyes, your standing has dropped to a contemptible zero."

The husky Californian secured the lightweight cotton, combination veil and turban well up over his face. Earlier, Crawford had shown him how to wind the ten-foot long, indigo-blue cloth around the head and features.

Isobel, of course, was unveiled, Tuareg fashion, and wore baggy trousers of black cotton held in place with a braided leather cord by way of drawstring and a gandoura upper-garment consisting of a huge rectangle of cloth some seven to eight feet square and folded over on itself with the free corners sewed together so as to leave bottom and most of both sides open. A V-shaped opening for her head and neck was cut out of a fold at the top, and a large patch had been sewed inside to make a pocket beneath her left breast. She wasn't exactly a Parisian fashion plate.

Even as they stepped down from the hovercraft, immediately after it had drifted to rest on the ground, an elderly man came from the tent entrance.

He looked at them for a moment, then rested his eyes exclusively on Homer Crawford.

"*La Bas*, El Hassan," he said through the cloth that covered his mouth.

Homer Crawford was taken aback, but covered the fact. "There is no evil," he repeated the traditional greeting. "But why do you name me El Hassan?"

A dozen veiled desert men, all with the Tuareg sword, several with modern rifles, had formed behind the Tuareg chief.

Melchizedek made a movement of hand to mouth, in a universal gesture of amusement. "Ah, El Hassan," he said, "you forget you left me the magical instrument of the Roumi."

Crawford was mystified, but he stood in silence. What the Tuareg paramount chief said now made considerable difference. As he recalled his former encounter with the Ahaggar leader, the other had been neither friendly nor antagonistic to the Reunited Nations team Crawford had headed in their role as itinerant desert smiths.

The Amenokal said, "Enter then my tent, El Hassan, and meet my chieftains. We would confer with you."

The first obstacle was cleared. Subduing a sigh of relief, Homer Crawford turned to Cliff. "This, O Amenokal of all the Ahaggar, is Clif ben Jackson, my Vizier of Finance."

The Amenokal bowed his head slightly, said, "*La Bas*."

Cliff could go that far in the Tuareg tongue. He said, "*La Bas*."

The Amenokal said, looking at Isobel, "I hear that in the lands of the Roumi women are permitted in the higher councils."

Homer said steadily, "This I have also been amazed to hear. However, it is fitting that my followers remain here while El Hassan discusses matters of the highest importance with the Amenokal and his chieftains. This is the Sitt Izubahil, high in the councils of her people due to the great knowledge she has gained by attending the new schools which dispense rare wisdom, as all men know."

The Amenokal courteously said, *"La Bas,"* but Isobel held her peace in decency amongst men of chieftain rank.

When Homer and the Tuaregs had disappeared into the tent, she said to Cliff, "Stick by the car, I'm going to circulate among the women. Women are women everywhere. I'll pick up the gossip, possibly get something Homer will miss in there."

A group of Tuareg women and children, the latter stark naked, had gathered to gape at the strangers. Isobel moved toward them, began immediately breaking the ice.

Under his breath, Cliff muttered, "What a gal. Give her a few hours and she'll form a Lady's Aid branch, or a bridge club, and where else is El Hassan going to pick up so much inside information?"

* * * * *

The tent, which was of the highly considered mouflon skins, was mounted on a wooden frame which consisted of two uprights with a horizontal member laid across their tops. The tent covering was stretched over this framework with its back and sides pegged down and the front, which faced south, was left open. It was ten feet deep, fifteen feet wide and five feet high in the middle.

The men entered and filed to the right of the structure where sheepskins and rugs provided seating. The women and children, who abided ordinarily to the left side, had vanished for this gathering of the great.

They sat for a time and sipped at green tea, syrup sweet with mint and sugar, the tiny cups held under the teguelmoust so as not to obscenely reveal the mouth of the drinker.

Finally, Homer Crawford said, "You spoke of the magical instrument of the Roumi which I gave you as gift, O Amenokal, and named me El Hassan."

Several of the Tuareg chuckled beneath their veils but Crawford could read neither warmth nor antagonism in their amusement.

The elderly Melchizedek nodded. "At first we were bewildered, O El Hassan, but then my sister's son, Guémama, fated perhaps one day to become chief of the Kel Rela and Amenokal of all the Ahaggar, recalled the tales told by the storytellers at the fire in the long evenings."

Crawford looked at him politely.

Melchizedek's laugh was gentle. "But each man has heard, in his time, O El Hassan, of the ancient Calif Haroun El Raschid of Baghdad."

Crawford's mind went into high gear, as the story began to come back to him. From second into high gear, and he could have blessed these bedouin for handing him a piece of publicity gobblydygook worthy of Fifth Avenue's top agency.

He held up a hand as though in amusement at being discovered. "Wallahi, O Amenokal, you have discovered my secret. For many months I have crossed the deserts disguised as a common Enaden smith to seek out all the people and to learn their wishes and needs."

"Even as Haroun el Raschid in the far past," one of the subchiefs muttered in satisfaction, "used to disguise himself as a lowborn dragoman and wander the streets of Baghdad."

"But how did you recognize me?" Homer said.

The Amenokal said in reproof, "But verily, your name is on all lips. The Roumi have branded you common criminal. You are to be seized on sight and great reward will be given he who delivers you to the authorities." He spoke without inflection, and Crawford could read neither support nor animosity-nor greed for the reward offered by El Hassan's enemies. He gathered the impression that the Tuareg chief was playing his cards close to his chest.

"And what else do they say?"

The elderly Melchizedek went on slowly, "They say that El Hassan is in truth a renegade citizen of a far away Roumi land and that he attempts to build a great confederation in North Africa for his own gain."

One of the others chuckled and said, "The Roumi on the magical instrument are indeed great liars as all can see."

Homer looked at him questioningly.

The other said, laughing, "Who has ever heard of a black Roumi? And you, O El Hassan, are as black as a Bela."

The Amenokal finished off the mystery of Crawford's recognition. "Know, El Hassan, that whilst you were here before, one of the slaves that served you for pay shamelessly looked upon your face in the privacy of your tent. It was this slave who recognized your face when the Roumi presented it on the magic instrument, calling upon all men to see you and to brand you enemy."

So that was it. The Reunited Nations, and probably all the rest, had used their radio and TV stations to broadcast a warning and offer a reward for Homer and his followers. Old Sven was losing no time. This wasn't so good. A Tuareg owes allegiance to no one beyond clan, tribe and confederation. All others are outside the pale and any advantage, monetary or otherwise, to be gained by exploiting a stranger is well within desert mores.

He might as well bring it to the point. Crawford said evenly, "And I have entered your camp alone except for two followers. Your people are many. So why, O Amenokal, have you not seized me for the reward the Roumi offer?"

* * * * *

There was a moment of silence and Homer Crawford sensed that the sub-chieftains had leaned forward in anticipation, waiting for their leader's words. Possibly they, too, could not understand.

The Tuareg leader finished his tea.

"Because, El Hassan, we yet have not heard the message which the Roumi are so anxious that you not be allowed to bring the men of the desert. The Roumi are great liars, and great thieves, as each man knows. In the memory of those still living, they have stolen of the bedouin and robbed him of land and wealth. So now we would hear of what you say, before we decide."

"Spoken like a true Amenokal, a veritable Suliman ben Davud," Homer said with a heartiness he could only partly feel. At least they were open to persuasion.

For a long moment he stared down at the rug upon which they sat, as though deep in contemplation.

"These words I speak will be truly difficult to hear and accept, O men of the veil," he said at last. "For I speak of great change, and no man loves change in the way of his life."

"Speak, El Hassan," Melchizedek said flatly. "Great change is everywhere upon us, as each man knows, and none can tell how to maintain the ways of our fathers."

"We can fight," one of the younger men growled.

The Amenokal turned to him and grunted scorn. "And would you fight against the weapons of the djinn and afrit, O Guémama? Know that in my youth I was distant witness to the explosion of a great weapon which the accursed Franzawi discharged south of Reggan. Know, that this single explosion, my sister's son, could with ease have destroyed the total of all the tribesmen of the Ahaggar, had they been gathered."

"And the Roumi have many such weapons," Crawford added gently.

The eyes of the tribal headmen came back to him.

"As each man knows," Crawford continued, "change is upon the world. No matter how strongly one wills to continue the traditions of his fathers, change is upon us all. And he who would press against the sand storm, rather than drifting with it, lasts not long."

One of the subchiefs growled, "We Tuareg love not change, El Hassan."

Crawford turned to him. "That is why I and my viziers have spent long hours in *ekhwan*, in great council, devoted to the problems of the Tuareg and how they can best fit into the new Africa that everywhere awakes."

They stirred in interest now. The Tuareg, once the Scourge of the Sahara, the Sons of Shaitan and the Forgotten of Allah, to the Arab, Teda, Moroccan and other fellow inhabitants of North Africa, were of recent decades developing a tribal complex. Robbed of their nomadic-bandit way of life by first the French Camel Corps and later by the efforts of the Reunited Nations, they were rapidly descending into a condition of poverty and defensive bewilderment. Not only were large numbers of former bedouin drifting to the area's sedentary centers, an act beyond contempt within the memory of the elders, but the best elements of the clans were often deserting Tuareg country completely and defecting to the new industrial centers, the dam projects, the afforestation projects, the new oases irrigated with the solar-powered pumps.

"Speak, El Hassan," the Amenokal ordered. And unconsciously, he, too, leaned forward, as did his subchiefs. The Ahaggar Tuareg were reaching for straws, unconsciously seeking shoulders upon which to lay their unsolvable problems.

"Let me, O chiefs of the Tuareg, tell of a once strong tribe of warriors and nomads who lived in the far country in which I was born," Crawford said. The desert man loves a story, a parable, a tale of the strong men of yesteryear.

Melchizedek clapped his hands in summons and when a slave appeared, called for *narghileh* water pipes. When all had been supplied, they relaxed, bits in mouths and looked again at Homer Crawford.

"They were called," he intoned, "the Cheyenne. The Northern Cheyenne, for they had a sister tribe to the South. And on all the plains of this great land, a land, verily, as large as all that over which the Tuareg confederations now roam, they were the greatest huntsmen, the greatest warriors. All feared them. They were the lords of all."

"Ai," breathed one of the older men. "As were the Tuareg before the coming of the cursed Franzawi and the other Nazrani."

"But in time," Crawford pursued, "came the new ways to the plains, and these men who lived largely by the chase began to see the lands fenced in for farmers, began to see large cities erected on what were once tribal areas, and to see the iron railroads of the new ways begin to spread out over the whole of the territory which once was roamed only by the Cheyennes and such nomadic tribes."

"Ai," a muffled mouth ejected.

Homer Crawford looked at the younger Targui, Guémama, the Amenokal's nephew. "And so," he said, "they fought."

"Wallahi!" Guémama breathed.

Homer Crawford looked about the circle. "Never has tribe fought as did the Cheyenne. Never has the world seen such warriors, with the exception, of course, of the Ahaggar Tuareg. Never were such raids, never such bravery, never such heroic deeds as were performed by the warriors of the Cheyennes and their women, and their old people and their children. Over and over they defeated the cavalry and the infantry of the newcomers who would change the old ways and bring the new to the lands of the Cheyennes."

The bedouin were staring in fascination, their water pipes forgotten.

"And then...?" the Amenokal demanded.

"The new ways taught the enemy how to make guns, and artillery, and finally Gatling guns, which today we call machine guns. And once a brave warrior might prevail against a common man armed with the weapons of the new ways, and even twice he might. But the numbers of the followers of the new ways are as the sands of the Great Erg and in time bravery means nothing."

"It is even so," someone growled. "They are as the sands of the erg, and they have the weapons of the djinn, as each man knows."

"And what happened in the end, O El Hassan?"

His eyes swept them all. "They perished," Homer said. "Today in all the land where once the Cheyenne pursued the game there is but a handful of the tribe alive. And they have become nothing people, no longer warriors, no longer nomads, and they are scorned by all for they are poor, poor, poor. Poor in mind and spirits, and in property and they have not been able to adjust to the ways of the new world."

Air went out of the lungs of the assembled Tuareg.

The Amenokal looked at him. "This is verily the truth, El Hassan?"

"My head upon it," Crawford said.

"And why do you tell us of these Cheyenne, these great warriors of the plains of the land of your birth? The story fails to bring joy to hearts already heavy with the troubles of the Tuareg."

It was time to play the joker.

Crawford said carefully, "Because there was no need, O Amenokal of all the Ahaggar, for the Cheyenne to disappear before the sandstorm of the future. They could have ridden before it and today occupy a position of honor and affluence in their former land."

They stared at him.

"And give up the old ways?" Guémama demanded. "Become no longer nomads, no longer honorable warriors, but serfs, slaves, working with one's hands upon the land and with the oil-dirty machines of the Roumi?"

The chiefs muttered angrily.

Crawford said hurriedly, "No! Never! In our great conferences, my viziers and I decided that the Tuareg could never so change. The Tuareg must die, as did the Northern Cheyenne before he would become a city dweller, a worker of the land."

"Bismillah!" someone muttered.

"Too often," Crawford explained, "do the bringers of these things of the future, be they Roumi or others, fail to utilize the potential services of the people of the lands they over-sweep."

"I do not understand you, El Hassan," Melchizedek grumbled. "There is no room for the Tuareg in this new world of bringing trees to the desert, of the great trucks which speed across the erg a score of time the pace of a *bejin* racing camel, of larger and ever larger oases with their great towns, their schools, their new industries. If the Tuareg remains Tuareg, he cannot fit into this new world, it destroys the old traditions, the old way which is the Tuareg way."

Homer Crawford now turned on the pressure. His voice took on overtones of the positive, his personality seemed to reach out and seize them, and even his physical stature seemed to grow.

"Some indeed of the ways of the bedouin must go," he entoned, "but the Tuareg will survive under my leadership. A people who have throve a millennium and more in the great wastes of the Sahara have strong survival characteristics and will blossom, not die, in my new world. Know, O Melchizedek, that it has been decided that the Ahaggar Tuareg will be the heart of my Desert Legion. In times of conflict, armed with the new arms, and riding the new vehicles, they will adapt their old methods of warfare to this new age. In times of peace they will patrol the new forests, watching for fire and other disaster, they will become herdsmen of the new herds and be the police and rescue forces of this wide area. As the Cheyennes of the olden times of the land of my birth could have become herdsmen and forest rangers and have performed similar tasks had they been shown the way."

Homer Crawford let his eyes go from one of them to the next, and his personality continued to dominate them.

The Amenokal ran his thin, aged hand through the length of his white beard beneath his teguelmoust and contemplated this stranger come out of the ergs to lead his people to still greater changes than those they had thus far rebelled against.

* * * * *

Crawford realized that the Targui was divided in opinion and inwardly the American was in a cold sweat. But his voice registered only supreme confidence. "Under my banner, all North

Africa will be welded into one. And all the products of the land will be available in profusion to my faithful followers. The finest wheat for cous cous from Algeria and Tunis, the finest dates and fruits from the oases to the north, the manufactured products of the factories of Dakar and Casablanca. For Africa has always been a poor land but will become a rich one with the new machines and techniques that I will bring."

The Amenokal raised a hand to stem the tide of oratory. "And what do you ask of us now, El Hassan?"

Instead of to the older man, Crawford turned his eyes to the face of Guémama, the leader of the young clansmen. "Now my people are gathering to establish the new rule. Teda from the east, Chaambra from the north, Sudanese from the south, Nemadi, Moors and Rifs from the west. We rendezvous in ten days from now at Tamanrasset where the Arab Legion dogs have seized the city as they wish to seize all the lands of the Sahara and Sudan for the corrupt Arab Union politicians."

Crawford came to his feet. His voice took on an edge of command. "You will address your scouts and warriors and each will ride off on the swiftest camels at your command to raise the Tuareg tribes. And the clans of the Kel Rela will unite with the Taitoq and the Tégéhé Mellet in a great harka at this point and we will ride together to sweep the Arab Legion from the lands of El Hassan."

Guémama was on his feet, too. "Bilhana!" he roared. "With joy."

The others were arising in excitement, all but Melchizedek, who still stroked his gray streaked beard beneath his teguelmoust. The Amenokal had seen much of desert war in his day and knew the horror of the new weapons possessed by the crack troops of the Arab Legion.

But his aged shoulders shrugged against the inevitable.

Crawford said, the ring of authority in his voice. "What does the Amenokal of all the Ahaggar say?" He had no intention of antagonizing the Tuareg chief by going over his head and directly to the people.

"Thou art El Hassan," Melchizedek said, his voice low, "and undoubtedly it is fated that the Tuareg follow you, for verily there is no way else to go, as each man knows."

"Wallahi!" Guémama crowed jubilantly.

V

Guémama, nephew of Melchizedek the Amenokal of the Ahaggar Tuareg confederation and fighting chief of the Kel Rela clan of the Kel Rela tribe, brought his Hejin racing camel to an abrupt halt with a smack of his mish'ab camel stick. He barked, *"Adar-ya-yan,"* in command to bring it to its knees, and slid to the ground before his mount had groaned its rocking way to the sand.

The Tarqui was jubilant. His dark eyes sparked above his teguelmoust veil and he presented himself before Homer Crawford with the elan of a Napoleonic cavalryman before his emperor. Were red leather fil fil boots capable of producing a clicking of heels, that sound would have rung.

Crawford said with dignity, "Aselamu, Aleikum, Guémama. Greeting to you."

"Salaam Aleikum," the tribesman got out breathlessly. "Your message spreads, O El Hassan. My men ride to eastward and westward and never a tent from here to Silet, from In Guezzam to Timissao but knows that El Hassan calls. The Taitoq and the Tégéhé Mellet ride!"

Homer Crawford was standing before the hovercraft. The Amenokal's tribesmen had set up two large goat leather tents for his use and the three Americans had largely withdrawn to their shelter. Crawford was aware of the dangers of familiarity.

Cliff Jackson, who as usual had been monitoring the radio, came from the hover-lorry and growled, "What's he saying?"

"The tribesmen are gathering as per instructions," Homer said in English.

Jackson grunted, somewhat self-conscious of the Targui's admiring gaze. The Tuareg is the handsomest physical specimen of North Africa, often going to six foot of wiry manhood, but there was nothing in all the Sahara to rival the build of Homer Crawford, not to speak of the giant Cliff Jackson.

Crawford turned back to the Tuareg chieftain. "You please me well, O Guémama. Know that I have been in conference with my viziers on the Roumi device which enables one to speak great distances and that we have decided that you are to head all the fighting clans of the Ahaggar, and that you will ride at the left hand of El Hassan, as shield on shoulder rides."

The Targui, overwhelmed, made adequate pledges of fidelity, flowering words of thanks, and then hurried off to inform his fellow tribesmen of his appointment.

Isobel emerged from her tent. She looked at Homer obliquely, the sides of her mouth turning down. "As shield on shoulder rides," she translated from the Tamaheq Berber tongue into English. "Hm-m-m." She cast her eyes upward in memory. "You aren't plagiarizing Kipling, are you?"

Crawford grinned at her. "These people like a well turned phrase."

"And who could turn them better than Rudyard?" she said. Her voice dropped the bantering tone. "What's this bit about making Guémama war-chief of the Tuareg? Isn't he on the young and enthusiastic side?"

Cliff scowled. "You mean that youngster? Why he can't be more than in his early twenties."

Crawford was looking after the young Targui who was disappearing into his uncle's tent on the far side of the rapidly growing encampment.

"You mean the age of Napoleon in the Italian campaign, or Alexander at Issus?" he asked. Isobel began to respond to that, but he shook his head. "He's the Amenokal's nephew, and traditionally would probably get the position anyway. He's the most popular of the young tribesmen, and it's going to be they who do the fighting. Having the appointment come from El Hassan, and at this early point, will just bind him closer. Besides that, he's a natural born warrior. Typical. Enthusiastic, bold, brave and with the military mind."

"What's a military mind?" Cliff said.

"He can take off his shirt without unbuttoning his collar," Homer told him.

"Very funny," Cliff grumbled.

Isobel turned to the big Californian. "What's on the radio, Cliff?"

"Let's go get a cup of coffee," he said. "All hellzapoppin."

* * * * *

They went into the larger of the two Tuareg tents, and Isobel poured water from a girba into the coffee pot which she placed on a heat unit, flicking its switch. She said sarcastically, from the side of her mouth, "A message, O El Hassan, from the Department of Logistics, subdepartment Commissary of Headquarters of the Commander in Chief. Unless you get around to capturing some supplies in the near future, your food is going to be prepared over a camel dung fire. This heat unit is fading out on me."

"Don't bother me with trivialities," Homer told her. "I've got *big* things on my mind."

She looked at him suspiciously. "Hm-m-m. Such as what?"

"Such as whether to put my face on the postage stamps profile or full."

She said, under her breath, "I shoulda known. Already, delusions of grandeur."

"Holy Mackerel," Cliff protested. "Aren't we ever serious around this place? You two will wind up gagging with the firing squad."

Crawford chuckled softly but let his face go serious. "Sorry, Cliff. What's on your mind?"

Cliff said impatiently, "From the radio reports, the Arab Union is consolidating its position. El Hassan is being discredited by the minute. Your followers were in control for a time in Mopti and Bamako, but they're falling away because of lack of direction. The best way I can put reports together, the Reunited Nations is in complete confusion. Everybody accusing everybody of double-dealing."

Isobel said dryly, "Any other good news?"

Cliff said glumly, "Rumors, rumors, rumors. Half the marabouts in North Africa are proclaiming a jehad in support of the Pan-Islam program of the Arab Union. Listen, Homer, we've got to get the backing of the Moslem leaders."

Homer Crawford grunted. "We need Islam in this part of the world like we need a hole in the head. That's one of the things already wrong with North Africa."

"What's wrong with Islam? It was probably the most dynamic religion ever to sweep the world."

"*Was* is right," Crawford growled, now on one of his favorite peeve subjects. "The Moslem religion exploded out of Arabia with some new concepts that set the world in ferment from India to Southern France. For all practical purposes Islam *invented* science. Sure, the Greeks had logic and the Romans had engineering-without applying the Greek-style logic. But the Arabs amalgamated the two concepts to yield experimental science. They were able to take the intellectual products of a dozen cultures and wield them into one. For a hundred years or so it looked as though they had something."

When he hesitated for a moment, Isobel said, questioningly, "And..."

"And they couldn't get away from that Q'ran of theirs. They took it seriously. They started off in their big universities, such as those at Fez, being the greatest scientists and scholars the world had ever seen. But the fundamentalists won out, and in a couple of hundred years the only thing being taught at Fez was the Q'ran. To even suggest that all necessary information isn't contained therein, is enough to have you clobbered. Islam became the most reactionary force to suppress progress in the civilized world. In fact, by this period in world history, we don't even think of the Moslem world as particularly civilized."

Cliff said defensively, "The Bible doesn't encourage original thinking either. A fundamentalist..."

"Sure," Crawford interrupted. "Those elements who take the Bible the way Islam took the Q'ran wind up in the same rut. But *as a whole*, Europe was sparked enough by the original Islamic explosion that the Renaissance resulted, with what world results we all know. Be..."

* * * * *

There was a roar of confusion outside. A blasting of guns, a shrieking of *Ul-Ul-Ul-Allah Akbar!*

Crawford came to his feet unhappily. "Another contingent of Tuareg," he said. "I'll have to give them a quick welcoming to the colors speech."

The guns outside continued their booming.

"Confound it," he growled, "I wish I could break them of that habit of blasting away their ammunition. They'll have better targets before the week is out."

He pushed open the tent flap and, followed by Isobel and Cliff, emerged into the stretch of clearing between his tents and the hovercraft, and the growing Tuareg encampment. His diagnosis had been correct. A contingent of possibly two score Tuareg camelmen had come a-galloping up, shaking rifles above their heads in a small scale gymhana, or fantasia as the Moors called them.

"At least it's a larger group than usual," Cliff said from behind. "But at this rate, it'll still take a month for us to equal the Arab Legion in Tamanrasset." He added in disgust, "And look at this bunch of ragamuffins. Half of them are carrying muzzleloaders."

The booming muskets and the cracking rifles suddenly began to fall off in intensity and the camelmen and the hordes of Tuareg women and naked children who had swarmed from the tents to greet them were falling silent. Here and there a hand pointed upward.

Homer, Cliff and Isobel swung their own eyes up to the sky in dreaded anticipation. The hover-lorry was camouflaged to blend in with the sands and rock outcroppings of this area, but it was possible that an aircraft might have determined that this was El Hassan's base, possibly through some act of a traitor, in which case...

They found the spot in the sky that the tribesmen were pointing out. It seemed to move slowly for a military craft, but for that matter it might be a helio-jet and considerably more dangerous, so far as they being spotted was concerned, than a fast moving fighter.

Guémama, was barking to his men to take cover. Two days before Crawford had checked out several of the more bright-eyed on the flac rifle and now three of them ran to where it was set up at a high point.

But hardly had the confused milling got under way than it fell off again. Movement stopped, and the Tuareg faced the approaching dot in the sky.

"Djinn...!"

"Afrit...!"

Cliff had darted back into the tent, now he emerged with binoculars.

"What the devil is it?" Crawford snapped. Desert trained eyes were evidently considerably more effective than his own. He couldn't see what the tribesmen were gaping at.

"It's the smallest heliohopper *I've* ever seen," Cliff snorted. "It's so small practically all you can see are the rotors and the passenger. He doesn't even look as though he's got a seat."

Guémama came hurrying up, his eyes wide beneath his teguelmoust. "El Hassan! A witchman ... come out of the sky!"

Homer said evenly, "It is nothing. Only post men ready to obey my commands."

Guémama hesitated as though to waver out another protest, but then spun and hurried off-military-like, glad to have an order to obey to keep his mind from the impossible.

"I'm beginning to have a sneaking suspicion —" Crawford began without finishing. "Come on Isobel, Cliff. We're going to have to make the most of this."

* * * * *

Rex Donaldson, ex-field man for the African Department of the British Commonwealth, dropped the lift lever of his heliohopper and settled to the ground immediately before Homer Crawford who stood there flanked by Isobel Cunningham and Cliff Jackson. Further back and in the form of a crescent were possibly two or three hundred Tuareg of all ages and both sexes.

Donaldson, in the garb of a Dogan juju man consisting of little more than a wisp of cloth about his loins, played it straight, not knowing the setup. On the face of it, he had just flown out of the sky *personally*. The size of his equipment so small as to be all but meaningless.

He unstrapped himself from the thin, bicyclelike seat, and, expressionlessly, folded the rotors of his tiny craft back over themselves and the engine, collapsed the whole thing into a manageable packet of some seventy-five pounds, the seat now becoming a handle, and then turned and faced Crawford.

Donaldson screwed his wizened face into an expression of respect and made a motion of obeisance. Then he waited.

Isobel said, "El Hassan bids you speak."

That was the tip-off, then. Crawford had already revealed himself to these people as El Hassan. Very well.

Donaldson spoke in Arabic, not knowing the Tamaheq tongue. "Aselamu, Aleikum, El Hassan. I come to obey your wishes."

A sigh had gone through the Tuareg. "Aiiiii." *Wallahi, even the djinn obeyed El Hassan!*

With dignity, Homer Crawford said, "Keif halak, all in my house is yours."

Rex Donaldson inclined his small bent body again, in respect.

Crawford said in English, "Let's not carry this *too* far. Come on into the tent."

Ignoring the Tuareg, who still gaped but held their distance, the four English-speaking Negroes headed for the larger of the two tents that had been set up for El Hassan.

As they passed Guémama who stood slightly aside from the other Tuareg with his uncle Melchizedek, the Amenokal, Crawford nodded and said, speaking to them both. "A messenger from my people to the south. Continue with your newly arrived warriors, O Guémama."

Cliff Jackson had picked up the folded heliohopper and was now carrying it easily.

Guémama looked at the device and blinked.

Crawford refrained from laughing at his commander of irregulars. "It is not a *kambu* device. My people deal not in magic. It is but one of the many of the things the new ways bring. One day, Guémama," Homer's face remained expressionless, "perhaps you will fly thus."

The teguelmoust hid the other's blanch.

In the tent, Homer turned to the Bahaman, motioned to what seating arrangements were available.

Isobel said, "I'll get some coffee."

Cliff blurted, "Holy Mackerel, if Donaldson, here, can drop in on us out of a clear sky, what keeps anybody else from doing it? Somebody with a couple of neopalm bombs in the way of calling cards."

The dried up little man grimaced in his equivalent of a grin and said, "Hold it, you chaps. I want to notify the others."

"The others? What others?" Crawford said.

Donaldson ignored him for a moment, unslung the small bag he carried over one shoulder and dipped into it for a tiny, two-way radio. He pressed the buzzer button, then held it up to his mouth. "Jack, Jimmy, Dave. Here we are. Took donkey's years, but I found them. You chaps zero-in here." He left the device on and set it to one side, then yawned and settled himself to the rug-covered ground, crosslegged, Dogon style.

Homer Crawford, even as he sat down himself on a footlocker, in lieu of a chair, rapped, "How did you find us? Who did you just radio? Where'd you come from?"

"I say, hold it," Donaldson chuckled sourly. "First of all, I've come to join up. I thought as far back as that time we co-operated in quelling the riots in Mopti that you ought to do this-proclaim yourself El Hassan. When I heard you'd taken the step, I came to join up."

"Oh, great," Cliff said. "What took you so long? We hardly get here, to our ultra-secret hideout, than here you are."

Isobel came with the coffee and handed it around, silently. Then she, too, settled to the rug which covered the sand of the floor.

Rex Donaldson turned to Cliff and there was a wrinkle of amusement in the older man's eyes. "I took so long, because I needed the time to recruit a few other chaps I knew would stand with us."

Crawford rapped, "That's who you just radioed?"

"Of course, old boy. I'd hardly bring the opposition down on us, would I?"

"Where are they?"

"In a couple of hovercraft, similar to your own, possibly twenty kilometers to the southwest."

"You still haven't told us how you found us?"

The little man shrugged. "After tendering my resignation to Sir Winton, I considered the possibilities, which narrowed down very quickly when I heard the Arab Legion had taken Tamanrasset."

"Why?" Isobel said.

Donaldson shot a glance at her. "Because, my dear, unless El Hassan is able to retake Tamanrasset, his movement has come a cropper." He turned his eyes back to Crawford, who was nervously running his hand through his hair. "I knew you had done considerable work in this area, so your whereabouts became obvious seeing that Tamanrasset is in Tuareg country. It was simply a matter of finding what Tuareg encampment was your base, and since your quickest manner of gathering support would be to swing the Amenokal to your banner, I headed for his usual encampment this time of year."

Cliff looked at Homer Crawford. "If Rex found us so easily, so will anybody else."

Isobel put in. "Not necessarily. Mr. Donaldson has information that most of El Hassan's opponents wouldn't."

* * * * *

Homer came to his feet unhappily and began pacing. "No, Isobel. Ostrander, for instance, has all the dope Rex has and is just as capable of working it through to a conclusion. It takes no great insight to realize El Hassan has to either put up or shut up when it comes to Tamanrasset. That's possibly why some of the other elements interested in North Africa have so far refrained from action against the Arab Union. They want to see what El Hassan is going to do-find out just what he has on the ball."

Rex Donaldson looked at him interestedly, "And? What are your plans?"

Homer Crawford's face worked. "My plans right at present are to stay alive, and you finding me so easily isn't heartening. However, it brings to mind some other problems which need solving, too."

The rest of them fell silent, looking at him. His usual casual humor had dropped away, and his personality gripped them.

He stopped his pacing, and frowned down at them.

"El Hassan is going to have to remain on the move. Always. There can be no capital city, no definite base, and it's going to be a poor idea to sleep twice in the same place." He shook his head emphatically as though to deny rebuttal, which they hadn't actually made. "El Hassan's enemies mustn't know his location within twenty miles."

"Twenty miles!" Cliff blurted.

Crawford stared at him, but unseeingly. "Yes. At least half a dozen of our opponents possess nuclear weapons."

Donaldson demured, sourly. "A nuclear weapon hasn't been exploded for donkey's years and —"

"Of course not," Homer snapped. "Nor would anyone dare, anywhere else except in the wastes of the Sahara. A nuclear explosion in the Ahaggar would not go undetected and a controversy might go up in the Reunited Nations. But who could prove who had done it? And who, actually, would care if in the explosion a common foe of all was eliminated? But let the Arab Union, or possibly the Soviet Complex, or even others, learn definitely where El Hassan is and a bomb could well devastate twenty square miles seeking him out." Crawford shook his head. "No, we've simply got to keep on the move."

Donaldson said, even as he nodded agreement, "And what other problems were you talking about?"

"Oh?" Homer said. "Well, keeping on the move will serve to add mystery to the El Hassan legend. It isn't good for this Tuareg encampment, for instance, to see too much of El Hassan. A leader claiming domination of half a continent looks small potatoes in a desert camp of a few score tents. On the move, showing up here, there, the other place, for only a day or two at a time, is another proposition."

He thought a moment. "Remember DeGaulle?"

"How could we forget?" Rex Donaldson said wryly.

"He had one angle that couldn't be more correct. He said a leader had to keep remote, ever mysterious. He can't afford to have real intimates. Napoleon, Hitler, Stalin. None of them had a real friend to their name. The nearest to friends that Adolph the Aryan ever had, his old comrades of the beerhall days, such as Rhoem, he butchered in the blood purge. And Stalin? He managed to do away with every Old Bolshevik he knew in the days before the Party came to power."

Cliff was staring at him. "Hey," he said. "The one other thing one of these mystical leader types needs is a belief in his own destiny. To the point of clobbering all his intimates if he thinks they stand in his way."

Homer broke into a sudden short laugh. "Any qualms, Cliff?"

Cliff growled, "I don't know. This dream of yours is growing. Where it might end —I don't know."

As they were talking the cries of *Ul-Ul-Ul-Allah Akbar!* had broken out again.

"Heavens to Betsy," Isobel said. "Another contingent of camelmen?"

* * * * *

But this time the newcomers were three in number and rode in air cushion hover-lorries, the twins of that used by Homer Crawford.

Rex Donaldson brought them up to the tent, saying, "I didn't think you chaps were quite so close."

Homer, Cliff and Isobel faced the new recruits. The three were dressed in khaki bushshirts, shorts and heavy walking shoes-British style. Two were so obviously relatives that they could have been twins except for an age discrepancy of two or three years. They were smaller in stature than the Americans present, almost chunky, but their faces held education and cultivation. The third was slight of build, almost as wiry as Rex Donaldson, and seemed ever at ease.

The small, bent Bahaman made introductions. "Gentlemen, let me present El Hassan-Homer Crawford to you-formerly of the Reunited Nations African Development Project, formerly of the United States of the Americas." His face twisted in his sour grimace of a grin. "Now running for the office of tyrant of North Africa."

"And these are two of his original and most trusted adherents, Isobel Cunningham and Cliff Jackson." Donaldson turned to the newcomers. "John and James Peters-that's Jack and Jimmy, of course-recently colleagues of mine with the African Department of the Commonwealth, working largely in the Nigeria area."

Homer shook hands, grinning. "You're a long way from home."

"Farther than that," the one labeled Jack said without a smile changing the seriousness of his face. "We're originally from Trinidad."

Donaldson said, "And this is David Moroka, late of South Africa."

The wiry South African said easily, "Not so very late. In fact, I haven't seen Jo-burg since I was a boy."

He was shaking hands with Isobel now. "Jo-burg?" she said.

"Johannesburg," he translated. "I got out by the skin of my teeth during the troubles in the 1950s."

"You sound like an American," Cliff said when it was his turn to shake.

"Educated in the States," Moroka said. "Best thing that ever happened to me was to be kicked out of the land of my birth."

Homer made a sweeping gesture at the floor and the few articles of furniture the tent contained that could be improvised as chairs. "I'm surprised you're up here instead of in your own neck of the woods," he said to the South African.

Moroka shrugged. "I was considering heading south when I ran into Jimmy and Jack, here. They'd already got the word on the El Hassan movement from Rex. Their arguments made sense to me."

Eyes went to the brothers from Trinidad and Jack Peters took over the position of spokesman. He said, seriously, as though trying to convince the others, "North Africa is the starting point, the beginning. Given El Hassan's success in uniting North Africa, the central areas and later even the south will fall into line. Perhaps one day there will be a union of *all* Africa."

"Or at least a strong confederation," Jimmy Peters added.

Homer nodded thoughtfully. "Perhaps. But we can't look that far forward now." He looked from one of the newcomers to the other. "I don't know to what extent you fellows understand what the rest of us have set out to accomplish but I suppose if you've been with Rex for the past week, you have a fairly clear idea."

"I believe so," Jack nodded, straight-faced.

Homer Crawford said slowly, "I don't want to give you the wrong idea. If you join up, you'll find it's no parade. Our chances were slim to begin, and we've had some setbacks. As you've probably heard, the Arab Union has stolen a march on us. And from what we can get on the radio, we have thus far to pick up a single adherent among the world powers."

"*Powers?*" Cliff snorted. "We haven't got a nation the size of Monaco on our side."

Moroka shot a quick glance at the big Californian.

Isobel caught it and laughed. "Cliff's a perpetual sourpuss," she said. "However, he's been in since the first."

The South African looked at her in turn. "We were hardly prepared to find a beautiful American girl in the Great Erg," he said.

Something about his voice caused her to flush. "We've all caught Homer's dream," she said, almost defensively.

* * * * *

David Moroka flung to his feet, viper fast, and dashed toward Homer Crawford, his hands extended.

Automatically, Cliff Jackson stuck forward a foot in an attempt to trip him-and missed.

The South African, moving with blurring speed, grasped the unsuspecting Crawford by the right hand and arm, swung with fantastic speed and sent the American sprawling to the far side of the tent.

Homer Crawford, old in rough and tumble, was already rolling out. Before the inertia of his fall had given way, his right hand, only a split second before in the grip of the other, was fumbling for the 9 mm Noiseless holstered at his belt.

Rex Donaldson, a small handgun magically in his hand, was standing, half crouched on his thin, bent legs. The two brothers from Trinidad hadn't moved, their eyes bugging.

Moroka was spinning with the momentum of the sudden attack he'd made on his new chief. Now there was a gun in his own hand and he was darting for the tent opening.

Cliff yelled indignantly, "Stop him!"

Isobel, on her feet by now, both hands to her mouth, was staring at the goatskin tent covering, against which, a moment earlier, Crawford had been gently leaning his back as he talked.

There was a vicious slash in the leather and even as she pointed, the razor-sharp arm dagger's blade disappeared. There was the sound of running feet outside the tent.

Homer Crawford had assimilated the situation before the rest. He, too, was darting for the tent entrance, only feet behind Moroka.

Donaldson followed, muttering bitterly under his breath, his face twisted more as though in distaste than in fighting anger.

Cliff, too, finally saw light and dashed after the others, leaving only Isobel and the Peters brothers. They heard the muffled coughing of a silenced gun, twice, thrice and then half a dozen times, blurting together in automatic fire.

Homer Crawford shuffled through the sand on an awkward run, rounding the tent, weapon in hand.

There was a native on the ground making final spasmatic muscular movements in his death throes, and not more than three feet from him, coolly, David Moroka sat, bracing his elbows on his knees and aiming, two-handed, as his gun emptied itself.

Crawford brought his own gun up, seeking the target, and clipping at the same time, "We want him alive —"

It was too late. Two hundred feet beyond, a running tribesman, long arm dagger still in hand, stumbled, ran another three or four feet with hesitant steps, and then collapsed.

Moroka said, "Too late, Crawford. He would have got away." The South African started to his feet, brushing sand from his khaki bush shorts.

The others were beginning to come up and from the Tuareg encampment a rush of Gué-mama's men started in their direction.

Crawford said unhappily, looking down at the dead native at their feet, "I hate to see unnecessary killing."

Moroka looked at him questioningly. "Unnecessary? Another split second and his knife would have been in your gizzard. What do you want to give him, another chance?"

Crawford said uncomfortably, "Thanks, Dave, anyway. That was quick thinking."

"Thank God," Donaldson said, coming up, his wrinkled face scowling unhappily, first at the dead man at their feet, and then at the one almost a hundred yards away. "Are these local men? Where were your bodyguards?"

Cliff Jackson skidded to a halt, after rounding the tent. He'd heard only the last words. "What bodyguards?" he said.

Moroka looked at Crawford accusingly. "El Hassan," he said. "Leader of all North Africa. And you haven't even got around to bodyguards? Do you fellows think you're playing children's games? Gentlemen, I assure you, the chips are down."

VI

El Hassan's Tuaregs were on the move. After half a century and more of relative peace the Apaches of the Sahara, the Sons of Shaitan and the Forgotten of Allah were again disappearing into the ergs to emerge here, there, and ghostlike to disappear again. They faded in and faded away again, and even in their absence dominated all.

El Hassan was on the move, as all men by now knew, and he, who was not for the amalgamation of all North Africa, was judged against him. And who, in the Sahara, could afford to be against El Hassan when his Tuaregs were everywhere?

Refugees poured into Tamanrasset for the security of Arab Legion arms, or into In Salah and Reggan to the north, or Agades and Zinder to the south. Refugees who had already taken their stand with the Arab Union and Pan-Islam. Refugees who were men of property and would know more of this El Hassan before risking their wealth. Refugees who took no stand, but dreaded those who drank the milk of war, no matter the cause for which they fought. Refugees who fled simply because others fled, for terror is a most contagious disease.

Colonel Midan Ibrahim of the crack motorized units of the Arab Legion which occupied Tamanrasset, was fuming. His task was a double one. First, to hold Tamanrasset and its former French stronghold Fort Laperrine; second, to keep open his lines of communication with Ghademès and Ghat, in Arab Union dominated Libya. To hold them until further steps were decided upon by his superiors in Cairo and the Near East-whatever these steps might be. Colonel Midan Ibrahim was too low in the Arab Union hierarchy to be in on such privy matters.

His original efforts, in pushing across the Sahara from Ghademès and Ghat, had been no more than desert maneuvers. There had been no force other than nature's to say him nay. The Reunited Nations was an organization composed possibly of great powers, but in supposedly acting in unison they became a shrieking set of hair-tearing women; the whole being less than any of its individual parts. And El Hassan? No more than a rumor. In fact, an asset because this supposed mystery man of the desert, bent on uniting all North Africa under his domination, gave the Arab Union, its alibi for stepping in with Colonel Ibrahim's men.

Yes, the original efforts had been but a drill. But now his Arab Legion troopers were beginning to face reality. The supply trucks, coming down under convoy from Ghademès, reported the water source at Ohanet destroyed. The major well would take a week or more to repair. Who had committed the sabotage? Some said the Tuareg, some said local followers of El Hassan, others, desert tribesmen resentful of *both* the Arab Union and El Hassan.

One of his routine patrols, feeling out toward Meniet to the north, had suddenly dropped radio communication, almost in mid-sentence. A relieving patrol had thus far found nothing, the armored car's tracks covered over by the sands.

And rumors, rumors, rumors, Colonel Midan Ibrahim, born of aristocratic Alexandrian blood, though trained to a sharp edge in Near Eastern warfare, was basically city bred. The gloss of desert training might take on him, but the bedouin life itself was not in his experience, and it was hard for him to trace the dividing line between possibility and fantasy.

Rumors, rumors, rumors. They seemed capable of sweeping from one end of the Sahara to the other in a matter of hours. Faster, it would seem than the information could be dispensed by radio. El Hassan was here. El Hassan was there. El Hassan was marching on Rabat, in

Morocco; El Hassan had just signed a treaty with the Soviet Complex; El Hassan had been assassinated by a disgruntled follower. Or El Hassan was a renegade Christian; El Hassan was a Moslem of Sheriffian blood, a direct descendant of the Prophet; El Hassan was a pagan come up from Dahomey and practiced ritual cannibalism; El Hassan was a Jew, a veteran of the Israel debacle.

But this Colonel Ibrahim knew-the Tuareg had gone over to the new movement en masse. Something there was in El Hassan and his dream that had appealed to the Forgotten of Allah. The Tuareg, for the first time since the French Camel Corps had broken their strength, were united-united and on the move.

The Tuareg were everywhere. In most sinister fashion-everywhere. And all were El Hassan's men.

Colonel Ibrahim fumed and wondered what kept his superiors from sending in additional columns, additional armored elements. And, above all, adequate air cover. Ha! Give the colonel sufficient aircraft and he'd begin snuffing out bedouin life like candles-and bring the Peace of Allah to the Ahaggar.

So Colonel Ibrahim fumed, demanded further orders from mum superiors, and put his legionnaires to work on bigger and better gun emplacements, trenches and pillboxes surrounding Fort Laperinne and Tamanrasset.

E

l Hassan's personal entourage numbered exactly twenty persons. Of these, five were his immediate English-speaking, Western-educated supporters, Cliff, Isobel and the new Jack and Jimmy Peters and Dave Moroka. Rex Donaldson had been sent south again to operate in Senegal and Mali, to take over direction of the rapidly spreading movement in such centers as Bamako and Mopti and later, if possible, in Dakar.

The other fifteen were carefully selected Tuareg, picked from among Guémama's tribesmen taking care to show no preference to any tribe or clan, and taking particular care to choose men who fought coolly, unexcitedly, and didn't froth at the mouth when in action; men who were slow to charge wildly into the enemy's guns-but slower still to retreat when the going was hot. El Hassan was prone to neither hero nor coward in his personal bodyguard.

They kept under movement. In Abelessa one day, almost in range of the mobile artillery of the Arab Legion; in Timassao the next, checking the wells that meant everything to a desert force; the following day as far south as the Tamesna region to rally the less warlike Irreguenaten, a half-breed Tuareg people largely held in scorn by those of the Ahaggar.

Homer Crawford was killing time whilst stirring up as much noise and dust as his handful of followers could manage. Killing time until Elmer Allen from the Chaambra country, Bey-ag-Akhamouk from the Teda, and Kenny Ballalou from the west could show up with their columns. He had no illusions of how things now stood. At best, he could hold together a thousand Tuareg fighting men. No more. The economics of desert life prevented him a larger force, unless he had the resources of the modern world at hand, and he didn't. Besides that, the Tuareg confederation could provide no larger number of fighting men and at the same time continue their desert economy.

He stood now with Isobel, Cliff and Dave Moroka in one of the western type tents which the Peters brothers had brought with them in their hover-lorries, and poured over the half-adequate maps which covered the area.

Dave Moroka traced with a finger. "If we could dominate these wells running to Djanet, our Arab Union friends would have only their one line of supply going through Temassinine to Ghademès. That's a long haul, Homer."

Homer Crawford scowled thoughtfully. "That involves only four wells. If Ibrahim's legionnaires staked out only three armored vehicles at each water hole, they could hold them. Our camelmen could never take armor."

Moroka frowned, too. "We've got to start *some* sort of action, or the men will start dribbling away."

Cliff Jackson said, "Bey and Kenny and Elmer should be coming soon. I heard a radio item this morning about a big pro-El Hassan movement starting in the Sudan among the Teda."

Moroka said, "We need some sort of quick, spectacular victory. The bedouin can lose interest as quickly as they can get steamed up, and thus far we haven't given them anything but words-promises."

"You're right," Homer growled, "but there's nothing we can do right now but mark time. Irritate the Arabs a bit. Keep them from spreading out."

Isobel brought coffee, handing around the small Moroccan cups. She said, "Well, one thing is certain. We get supplies soon or start eating jerked goat and camel milk curds."

Moroka said in irritation, "It's not funny."

Isobel raised her eyebrows. "I didn't mean it to be. Have you ever been on a camel curd diet?"

"Yes, I have," Moroka said impatiently. He turned back to Homer Crawford. "How about waylaying an armored car or so, just in the way of giving the men something exciting to do?"

Crawford ran a hand back through his short hair. "Confound it, Dave, can you picture what a Recoilless-Brenn gun would do to a harka of our charging camelmen? We can't let these people be butchered."

"I wasn't thinking of wild charges," Moroka argued.

They had both turned away from Isobel, in their discussion. Now she looked at them, strangely. And especially at Homer Crawford. His brusqueness toward her didn't seem the old Homer.

* * * * *

There was a bustle from outside and a guardsman stuck his head in the tent entrance and reported in Tamaheq that a small camel patrol approached.

The four of them went out. Coming up were a dozen Tuareg and two motor vehicles.

Cliff said, "Something new."

Moroka said, "We can use the transport."

"Let's see who they are, before we start requisitioning their property," Homer said dryly.

The two desert trucks had hardly come to a halt before the camouflaged tents and hover-lorries of El Hassan's small encampment before a heavy-set, gray haired Negro, whose energy belied his weight, bounced down from the seat adjacent to the driver's in the lead vehicle and stomped belligerently to the group before the tent.

"What is the meaning of this?" he snapped.

Homer Crawford looked at him. "I'm sure I don't know as yet, Dr. Smythe. Neither you nor these followers of mine have informed me as to what has transpired. Won't you enter my quarters here and we'll go into it under more comfortable conditions?" He glanced upward at the midday Saharan sun.

The other seemed taken aback at Crawford calling him by name. He squinted at the man who was seemingly his captor.

"Crawford!" he snapped. "Dr. Homer Crawford! See here, what is the meaning of this?"

Homer said, "Dr. Warren Harding Smythe, may I present Isobel Cunningham, Clifford Jackson and David Moroka, of my staff?"

"Huuump. I met Miss Cunningham and, I believe, Mr. Jackson at that ridiculous meeting in Timbuktu, a short time ago." The doctor peered over his glasses at Moroka.

The wiry South African nodded his head. "A pleasure, Doctor." He held open the tent entrance.

Smythe snorted again and stomped inside to escape the sun's glare.

In the shade of the tent's interior, Isobel clucked at him and hurried to get a drink of water from a moist water cooler. Homer Crawford motioned the other to a seat, and took one himself. "Now then, Dr. Smythe."

The indignant medic blurted, "Those confounded bandits out there —"

"Irregular camel cavalry," Crawford amended gently.

"They've kidnapped me and my staff. I demand that you intercede, if you have any influence with them."

"What were you doing?" Crawford was frowning at the other. Actually, he had no idea of the circumstances under which the probably overenthusiastic Tuareg troopers had rounded up the American medical man.

"Doing? You know perfectly well I represent the American Medical Relief. My team has been in the vicinity of Silet, working with the nomads. The country is rife with everything from rickets to syphilis! Eighty per cent of these people suffer from trachoma. My team —"

"Just a moment," Moroka said. "You mean out in those two trucks you have a complete American medical setup? Assistants and all?"

Smythe said stiffly, "I have two American nurses with me and four Algerians recruited in Oran. This sort of interference with my work is insufferable and —"

The South African was staring at Homer Crawford.

Cliff Jackson cleared his throat. "It seems as though El Hassan has just acquired a Department of Health."

"El Hassan?" Smythe stuttered. "What, what?"

Isobel said softly, "Dr. Smythe, surely you have heard of El Hassan."

"Heard of him? I've heard of nothing else for the past month! Confounded ignorant barbarian. What this part of the world needs is *less* intertribal, interracial, international fighting, not more. The man's a raving lunatic and —"

Isobel said gently, "Doctor ... may I introduce you to El Hassan?"

"What ... what —?" For the briefest of moments, there was an element of timorness in the sputtering doctor's voice. Then suddenly he comprehended.

He pointed at Homer Crawford accusingly. "You're El Hassan!"

Homer nodded, seriously, "That's correct, Doctor."

The doctor's eyes went around the four of them. "You've done what you were driving at there at that meeting in Timbuktu. You're trying to unite these people in spite of themselves and then drag them, willy-nilly, into the twentieth century."

Homer still nodded.

Smythe shook an indignant finger at him. "I told you then, Crawford, and I tell you now. These natives are not suited for such sudden change. Already they are subject to mass neurosis because they cannot adjust to a world that changes too quickly."

"I wonder if that doesn't apply to the rest of us as well," Cliff said unhappily. "But the changes go on, if we like them or not. Can you think of any way to turn them off?"

The doctor snorted.

Homer Crawford said, "Dr. Smythe, the die is already cast. The question now becomes, will you join us?"

"Join you! Certainly not!"

Crawford said evenly, "Then I might suggest that, first, you will not be allowed to operate in my territory." He considered for a moment, grinning inwardly, but on the surface his expression serene. He added, "And second, that you will probably have difficulties procuring an exit visa from my domains."

"Exit visa! Are you jesting? See here, my good man, you realize I am a citizen of the United States of the Americas and —"

"A country," Homer yawned, "with which I have not as yet opened diplomatic relations, and hence has little representation in North Africa."

The doctor was bug-eying him. He began sputtering again. "This isn't funny. You're an American citizen yourself. And you, Miss Cunningham and —"

Isobel said sadly, "As a matter of fact, the last we heard, the State Department representative told us our passports were invalid."

Crawford leaned forward. "Look here, Doctor. You don't see eye to eye with us on matters socio-economic. However, as a medical man, I submit that joining my group ... ah, that is, until you can secure an exit visa from my authorities ... will give you an excellent opportunity to practice your science here in the Sahara under the wing of El Hassan. I'll assign a place for your trucks and tents. Please consider the question and let me have your answer at your leisure. Meanwhile, we will prepare a desert feast suitable to the high esteem in which we hold you."

* * * * *

They looked after the doctor, as he left, and Moroka chuckled. However, Isobel was watching Homer Crawford quizzically.

She said finally, "We rode over him a little in the roughshod manner, didn't we?"

Homer Crawford growled uncomfortably, "Particularly when we finally have our showdown with the Arab Legion, a medic will be priceless."

Isobel said softly, "And the end justifies the means —"

Homer shot a quick, impatient look at her. "The good doctor and his people are in the Sahara to work with the Tuareg and the Teda and the rest of the bedouin. Beyond that, he has the same dream we have-of developing this continent of our racial background."

"But he doesn't believe in your methods, Homer, and we're forcing him to follow El Hassan's road in spite of his beliefs."

Moroka had been peering at the two of them narrowly. "You don't make omelets without breaking eggs," he said, his voice on the overbearing side.

She spun on him. "But the omelets don't turn out so well if some of the eggs you use are rotten."

The South African's voice turned gentle. "Miss Cunningham," he said, "working in the field, like this, can have its rugged side for a young and delicate woman —"

"*Delicate!*" she snapped. "I'll have you know —"

"Hey, everybody, hold it," Cliff injected. "What goes on?"

Dave Moroka shrugged. "It just seems to me that Isobel might do better back in Dakar, or in New York with your friend Jake Armstrong. Somewhere where her sensibilities wouldn't be so bruised, and where her assets" —his eyes went up and down her lithe body —"could be put to better use."

Isobel's sepia face had gone a shade or more lighter. She said, very flatly, "My assets, Mr. Moroka, are in my head."

Homer Crawford said disgustedly, "O.K., O.K., let's all knock it off."

His eyes flicked back and forth between them, in definite command. "I don't want to hear any more in the way of personalities between you two."

Moroka shrugged again. "Yes, sir," he said without inflection.

Isobel turned away and took up some paperwork, without further words. She suppressed her feeling of seething indignation.

Homer Crawford, under his pressures, was changing. Possibly, she had told herself before, it was change for the better. The need was for a *strong* man, perhaps even a ruthless one.

The Homer Crawford she had first known was an easier going man than he who had snapped an abrupt order to her a moment ago. The Homer she had first known requested things of his teammates and friends. El Hassan had learned to command.

The Homer she had first known could never have ridden, roughshod, over the basically gentle Dr. Smythe.

The Homer she had first known, when the El Hassan scheme was still aborning, had thought of himself as a member of a team. He was quick to ask advice of all, and quick to take it if it had validity. Now Homer, as El Hassan, was depending less and less upon the opinions of those surrounding him, more and more upon his own decisions which he seemed to sometimes reach purely through intuition.

The El Hassan dream was still upon her, but, womanlike, she wondered if she liked the would-be tyrant of all North Africa as well as she had once liked the easy-going American idealist, Homer Crawford.

Jack and Jimmy Peters, the brothers from Trinidad, entered, the former carrying a couple of books.

They'd evidently failed to note the raised voices and wore their customary serious expressions. Jack looked at Homer and said, "*Cu vi scias Esperanton?*"

Homer Crawford's eyebrows went up but he said, "*Jes, mi parolas Esperanto tre bona, mi pensas.*"

"*Bona,*" Jack said, "*Tre bona.*"

"*Jes, estas bele,*" his brother said.

Moroka was scowling back and forth from one of them to the other. "I thought I had a fairly good working knowledge of the world's more common languages," he said, "but that goes by me. It sounds like a cross between Italian and pig-Latin."

Homer said to the Peters brothers, "Let's drop Esperanto so that Dave, Isobel and Cliff can follow us. We can give it a whirl later, if you'd like, just for the practice."

Isobel said slowly, "*Mi parolas Esperanto, malgranda.*" Then in English, "I took it for kicks while I was still in school. Kind of rusty now, though."

"Esperanto?" Cliff said. "You mean that gobblydygook so-called international language?"

Jack Peters looked at him, serious faced as always. "What is wrong with an international language, Mr. Jackson?"

Cliff was taken aback. "Search me. But it doesn't seem to have proved very practical. It didn't catch on."

"Well, more than you might think," Isobel told him. "There are probably hundreds of thousands of persons in one part of the world or another who can get along in Esperanto."

Moroka said impatiently, "What're a few hundred thousands of people in a world population like ours? Cliff's right. It never took hold."

Homer said, "All right, Jack and Jimmy. You boys evidently have something on your minds. Let everybody sit down and listen to it."

* * * * *

Even before they got thoroughly settled, Jack Peters was launching into his pitch.

"We need an official language," he said. "The El Hassan movement has set as a goal the uniting of all North Africa. We might start here in the Sahara, but it's just a start. Ultimately, the idea is to reach from Morocco to Egypt and from the Mediterranean to ... to where? The Congo?"

"Actually, we've never set exact limits," Homer said.

"Ultimately *all Africa,*" Dave Moroka muttered softly. He ignored the manner in which Isobel contemplated him from the side of her eyes.

"All right," the West Indian said. "There are more than seven hundred major languages, not counting dialects, in Africa. Sooner or later, we need an official language, what is it going to be?"

"Why *one* official language? Why not several?" Cliff scowled. "Say Arabic, here in this area. Swahili on the East coast. And, say, Songhoi along the Niger, and Wolof, the Senegalese lingua franca, and —"

"You see," Peters interrupted. "Already you have half a dozen and you haven't even got out of this immediate vicinity as yet. Let me develop my point."

138

Homer Crawford was becoming interested. "Go on, Jack," he said.

Jack Peters pointed a finger at him. "To be the hero-symbol we have in mind, El Hassan is going to have to be able to communicate with *all* of his people. He's not going to be able to speak Arabic to, say, a Masai in Kenya. They hate the Arabs. He's not going to be able to speak Swahili to a Moroccan, they've never heard of the language. He can't speak Tamaheq to the Imraguen, they're scared to death of the Tuareg."

Homer said thoughtfully, "A common language would be fine. It'd solve a lot of problems. But it doesn't seem to be in the cards. Why not adopt as our official language the one in which the *most* of our people will be able to communicate? Say, Arabic?"

Jack was shaking his head seriously. "And antagonize all the Arab hating Bantu in Africa? It's no go, Homer."

"Well, then, say French-or English."

"English is the most international language in the world," Moroka said. But his face was thoughtful, as those of the others were becoming.

The West Indian was beginning to make his points now. "No, any of the European languages are out. The white man has been repudiated. Adopting English, French, Spanish, Portuguese or Dutch, as our official language would antagonize whole sections of the continent."

"Why Esperanto?" Cliff scowled. "Why not, say, Nov-Esperanto, or Ido, or Interlingua?"

Jimmy Peters put in a word now. "Actually, any one of them would possibly do, but we have a head start with Esperanto. Some years ago both Jack and I became avid Esperantists, being naïve enough in those days to think an international language would ultimately solve all man's problems. And both Homer and Isobel seem to have a working knowledge of the language."

Homer said, "So have the other members of my former Reunited Nations team. That's where those books you found came from. Elmer, Bey, Kenny ...and Abe ...and I used to play around with it when we were out in the desert, just to kill time. We also used it as sort of a secret language when we wanted to communicate and didn't know if those around us might understand some English."

"I still don't get the picture," Cliff argued. "If we picked the most common half a dozen languages in the territory we cover, then millions of these people wouldn't have to study a second language. But if you adapt Esperanto as an official language then *everybody* is going to have to learn something new. And that's not going to be easy for our ninety-five per cent illiterate followers."

Isobel said thoughtfully, "Well, it's a darn sight easier to learn Esperanto than any other language we decided to make official."

"Why?" Cliff said argumentatively.

* * * * *

Jack Peters took over. "Because it's almost unbelievably easy to learn. English, by the way, is extremely difficult. For instance, spelling and pronunciation are absolutely phonetic in Esperanto and there are only five vowel sounds where most national languages have twenty or so. And each sound in the alphabet has one sound only and any sound is always rendered by the same letter."

Dave Moroka said, "Actually, I don't know anything at all about this Esperanto."

The West Indian took him in, with a dominating glance. "Take grammar and syntax which can take up volumes in other languages. Esperanto has exactly sixteen short rules. And take vocabularies. For instance, in English we often form the feminine of a noun by adding *ess-actor-actress, tiger-tigress*. But not always. We don't say *bull-bulless* or *ghost-ghostess*. In Esperanto you simply add the feminine ending to any noun-there's no exception to any rule."

Jack Peters was caught up in his subject. "Still comparing it to English, realize that spelling and pronunciation in English are highly irregular and one letter can have several different sounds, and one sound may be represented by different letters. And there are even silent letters which are written but not pronounced like the *ugh* in *though*. There are none of these irregularities in Esperanto. And the sounds are all sharp with none of such subtle differences as, say, *bed/bad/bard/bawd*, that sort of thing."

Jimmy Peters said, "The big item is that any averagely intelligent person can begin speaking Esperanto within a few hours. Within a week of even moderate study, say three or four hours a day, he's astonishingly fluent."

Isobel said thoughtfully, "There'd be international advantages. It's always been a galling factor in Africans dealing with Europeans that they had to learn the European language involved. You couldn't expect your white man to learn kitchen kaffir, or Swahili, or whatever, not when you got on the diplomatic level."

Cliff Jackson was thinking out loud. "So far, El Hassan is an unknown. Rumor has it that he's everything from a renegade Egyptian, to an escaped Mau-Mau chief, to a Senegalese sergeant formerly in the French West African forces. But when he starts running into the press and they find that Homer and his closest associates all speak English, and most of them with an American accent, there's going to be some fat in the fire."

"And El Hassan will have lost some of his mysterious glamour," Homer added thoughtfully.

Even Moroka, the South African, was beginning to accept the idea. "If El Hassan, himself, refused in the presence of foreigners ever to speak anything but Esperanto, the aura of mystery would continue."

Jimmy Peters, elaborating and obviously pushing an opinion he and his brother had already discussed, said, "We make it a rule that every school, both locally taught and foreign, must teach Esperanto as a required subject. All El Hassan governmental affairs would be conducted in that language. Anybody at all trying to get anywhere in the new regime would have to learn the official inter-African tongue."

"Oh, brother," Cliff groaned, "that means me." He brightened. "We haven't any books or anything, as yet."

Isobel laughed at him. "I'll take on your studies, Cliff. We have a few books. Those that Homer and his team used to kill time with. And as soon as we're in a position to make requests for foreign aid of the great powers, Esperanto grammars, dictionaries and so forth can be high on the list."

With a sharp cry, almost a bark, a figure jumped into the entrance and with a bound into the center of the tent, sub-machinegun in hand. *"All right, everybody. On your feet. The place is raided!"*

Dave Moroka leaped to his feet, his hand tearing with blurring speed for his holstered hand gun. "Where's that bodyguard?" he yelled.

VII

Hold it," Homer Crawford roared, jumping to his own feet and grabbing the South African in his arms. He glared at the newcomer. "Kenny, you idiot, you're lucky you don't have a couple of holes in you."

Kenny Ballalou, grinning widely, stared at Dave Moroka. "Jeepers," he said, "you got that gun out fast. Don't you ever stick 'em up when somebody has the drop on you?"

Dave Moroka relaxed, the side arm dropping back into its holster. Homer Crawford released him and the South African ran a hand over his mouth and shook his head ruefully at Kenny.

Isobel and Cliff crowded up, the one to kiss Kenny happily, the other to pound him on the back.

Homer made introductions to Dave Moroka and the Peters brothers.

"I've told you about Kenny," he wound it up. "I sent him over to the west to raise a harka of Nemadi to help in taking Tamanrasset." He joined Cliff Jackson in giving the smaller man an affectionate blow on the shoulder. "What luck did you have, Kenny?"

Kenny Ballalou rubbed himself ruefully. "If you two will stop beating, I'll tell you. I didn't recruit a single Nemadi."

Homer Crawford looked at him.

Kenny said to the tent at large. "Anybody got a drink around here? Good grief, have I been covering ground."

Isobel bustled off to a corner where she'd amassed most of their remaining European type supplies, but she kept her attention on him.

Dave Moroka said, his voice unbelieving, "You mean you haven't brought any assistance *at all?*"

Kenny grinned around at them. "I didn't say that. I said I didn't recruit any of the Nemadi. I never even got as far as their territory."

Homer Crawford sank back onto the small crate he'd been using as a chair before Kenny's precipitate entrance. "O.K.," he said, "stop dramatizing and let us know what happened."

Kenny spread his hands in a sweeping gesture. "The country's alive from here to Bidon Cinq and south to the Niger. Bourem and Gao have gone over to El Hassan and a column of followers was descending on Niamey. They should be there by now. I never got as far as Nemadi country. I could have recruited ten thousand fighting men, but I didn't know what we'd do with them in this country. So I weeded through everybody who volunteered and took only veterans. Men who'd formerly been in the French forces, or British, or whatever. Louis Wallington and his team were in Bourem when I got there and—"

"Who is Louis Wallington?" Jack Peters said.

Homer looked over at the Peters brothers and Dave Moroka. "Head of a six-man Sahara Development Project team like the one I used to head." His eyes went back to Kenny. "What about Louis?"

"He's come in with us. Didn't know how to get in touch, so he was working on his own. And Pierre Dupaine. Remember him, the fellow from Guadeloupe in the French West Indies, used to be an operative of the African Affairs sector of the French Community? Well, he and a half dozen of his colleagues have come in and were leading an expedition on Timbuktu. But Timbuktu had already joined up too, before they got there—"

"Wow," Homer said. "It's really spreading."

Cliff said, "Why isn't all this on the radio?"

Isobel had brought Kenny a couple of ounces of cognac from their meager supply. He knocked it back thankfully.

Kenny said to Cliff, "Things are moving too fast, and communications have gone to pot." He looked at Homer. "Have any of these journalists found you yet?"

"What journalists?"

Kenny laughed. "You'll find out. Half the newspapers, magazines, newsreels and TV outfits in the world are sending every man they can release into this area. They're going batty trying to find El Hassan. Man, do you realize the extent of the country your followers now dominate?"

Homer said blankly, "I hadn't thought of it. Besides, most of what you've been saying is news to us here. We've been keeping on the prod."

Kenny grinned widely. "Well, the nearest I can figure it, El Hassan is ruler of an area about the size of Mexico. At least it was yesterday. By today, you can probably tack on Texas."

Jimmy Peters, serious faced as usual, said, "Things are moving so fast, we're going to have to run to keep ahead of El Hassan's followers. One thing, Homer, we're going to have to have a press secretary."

"Elmer Allen was going to handle that, but he's still up north," Isobel said.

"I'll do it. Used to be a newspaperman, when I was younger," Dave Moroka said quickly.

Isobel frowned and began to say something, but Homer said, "Great, you handle that, Dave." Then to Kenny, "Where're your men and how well are they armed?"

"Well, that's one trouble," Kenny said unhappily. "We requisitioned motor transport from some of the Sahara Afforestation Project oases down around Tessalit. In fact, Ralph Sandell, their chief mucky-muck in those parts, has come over to us. But we haven't got much in the way of shooting irons."

Homer Crawford closed his eyes wearily. "What it boils down to, still, is that a hundred of those Arab Legionnaires, with their armor, could finish us all off in ten minutes if it came to open battle."

* * * * *

El Hassan continued moving his headquarters, usually daily, but he eluded the journalists only another twelve hours. Then they were upon the mobile camp like locusts.

And David Moroka took over with a calm efficiency that impressed all. In the first place, he explained, El Hassan was much too busy to handle the press except for one conference a week. In the second place, he spoke only Esperanto to foreigners. Meanwhile, he, Dave Moroka, would handle all their questions, make arrangements for suitable photographs, and for the TV and newsreel boys to trundle their equipment as near the front lines as possible. And, meanwhile, James and John Peters of El Hassan's staff had prepared press releases covering the El Hassan movement and its program.

Homer, to the extent possible, was isolated from the new elements descending upon his encampment. Attempting anything else would have been out of the question. At this point, he was getting approximately four hours of sleep a night.

Kenny Ballalou was continually coming and going in a mad attempt to handle the logistics of supplying several thousand men in a desert area all but devoid of either water or graze, not to speak of food, petroleum products and ammunition.

Isobel and Cliff were thrown into the positions of combination secretaries, ministers of finance, assistant bodyguards, and all else that nobody else seemed to handle, *including* making coffee.

It was Isobel who approached a subject which had long worried her, as they drove across country, the only occupants of one of the original hover-lorries, during a camp move.

She said, hesitantly, "Homer, is it a good idea to give Dave such a free hand with the press? You know, there are some fifty or so of them around now and they must be influencing the TV, radio, magazines and newspapers of the world."

"He seems to know more about it than any of the rest of us," Homer said, his eyes on the all but sand-obliterated way. "We're going to have to move more of the men south. We simply haven't got water enough for them. There'd be enough in Tamanrasset, but not out here. Make a note to cover this with Kenny. I wonder where Bey is, and Elmer."

Isobel made a note. She said, "Yes, but the trouble is, he's a comparative newcomer. Are you *sure* he's in complete accord with the original plan, Homer? Does the El Hassan dream mean the same to him as it does to you, and …well, me?"

He shot her an impatient glance, even as he hit the lift lever to raise them over a small dune. "You and Dave don't hit it off very well. He's a good man, so far as I can see."

Her delicate forehead wrinkled and her pixie face showed puzzlement. "I don't know why. I get along with most people, Homer."

He patted her hand. "You can't please everybody, Isobel. Listen, something's got to be done about this king-size mob of camp followers we've got. Did you know Common Europe sent in a delegation this morning?"

"Delegation? Common Europe —?"

"Yeah. Haven't had time to discuss it with you. They found us just before we raised camp. Evidently, the British Commonwealth and possibly the Soviet Complex-some Chinese, I think- are also trying to locate us. Half of these people are without their own equipment and supplies, but that's not what worries me right now. We used to be able to camouflage our headquarters camp. Dig into the desert and avoid the aircraft. But if a group of bungling Common Market diplomats can locate us, what's to keep the Arab Legion from doing it and blessing us with a stick of neopalm bombs?"

Isobel said, "Look, before we leave Dave. Did you know he was confiscating all radio equipment brought into our camp by the newsmen and whoever else?"

Homer frowned. "Well, why?"

"Espionage, Dave says. He's afraid some of these characters might be in with the Arab Union and inform on us."

"Well, that makes some sense," Homer nodded.

"Does it?" Isobel grumbled.

He shot an irritated glance at her again and said impatiently, "Can't the poor guy do anything right?"

"My woman's intuition is working," Isobel grumbled.

* * * * *

Dave Moroka came into headquarters tent without introduction. He was one of the half dozen who had permission for this. He had a sheaf of papers in his left hand and was frowning unhappily.

"What's the crisis?" Homer said.

"Scouts coming up say your pal Bey-ag-Akhamouk is on the way. Evidently, with a big harka of Teda from the Sudan."

"Great." Homer crowed. "Now we'll get going."

"Ha!" Dave said. "From what we hear, a good many are camel mounted. How are we going to feed them? Already some of the Songhai Kenny brought up from the south have drifted away, unhappy about supplies."

"Bey's a top man," Homer told him. "The best. He'll have some ideas on our tactics. Meanwhile, we can turn over most of his men to one of the new recruits, and head them down to take Fort Lamy. With Fort Lamy and Lake Chad in our hands we'll control a chunk of Africa so big everybody else will start wondering why they shouldn't jump on the bandwagon while the going is good."

Dave said, "Well, that brings up something else, Homer. These new recruits. In the past couple of days, forty or fifty men who used to be connected with African programs sponsored by everybody from the Reunited Nations to this gobblydygook outfit Cliff and Isobel once worked for, the AFAA, have come over to El Hassan. The number will probably double by tomorrow, and triple the next day."

"Fine," Homer said. "What's wrong with that? These are the people that will really count in the long run."

"Nothing's wrong with it, within reason. But we're going to have to start becoming selective, Homer. We've got to watch what jobs we let these people have, how much responsibility we give them."

Homer Crawford was frowning at him. "How do you mean?"

"See here," the wiry South African said plaintively, "when El Hassan started off there were only a half dozen or so who had the dream, as you call it. O.K. You could trust any one of them. Bey, Kenny, Elmer, Cliff, this Jake Armstrong that you've sent to New York, Rex Donaldson, then Jimmy and Jack Peters and myself. We all came in when the going was rough, if not impossible. But now things are different. *It looks as though El Hassan might actually win.*"

"So?" Homer didn't get it.

"So from now on, you're going to have an infiltration of cloak and dagger lads from every outfit with an interest in North Africa. Potential traitors, potential assassins, subversives and what not."

Homer was scowling at him. "Confound it, what do you suggest? That these Johnny-Come-Latelies be second-class citizens?"

"Not exactly that, but this isn't funny. We've got to screen them. The trouble with this movement is that it's a one-man deal, and has to be. The average African is either a barbarian or an actual savage, one ethnic degree lower. He wants a hero-symbol to follow. O.K., you're it. But remember both Moctezuma and Atahualpa. Their socio-economic systems pyramided up to them. The Spanish conquistadores, being old hands at sophisticated European-type intrigue, quickly sized up the situation. They kidnaped the hero-symbol, the big cheese, and later killed him. And the Inca and the Aztec cultures collapsed."

Homer was scowling at him unhappily.

Dave summed it up. "All we need is one fuzzy minded commie from the Soviet Complex, or one super-dooper democrat who thinks that El Hassan stands in the way of *freedom*, whatever that is, and bingo a couple of bullets in your tummy and the El Hassan movement folds its tents like the Arabs and takes a powder, as the old expression goes."

"You have your point," Homer Crawford admitted. "Follow through, Dave. Figure out some screening program."

* * * * *

Cliff came in. "Hey, Homer. Guess what old Jake has done."

"Jake Armstrong?"

"He's swung the Africa for Africans Association in New York over to us. They've raised a million bucks. What'll we do with it? How can he get anything to us?"

"We'll have him plow it back into publicity and further fund raising campaigns," Homer said. "That's the way it's done. You raise some money for some cause and then spend it all on a bigger campaign to raise still more money, and what you get from that one you plow into a still bigger campaign."

Cliff said, "Don't you *ever* get anything out of it?"

Dave and Homer both laughed.

Cliff said, "I've got some still better news."

"Good news, we can use," Homer said.

* * * * *

The big Californian looked at him in pretended awe. "A poet no less," he said.

"Shut up," Homer said. "What's the news?"

The fact of the matter was, he was becoming increasingly impatient of the continual banter expected of him by Cliff and even the others. As original members of the team, they expected an intimacy that he was finding it increasingly difficult to deliver. Among other things, he wished that Cliff, in particular, would mind his attitude when such followers as Guémama were present. The El Hassan posture could be maintained only in never to be compromised dignity.

Bey had once compared him to Alexander, to Homer's amusement at the time. But now he was beginning to sympathize with the position the Macedonian leader had found himself in, betwixt the King-God conscious Persians, and the rough and ready Companions who formed his bodyguard and crack cavalry units. A King-God simply didn't banter with his subordinates, not even his blood-kin.

Cliff scowled at him now, at the sharpness of Homer's words, but he made his report.

"Our old pal, Sven Zetterberg. He's gone out on a limb. Because of the great danger of this so-far localized fight spreading into world-wide conflict-says old Sven-the Reunited Nations will not tolerate the combat going into the air. He says that if *either* El Hassan or the Arab Legion resort to use of aircraft, the Reunited Nations will send in its air fleet."

"Wow," Homer said. "All the aircraft we've got are a few slow-moving heliocopters that Kenny brought up with him."

Dave Moroka snapped his fingers in a gesture of elation. "That means Zetterberg is throwing his weight to our side."

Homer was on his feet. "Send for Kenny and Guémama and send a heliocopter down to pick up Bey and rush him here. He shouldn't be more than a day's march away. I wonder what Elmer is up to. No word at all from him. At any rate, we want an immediate council of war. With Arab Legion air cover eliminated, we can move in."

Cliff said sourly, "It's still largely rifles against armored cars, tanks, mobile artillery and even flame throwers."

* * * * *

All the old hands were present. They stood about a map table, Homer and Bey-ag-Akhamouk at one end, the rest clustered about. Isobel sat in a chair to the rear, stenographer's pad on her knees.

Bey was clipping out suggestions.

"We have them now. Already our better trained men are heading up for Temassinine to the north and Fort Charlet to the east. We'll lose men but we'll knock out every water hole between here and Libya. We'll cut every road, blow what few bridges there are."

Jack Peters said worriedly, "But the important thing is Tamanrasset. What good —"

"We're cutting their supply line," Bey told him. "Can't you see? Colonel Ibrahim and his motorized column will be isolated in Tamanrasset. They won't be able to get supplies through without an air lift and Sven Zetterberg's ultimatum kills that possibility. They're blocked off."

Jimmy Peters was as confused as his brother. "So what? to use the Americanism. They have both food and water in abundance. They can hold out indefinitely. Meanwhile, our forces are undisciplined irregulars. We gain a thousand recruits a day. They come galloping in on camel-back or in beat-up old vehicles, firing their hunting rifles into the air. But we also lose a thousand a day. They get bored, or hungry, and decide to go back to their flocks, or their jobs on the new Sahara projects. At any rate, they drift off again. It looks to me that, if Colonel Ibrahim can hold out another week or so, our forces might melt away-all except the couple of hundred or so European and American educated followers. And, cut down to that number, they'll eliminate us in no time flat."

Homer Crawford was eying him in humor. "You're no fighting man, Peters. Tell me, what is the single most fearsome enemy of an ultra-mechanized soldier with the latest in military equipment and super-firepower weapons?"

Jimmy Peters was blank. "I suppose a similarly armed opponent."

Homer smiled at him. "Rather, a man with a knife."

The expressions of the Peters brothers showed resentment. "We weren't jesting."

"Neither was I," Homer rapped. He looked around at the rest, including Bey and Kenny. "What happens to a modern mechanized army when it runs out of gasoline? What happens to a water-cooled machine gun when there is no water? What use is a howitzer when the target is a single man in ten acres of cover? Gentlemen, have any of you ever studied the tactics of Abd-el-Krim or, more recently still, Tito? Bey, I assume you have."

He had their attention.

"During the Second War," Homer continued, "this Yugoslavian Tito tied up two Nazi army corps with a handful of partisans-guerrillas. The most modern army in the world, the German Panzers, tried to ferret him out for five years, and couldn't. There are other examples. The Chinese operating against the Japs in the same war. Or one of the classic examples is Abd-el-Krim destroying two different Spanish armies in the Moroccan Rif in the 1920s. His barefoot men, armed with rifles, took on Primo de Rivera's modernized Spanish armies and trounced them."

Bey said, "Homer's right. Our only tactics are guerrilla ones."

Homer Crawford looked at Guémama, who had been standing in the background, unfamiliar with the language these others spoke, but holding his dignity. Crawford said, diplomatically, "And what sayest thou, O chieftain of the Tuareg?"

Guémama was gratified at the attention. He said in Tamaheq, "As all men know, O El Hassan, we now outnumber by thrice the Arab *giaours* may they burn in Gehennum. Therefore, let us rush in and kill them all."

Bey shuddered.

Homer Crawford nodded seriously. "Ai, Guémama, that would be the valorous way of the Tuareg. But the heart of El Hassan forbids him to sacrifice the lives of his people. Consequently, we shall use the tactics of the desert jackal. Instruct those of your people who are most cunning, to infiltrate Tamanrasset in the night. Let them not carry arms for they may well be searched by the Arab *meleccha*."

The Tuareg chieftain was intrigued. "And what shall they do in Tamanrasset, El Hassan? Suddenly seize arms, one night, and rise up in wrath against the Arab dogs and kill them all?"

Homer was shaking his head. "They will address themselves to the Haratin serfs and spread to them the message of El Hassan. They will be told that in the world of El Hassan each man shall be free to seek his own destiny to the extent his mind and abilities allow. And no man shall be the less because he was born a serf, and no man the more because he was born to wealth or power in the old days."

"Aiii," Guémama all but moaned. "But such a message —"

"Is the message of El Hassan, as all men know," Homer Crawford said flatly. He turned to Kenny Ballalou. "Kenny, take over this angle. We want as many propagandists in that town as possible. It's already choked with refugees, most of them not knowing what they're fleeing. We might get recruits there, too. But mostly we want to appeal to the sedentary natives in town. They've got to get the dreams, too. Promise them schools, land ... I don't have to tell you."

"Right," Kenny said.

Isobel said, "Maybe I ought to get in on this, too. The women might do a better job than men on this slant. It's going to take a lot to get a Tuareg bedouin to sink to talking to a Haratin on an equal basis."

Bey and Homer had bent back over the maps, but before they could get back into the details of guerrilla warfare against Colonel Ibrahim and his legionnaires, they were halted by a controversy from without.

"What now?" Homer growled. "This camp is getting to be like a three-ring circus."

The entrance flap was pushed aside and three of Bey's Sudanese tribesmen half escorted, half pushed a newcomer front and center.

It was Fredric Ostrander, natty as usual, but now in khaki desert wear. He was obviously in a rage at the three rifle-carrying nomads who had him in charge.

Bey spoke to the Teda warriors in their own tongue. Then to Homer in Tamaheq, which he assumed the C.I.A. man didn't know, "They picked him up in the desert in a hover-jeep. He was evidently looking for our camp." He dismissed the three bedouin with a gesture.

Ostrander was outraged. He snapped at Homer Crawford, "I demand an explanation of this cavalier attack upon —"

His face expressionless, Homer held up a hand to quiet the smaller man. He looked at Jack Peters and raised his eyebrows. *"Kion li la fremdul diras?"*

Jack, serious as ever, replied in Esperanto, then turned to the American C.I.A. man and said, "El Hassan has requested that I translate for him. He speaks only the official language of North Africa to foreign representatives. Undoubtedly, sir, you have proper credentials?"

Had Fredric Ostrander been of lighter complexion, his color would have undoubtedly gone dark red.

"Look here, Crawford," he snapped. "I'm in no mood for nonsense. The State Department has sent me to your headquarters to make another attempt to bring some sense home to you. As an American citizen, owing alliance —"

Homer Crawford spoke in Esperanto to Jack Peters who nodded seriously and said to Ostrander, "El Hassan informs you he owes alliance only to the people of North Africa whose chosen leader he is."

Ostrander knew they were kidding him, but at the same time the stand being taken was actuality. He glared at the Americans present whom he knew, Bey, Isobel, Cliff and Kenny. He snapped, "Very well, but I repeat what I told you when last we met. The State Department of the United States of the Americas will not stand idly by and see this area taken over by elements dominated by red subversives."

"Holy Mackerel," Cliff growled, "are you still tooting that horn?"

Dave Moroka said sarcastically, "It's an old wheeze. The definition of a red subversive is anybody who doesn't see eye to eye with the United States. They've been pulling the gag for decades. Remember Guatemala and Cuba? Do anything that interferes with American business abroad and the cry goes up, *he's an enemy of the free world!*"

Ostrander spun on him, his eyes narrowing.

Dave laughed. "The definition of members of the free world, of course, being anybody who follows the American line. Anybody is free, Spanish and Portuguese dictators, absolute monarchs in Arabia, Chinese warlords, if they're on the American side."

Ostrander snapped, "I don't believe we've met."

Moroka made a sweeping bow. "I'm afraid we don't move in the same circles. I've spent possibly a third of my life in prison —"

"Undoubtedly," Ostrander snorted.

"...Put there by people such as yourself-in various countries-because I was fighting for my own version of freedom."

"Communism, undoubtedly!"

Moroka said softly, "I'm a South African, sir. Both my parents were killed in the 1960 riots. It seems that they had dark skins-even as you and I —and weren't able to see why that should keep them from *freedom*."

Fredric Ostrander spun back to Homer Crawford. "I'm not here to quibble with self-confessed malcontents. I've been sent to represent the State Department, to report to them, and, above all, to do what I can to prevent your activities from redounding to the further advantage of the Soviet Complex. I assume you can assign me quarters."

Straight-faced, Jack Peters translated this into Esperanto, and, straight-faced, Homer answered in the same language.

Jack turned back to the impatient C.I.A. man. "El Hassan welcomes the representative of the United States of the Americas and hopes this will be the first step toward diplomatic recognition between North Africa and your great country. He has instructed me to find you quarters, which, possibly you may have to share with delegations from Common Europe or" —Peters cleared his throat —"the Soviet Complex. He further suggests that it might be well, if you maintain communications with your superiors, to have sent to you books on Esperanto, the official language of North Africa."

Dave Moroka put in, "By the way, we'll have to go through your things. We can't allow any radio communication from El Hassan's camp, except through official El Hassan channels-for obvious military reasons."

Ostrander snorted, stared indignantly at Homer again, spun on his heel and stalked from the tent. Jack Peters followed him but not before tipping an uncharacteristic wink at Homer.

When they were gone, Homer sighed and looked at Dave Moroka. "That reminds me, how are our other delegations coming?"

The South African grinned ruefully. "They're playing it cool. Waiting to see what way to jump. Give El Hassan some real success, and they'll probably jump at the chance to be first to recognize him. Especially these Soviet Complex opportunists. They'd just love to suck you into their camp."

Isobel looked at him. "After that tearing down you gave poor Ostrander about the United States, now you rip into the Soviet Complex. Just where do you stand, Dave?"

Dave shrugged her question off, as though there were more important things. "I'm an El Hassan man," he said. "Let those two overgrown powers handle their own troubles."

Jimmy Peters spoke up for the first time since Ostrander entered the tent. "You know," he said, seriously, "I'm beginning to wonder if the world can afford nationalistic patriotism. Haven't we gone too far along the road to think of ourselves any longer as Americans, or Russians, or French, or West Indians, or whatever? Hasn't the human race grown up beyond that point?"

Kenny said mockingly, "What! Aren't you proud of being a West Indian, and a loyal subject of Her Majesty?"

Peters ignored his tone. "Why should I be proud of my country? It was an accident of birth with which I had nothing to do, that made me a West Indian, rather than a Canadian, a Chinese, a Norwegian, or whatever. Intelligently, I should be proud only of things that I, myself, have accomplished."

Bey said, "If we can stop waxing philosophic for a while and get back to how most efficiently to clobber these Arabs —"

* * * * *

The Hindu entered Kirill Menzhinsky's small office behind the Indian souvenir shop in the Tangier Zocco Chico and said, "The operative Anton is on the receiver."

The agent superior of the *Chrezvychainaya Komissiya* for North Africa looked up from his desk and grunted acceptance of the message. He came to his feet and followed the other into a back room and took his place before a mouthpiece and screen.

The man whose party name was Anton nodded a greeting.

Kirill Menzhinsky said, "It's about time I heard from you, Anton."

"Yes. But the situation has been such that it was not easy to report."

"And now?"

"Briefly, I am at El Hassan's headquarters. You were correct. He is in actuality Homer Crawford. The others you mentioned are also with him, including the traitor Isobel Cunningham."

The Soviet Complex's agent allowed his eyebrows to rise.

Anton said flatly, "The dame has evidently renounced the party and now holds high rank in Crawford's inner circle."

"And you?"

"I am rapidly becoming his right-hand man. I am his press secretary and in charge of communications. Early in our acquaintanceship I was able to engineer an attempted assassination. I was able to, ah, save the life of El Hassan."

The Russian's eyes narrowed. "The assassins? Is there any chance that they might reveal your little trick?"

Anton grimaced. "I am not a fool, Kirill. Both of them were killed in the assassination attempt. El Hassan was most grateful."

"I see. And how would you sum up the present situation?"

"This area is swinging rapidly to El Hassan, but any sort of defeat and undoubtedly his followers would melt away. The bedouin are too volatile. Before he ever makes any real headway he will have to take the major commercial and industrial cities such as Dakar, Kano, Lagos, Accra, Freetown, Khartoum, and eventually, of course, Cairo, Casablanca, Algiers and so forth."

"And our friend El Hassan leans not at all in our direction?"

The man the Party called Anton shook his head. "He leans in no direction, except that which will unite and modernize North Africa. Neither do his immediate followers. They're a well-knit group and it seems unlikely that I could pry any of them away from him in case it became desirable."

"I see," Kirill Menzhinsky muttered. "I understand that a delegation from Moscow has arrived in El Hassan's camp. Have you contacted them?"

"Certainly not. My orders were to rise in the El Hassan hierarchy and await further orders. None of my current, ah, colleagues have any suggestion that I am identified with the Party. Which reminds me, an American C.I.A. man, Fredric Ostrander, has shown up. The fool seems to be under the impression that El Hassan is a Party tool."

"I know this Ostrander. Don't underestimate him, Anton. He's an extremely competent operative in the clutch, as the Americans call it."

"Perhaps. But nevertheless, there is no indication that the El Hassan movement leans either to East or West, nor do I see any signs that it is apt to in the future."

The Russian was scowling. "I see. Then perhaps it will be necessary for us to do something to topple our El Hassan before he becomes much stronger, and to find another to unite North Africa."

Anton frowned in his turn. "I don't know. This man Crawford-and his followers, for that matter-are motivated by high ideals. As you have said, North Africa is not ready for our socioeconomic system. Men of the caliber of Homer Crawford could bring it into the modern age perhaps more quickly than another."

Menzhinsky chuckled. "Don't worry about it, Anton. Such matters of policy will be decided by others than you, or even me. Keep in touch with me more often, in the future, Anton."

"Yes, Comrade." His face faded from the screen.

* * * * *

Tamanrasset lies at an altitude of approximately 4,600 feet, about average for the Ahaggar plateau. Around it, such peaks as the Tahat reach 9,600 feet above sea level. The country is rugged, jagged, bleak beyond belief. With the possible exception of Southern Afghanistan in the Khyber area, there is no place in the world more suited for guerrilla warfare, less suited for the proper utilization of modern armor, particularly when the latter is forced to work without air cover.

Homer Crawford, equipped with an old-style telescope, was spread-eagled on top a rock outcropping, his only companion Isobel Cunningham. Directly before him, possibly two miles in distance, was the desert city of Tamanrasset, to the right, a kilometer or so, Amsel where palatable water was to be found at eighteen meters depth.

"Our friend, the colonel, is up to something," he grumbled.

She had a pair of binoculars, of considerably less power than his glass.

"It looks as though Guémama's boys are on the run," she said.

"As per orders. The primary theory of partisan warfare is not to get killed. The guerrilla never stands and fights. If the regular forces he opposes can bring him to bay, they've got him." He interrupted himself to clip out, "Look at that tank, darling! There on the left!"

Isobel tightened, looked at him quickly from the side of her eyes. No. He'd said it inadvertently, his mind concentrated on the fighting men below. She had often wondered where she stood with Homer Crawford the man, as opposed to El Hassan the idealist. The tip of her tongue licked the side of her mouth, as she surreptitiously took him in. But Crawford the man would have to wait, there was no time, no time.

Isobel swung her glasses. "The one starting to go in a circle? There, it stopped."

"One of the snipers got its commander," Homer said. "You can't fight a tank without the commander's head being up through the hatch. That's a popular fallacy. You can't see well enough to fight your tank unless you've got your head up. And that's suicide when you're against guerrillas. The colonel ought to send his infantry out first."

Isobel said, "What did you mean when you said that he's up to something?"

Homer's eye was still glued to the eyepiece of his glass. "He's leaving his entrenchments and sending his vehicles out to capture our ... our strong points."

"You mean our water, don't you?"

Bey came snaking up to them on his belly. He came abreast of Homer and brought forth his own binoculars. He watched for a moment and then muttered a curse under his breath.

"Guémama better start pulling back those men more quickly," he said.

"He will. He's a good man," Homer told him. "What's up?"

"Evidently, Colonel Ibrahim has decided to come out of retirement. He's sent small motorized elements to Effok, In Fedjeg, Otoul and even to Tahifet."

"And —?"

"And has taken them all, of course. Our men fall back, fighting a stubborn rear-guard action, taking as few casualties as possible."

"I don't get it," Homer bit out. "He's using up his fuel and ammunition and losing more men than we are. Certainly he can't figure, with the thousand odd troops he has, to be able to take and hold enough of the oases and water holes in this vicinity to push us out completely."

Bey said, "What worries me is the possibility that he knows something we don't. That he's figuring on being relieved or has a new source of fuel, ammunition and men on tap."

"The roads are cut. Our men hold every source of water from here to Libya and the Reunited Nations has put thumbs down on aircraft which eliminates an air lift."

"Yeah," Bey said, unhappily.

* * * * *

That evening, following the day's last meal, Cliff came into the headquarters tent grinning, broadly. "Hey, guess what we've liberated."

"A bottle of Scotch?" Kenny said hopefully.

"A king-size portable radio transmitter. Ralph Sandell knew about it. The Sahara Afforestation Project people were going to use it to propagandize the tribesmen into coming in and taking jobs in the new oases."

Dave Moroka, who'd been censoring press releases, shook his head. "That's why we need an El Hassan in this country," he complained. "They put a couple of million dollars into a radio transmitter, never asking themselves how many of the bedouin own radios."

Jack Peters said, "Wait a moment, you chaps. Didn't Bey capture a couple of Arab Legion radio technicians today?"

"They defected to us," Homer Crawford said, looking up from an improvised desk where he was poring over some supply papers with Isobel. "What did you have in mind, Jack?"

"There are radios in Tamanrasset. In fact, there's probably a radio in every one of those military vehicles of Ibrahim's. Why can't we blanket these Arab Union chaps with El Hassan propaganda? Quite a few of them are from Libya, Tunisia and Egypt. In short, they're Africans and susceptible to El Hassan's dream."

"Good man. Take over the details, Jack," Homer said. He went back to his work with Isobel.

Jimmy Peters entered with some papers in hand. He said, seriously, "The temperature is rising in the Reunited Nations-and everywhere else, for that matter. Damascus and Cairo have been getting increasingly belligerent. Homer, it looks as though the Arab Union is getting ready to go out on a limb. Weeks have passed since Colonel Ibrahim first took Tamanrasset and the Reunited Nations, the United States, the Soviet Complex and all others interested in North Africa, have failed to do anything. Everybody, evidently, afraid of precipitating something that couldn't be ended."

All eyes went to Homer Crawford who ran a black hand back over his hair in weariness. "I know," he said. "Something is about to blow. Dave has sent some of his best men into Tamanrasset to pick up gossip in the souks. Morale was dragging bottom among the legionnaires just a couple of days ago. Now they seem to have a new lease."

"In spite of the sabotage our people have been committing?" Isobel said.

"That's falling off somewhat," Cliff said. "At first our more enthusiastic followers were able to pull everything from heaving Molotov Cocktails into tanks, to pouring sugar in hover-jeep gas tanks, but the legionnaires have both smartened up and gotten very tough."

"Good," Dave Moroka said now.

They looked at him.

"Atrocities," he said. "In order to guard against sabotage, the legionnaires will be taking measures that will antagonize the people in Tamanrasset. They'll shoot a couple of teenage kids, or something, then they'll have a city-wide mess on their hands."

Isobel said unhappily, "It seems a nasty way to win a war."

Dave grunted his contempt of her opinion. "There is no way of winning a war other than a nasty one."

Bey came in, yawning hugely. His energy was inconceivable to the others. So far as was known, he hadn't slept, other than sitting erect in a moving vehicle, for the past four days. He said to Homer, "Fred Ostrander has been bending my ear for the past hour or so. Do you want to talk to him?"

"About what?" Homer said.

"I don't know. He has a lot of questions. I think he's beginning to suspect-just *suspect*, understand-that possibly the whole bunch of us aren't receiving our daily instructions from either Moscow or Peking."

Dave and Cliff both laughed.

Homer sighed and said, "Show him in. He's the only thing we have in the way of a contact with the United States of the Americas and sooner or later we're going to have to make our peace with both them and the Soviet Complex. In fact, what we're probably going to have to do is play one against the other, getting grants, loans, economic assistance —"

"Technicians, teachers, arms," Bey continued the list.

Kenny Ballalou looked at him and snorted. "Arms! If there's anything this part of the world doesn't need it's more arms. In fact, that goes for the rest of the world, too. In the old days when the great nations were first beginning to attempt to line up the neutrals they sent aid to such countries by the billions-and most of it in arms. How ridiculous can you get? Putting arms in the hands of most of the governments of that time was like handing a loaded pistol to an idiot."

Bey hung his head in mock humility. "I bow before your wisdom," he said. He left the room to get Ostrander.

*   *   *   *   *

The C.I.A. man had lost a fraction of his belligerence, but none of his arrogance and natty appearance. Homer wondered vaguely how the other managed to remain so spruce in the inadequate desert camp.

Jack Peters said, "What did you wish to ask El Hassan? I will translate."

"Never mind that, Jack," Homer said. "We'll get tougher about using our official language when we've gone a little further in building our new government." He said to Ostrander, "What can I do for you? Obviously, my time, is limited."

Fredric Ostrander said, "I've been gathering material for reports to my superiors. I've been doing a good deal of questioning, and, frankly, even prying around."

Cliff grunted.

Ostrander went on. "I've also read the various press releases, manifestoes and so forth that your assistants have been compiling."

"We know," Homer said. "We haven't put any obstacles in your way. We haven't any particular secrets, Mr. Ostrander."

"You disguise the fact that you are an American," the C.I.A. man said accusingly.

Homer said slowly, "Only because El Hassan *is not* an American, Mr. Ostrander. He is an African with African solutions to African problems. That is what he must be if he is to accomplish his task."

Ostrander seemed to switch subjects. "See here, Crawford, the State Department is not completely opposed to the goal of uniting North Africa. It would solve many problems, both African and international."

Kenny Ballalou laughed softly. "You mean, you're on our side?"

Ostrander turned to him, for once not incensed at being needled. "Possibly more than you'd think," he rapped. He turned back again to Homer Crawford. "The question becomes, why do you think that *you* are the man for the job? Who gave *you* the go-ahead?"

Bey, who had settled down into a folding camp chair, now came to his feet, his tired face angry.

But Homer waved him to silence. "Hold it," he said. Then to Ostrander. "It doesn't work that way. It's not something you decide to do because you're thirsty for power, or greedy for money. You're pushed into it. Do you think Washington, a retired Virginian planter wrapped up in his estate and his family, wanted to spend years leading the revolutionary armies through the wilderness that was America in those days? He was thrust into the job, there was no one else more competent to take it. Men make the times, Ostrander, but the times also make the men. Look at Lenin and Trotsky. Three months before the October Revolution, Lenin wrote that he never expected to see in his lifetime the Bolsheviks come to power. Within those months he was at the head of government and Trotsky, a former bookworm who had never fired a gun in his life, was head of the Red Army and being proclaimed a military genius."

Ostrander was scowling at him, but his face was thoughtful.

Homer said quietly, "It's not always an easy thing, to have power thrust into your hands. Not always a desirable thing." His voice went quieter still. "Only a short time ago it led me to the necessity of ... killing ... my best friend."

154

"And mine," Isobel said softly, almost under her breath.

Dave Moroka said, "Abe Baker," before he caught himself.

Kenny Ballalou looked at him strangely. "Did you know Abe?"

The South African recovered. "I've heard several of you mention him from time to time. He was a commie, wasn't he?"

"Yes," Homer said without inflection. "And a man. He saved my life on more than one occasion. As long as we worked together with only Africa in mind, there was no conflict. But Abe had a further, and, to him, greater alliance."

He turned his attention back to the C.I.A. man. "A man does what he must do," he finished simply. "I did not ask to become El Hassan."

Ostrander said, "Your motivation is possibly beside the point. The thing is that the battle for men's minds continues and your program, eventually, must align with the West."

"And get clobbered in the stampeding around between the two great powers," Kenny said dryly.

"You've got to take your stand," Ostrander said. "I'd rather die under the neutron bomb, than spend the rest of my life on my knees under a Soviet Complex government. Wouldn't you?" His eyes went from one of them to the other, defiantly.

Homer said slowly. "No, even though that was the only alternative, which is unlikely. Not if it meant finishing off the whole human race at the same time." He shook his head. "If it were only me, it might be different. But if it was a matter of nuclear war the whole race might well end. Given such circumstances, I'd be proud to remain on my knees the rest of my life. You see, Ostrander, you make the mistake of thinking the Soviet socio-economic system is a permanent thing. It isn't. It's changing daily, even as our own socio-economic system is. Even if the Soviet Complex were to dominate the whole world, it would be but a temporary phase in man's history. Their regime, in its time, right or wrong, will go under in man's march to whatever his destiny might be. Some day it will be only a memory, and so will the socio-economic systems of the West. No institutions are less permanent than politico-economic ones."

"I don't agree with you," Ostrander snapped.

"Obviously," Homer shrugged. "However, this is another problem. El Hassan deals with North Africa. The other problems you bring up we admit, but at this stage are not dealing with them. Our dream is in Africa. Perhaps the Africans will be forced to taking other stands, to dreaming new dreams, twenty or thirty years from now. When that time comes, I assume the new problems will be faced. By that time there will probably be no need for El Hassan."

Ostrander looked at him and bit his lip in thought.

It came to him now that he had never won in his contests with Homer Crawford, and that he would probably never win. No matter how strong his convictions, in the presence of the other man, something went out of him. There was strength in Crawford that must be experienced to be understood. When he talked, he held you, and your own opinions became nothing-stupidities on your lips. He had a dream, and in conversation with him, all other things dropped away and nothing was of importance but that dream. A dream? Possibly *disease* was the better word. And so highly contagious.

While they talked, an aide had entered and handed a report to Bey-ag-Akhamouk. He read it and closed his eyes in weariness.

"What's up, Bey," Homer asked.

"I don't know. Colonel Ibrahim has stepped up his attacks in all directions. At least two thirds of his force is on the offensive. It doesn't make much sense. But it must make sense to *him*, or he wouldn't be doing it."

Ostrander said, and to everyone's surprise there seemed to be an element of worry in his voice too, "I know Colonel Midan Ibrahim, met him in Cairo and in Baghdad on various occasions. He's considered one of the best men in the Arab Legion. He doesn't make military blunders."

Bey said, "Come on, Kenny. Let's round up Guémama and take a look at the front." He led the way from the tent.

* * * * *

There was a guard posted before the tent which doubled as press and communications center, and the private quarters of David Moroka.

The figure that approached timidly was garbed in the traditional clothing of the young women of the Tégéhé Mellet tribe of the Tuareg and bore an *imzad* in her left hand, while her right held a corner of her gandoura over her face.

The guard, of the Kel Rela tribe, eyed the one-stringed violin with its string of hair and sounding box made of half a gourd covered with a thin membrane of skin, and grinned. A Tuareg maid was accustomed to sing and to make the high whining tones of desert music on the *imzad* before submitting to her lover's embrace. *Wallahi!* but these women of the Tégéhé Mellet were shameless.

"Where do you go?" he said gruffly. "El Hassan's vizier has ordered that he is occupied and none should approach."

"He awaits me," she wavered. There was *kohl* about her eyes, and indigo at the corners of her mouth. "We met at the *tendi* last night and he bid me come to his tent. It is for me he waits."

Wallahi! but his leader had taste, the sentry decided.

"Pass," he said gruffly. Even a vizier of such importance as this one must need solace at times, he decided philosophically.

She slipped past silently to the tent entrance where the Tuareg guard noticed she paused for a long moment before entering. He grinned into his teguelmoust. Aiii, the little bird was timid before the hawk.

She stood for a moment listening, and then slipped inside, dropping the desert musical instrument to the ground. Dave Moroka's back was to her and even as she entered he flicked off the switch of the video-radio into which he had been speaking and scowled at it.

When he stood and began to turn, she covered him with the small pocket pistol. She had an ease in handling it which denoted competence.

His eyebrows went up, but he remained silent, waiting for her gambit.

Isobel said evenly, "You're a Party member, aren't you, Dave?"

"Why do you say that?"

She nodded infinitesimally to the set. "You were reporting just now. I heard enough just as I came in."

He took in her disguise. "My guard isn't as efficient as I had thought," Dave said wryly.

Isobel said, "You knew Abe Baker, didn't you?"

He looked at her, expressionlessly.

She said, "I already knew you belonged to the Party, Dave. No matter how competent an agent, it's something difficult to hide from any other long-time member. There's a terminology you use–such as calling it the Soviet Union, rather than Russia. No commie ever says Russia, it's always *the Soviet Union*. You can tell, just as a Roman Catholic can tell a person raised in the Church, even though the other has dropped away, or even as one Jew can tell another. Yes, I've known you were a Party member for some time, Dave."

"And?" the South African said.

"Why are you here?"

Dave Moroka said, "For the same reason you are, to further the El Hassan dream, the uniting and modernization of the continent of my racial heritage."

"But you are still a Party member and still report to your superiors."

Dave Moroka looked at the tiny gun she held in her hand.

"Don't try it," she said. "I have seen you in action, Dave. I have never seen a man move so ruthlessly fast ... but don't try it."

"No reason to," he bit out. "Come on, let's go see Homer."

She was slightly taken aback, but not enough to release her control for even a split second. "Lead the way," she said.

* * * * *

Even at this time of evening, the headquarters tent was brightly lit and most of the immediate El Hassan staff still at work. Homer Crawford looked up as they entered.

Cliff Jackson saw the gun first and said, "Holy Mackerel, Isobel."

Fredric Ostrander was sitting to one side in discussion with the sober faced Jack Peters. He took in the gun and slowly came to his feet, obviously expecting climax.

Isobel said, "Dave's taking over control of communications had method. I just found him reporting to what must have been a superior ... in the Party."

Homer Crawford looked from the South African to Isobel, then back to Dave again, without speaking. His eyes were questioning.

Dave said, his voice sharp. "I haven't time for details now. Isobel's right. I was a Party member."

"Was?" Ostrander chuckled. "That's the understatement of the year. I hadn't got around to revealing the fact as yet, but our friend Dave is the notorious Anton, one of the Soviet Complex's most competent hatchetmen."

Dave looked at him only briefly. "Was," he reiterated. He turned his attention to Homer and to Bey, who was staring tired dismay at this new addition to the load.

Homer still held his peace, waiting for the other to go on.

"I found out tonight why Colonel Ibrahim is attacking, instead of pulling in his horns as reason would dictate." Dave paused for emphasis. "The Soviet Complex has thrown its weight, in this matter at least, on the side of the Arab Union. They have insisted that Sven Zetterberg be dismissed as head of the Sahara Division of the African Development Project and that his threat to use Reunited Nations aircraft if the local fighting spreads to the air, be repudiated."

Kenny blurted, "Good grief ... that means —"

Dave looked around at them, one by one. "It means," he said, "that the Arab Legion is going to be reinforced tomorrow morning by a full regiment of paratroopers."

"Holy Mackerel," Cliff groaned. "We've had it. Another regiment of crack troops in Tamanrasset and we'll *never* take the town."

Dave shook his head. "That's not the big thing. The paratroopers aren't going to drop in Tamanrasset. They're going to hit every oasis, every water hole, in a circumference of two hundred miles."

There was an empty silence.

Homer Crawford said finally, evenly, "In the expectation that every follower of El Hassan in the Sahara will either surrender or die of thirst, eh?" He didn't seem sufficiently impressed by the threatening disaster. He looked at Dave questioningly. "Why do you bother to tell us, Dave, if you're on the other side?"

Dave grunted sour amusement. "Because I've just become a full member of the team. I resigned from the Party tonight."

"Brother," Bey said, "you sure pick a helluva time to join up." He obviously was expressing the opinions of the majority.

Homer Crawford came to his feet and looked around at them. "All right," he said. "A new complication. Let's face up to it. There's always an answer. We're in the clutch, let's fight our way out."

Largely, they stared at him, but he ignored their dismay. He looked from one to the other. "We need some ideas. Let's kick it around. Isobel, Cliff, Jack, Kenny —?" His eyes went from one to the other. Obviously his own mind was churning.

They shook their heads dumbly.

Kenny said, "Ideas! We've had it, Homer!"

Homer Crawford spun on him and now the force they all knew was emanating from him. He laughed his scorn. "A month ago we were half a dozen fugitives. Now we're an army besieging a city. And you say we've had it? Listen, Kenny, if we have to we'll go back to being half a dozen fugitives again-those of us that are left. But the dream goes on! However, we're not going to have to. We're too near victory in this stage of the operation to sit down on the job because of a threatened reverse. Now then, let's kick it around. Jimmy! Dave! Kenny! Ostrander!"

Fredric Ostrander raised his eyebrows only slightly at being included in their number.

* * * * *

Bey, for once, was seemingly too exhausted to be brought to new enthusiasm. He tossed a detail map of Tamanrasset to the table. "And I'd just worked out a bang-up scheme for infiltrating into town, joining up with our adherents there, and seizing it while most of Ibrahim's men were out in the desert, trying to capture our nearer water holes."

Homer snapped, "It sounds like it still might have possibilities."

Ostrander looked down at the map, his face very tight. "How long would it take?"

Bey scowled at him, defeat dulling his mind. "What?"

"How long do you figure it would take to infiltrate Tamanrasset and capture it? Behind Ibrahim's back, so to speak."

Bey grunted. "A couple of hours in the early morning. I had a beautiful picture of the colonel's armor out in the desert, cut off from its petroleum supplies and ammunition dump while we held the town. Some of our men, the former veterans of the French West African forces, could have even operated the antitank guns he has mounted at Fort Laperrine."

The C.I.A. man's mouth worked.

Homer Crawford's eyes pierced him.

Ostrander walked over to the radio before which Kenny Ballalou sat. "See if you can raise Colonel Ibrahim for me."

Kenny scowled at him. "Why?"

"Do it."

Kenny looked at Homer Crawford.

Homer said, "O.K. Do it."

Kenny shrugged and turned to the set. While the others watched, Crawford's face alert, his eyes narrowed, the rest of them dull in apathy, the face of Colonel Ibrahim finally faded in on the screen.

Fredric Ostrander took his place at the instrument. He nodded, formally. "Greetings, Colonel, it seems a long time since last we met in Amman."

The Arab Legion officer smiled politely. "I had heard that you represented the State Department in this area, Mr. Ostrander, and have been somewhat surprised that you failed to make Tamanrasset your headquarters. It would have been pleasant to have renewed old friendship."

Ostrander cleared his throat. "I am afraid that would have been difficult, Colonel, particularly in view of the stand of my government at this time."

On the screen, the other's eyebrows went up.

Ostrander said evenly, "Colonel, we have just been informed that a regiment of paratroopers has been put at your disposal and that they plan to land at various points in the Sahara in the morning."

The colonel said stiffly, "This is military information which I am not free to discuss, Mr. Ostrander."

Frederic Ostrander went on, his voice still even. "We have further been informed that the Reunited Nations has withdrawn its ban on aircraft, which would seem to free your paratroop carrying planes."

The colonel remained silent, waiting for the bombshell. It was obvious that he expected a bombshell.

Ostrander said, "As representative of the State Department I warn you that if these paratroop carrying planes take off tomorrow morning, the Seventh Airfleet of the United States of the Americas will enter the conflict on the side of El Hassan. Good evening, Colonel."

The C.I.A. man reached out and flicked the switch that killed the set. Then he took the snowy white handkerchief from the breast pocket of his jacket and wiped his mouth.

Isobel said, "Heavens to Betsy."

Kenny said indignantly, "Good grief, you fool, it won't take more than hours for your superiors to repudiate you. Then what happens?"

"By then, I assume, the battle will be over and Tamanrasset in El Hassan's hands. The Arab Union will then think twice before committing their paratroopers, particularly with captured armor in El Hassan's hands."

"And your name will be mud," Kenny blurted.

Ostrander looked at Homer Crawford. "Gentlemen, you must remember that I, too, am an African. I had thought that perhaps there would be a position for me on El Hassan's staff."

Crawford reached for the Tommy-Noiseless that leaned up against the improvised desk at which he worked. He said, "Let's get moving, Bey. We haven't much time. We're going to have to be able to announce its capture *from* Tamanrasset in a couple of hours."

"Not you," Bey said, grabbing up his own weapon and motioning with his head for Kenny and Cliff to come along. "You're El Hassan and can't be risked."

"I'm coming," Homer said flatly. "It's about time El Hassan began taking some of the same risks his followers seem to be willing to face. Besides, the men will fight better with me out in front. Got a gun, Fred?"

Ostrander said, "No. Where am I issued one?"

"I'll show you," Homer said, stuffing extra clips in his bush jacket pockets. "Come on, Dave."

The whole group began heading for the open air, Bey already yelling orders.

Fredric Ostrander looked at Dave Moroka. "Strange bedfellows," he said.

Moroka grinned wryly. "My long view hasn't changed," he said. "It's just that this African matter takes precedence right now."

"Nor mine, of course," Ostrander said. He cleared his throat. "However, I hope you last out the night. El Hassan needs strong men."

"Same to you," Moroka said gruffly. "Let's get going, or the fight will be over while we hand each other flowers."

Epilogue

El Hassan stood in the smoking, war-wasted ruin of Fort Laperine, his mind empty. The body of Jack Peters was ten feet to his left, burned beyond recognition and crumpled over a flame thrower which he'd eliminated in the last few moments of the fighting. Had he let his eyes go out the gun port before which he stood, it might have been possible for El Hassan to have picked out the bodies of David Moroka and Fredric Ostrander amidst those of the several hundred Haratin serfs who had swarmed out of the souk area at the crucial moment and stormed the half manned fort-unarmed save for knives and farm implements.

To his right, Dr. Warren Harding Smythe supervised two Tuareg who were carrying off the broken body of Kenny Ballalou; there was still faint life in it.

The doctor looked at him. "You are satisfied, I assume?"

El Hassan failed to hear him.

Smythe turned and stomped off, following his impressed nurses.

In the distance, Bey-ag-Akhamouk called hoarse orders from an over-strained throat, placing guns for a counterattack that would never come. The Arab Legion was broken and Colonel Ibrahim a prisoner. Large numbers of the survivors were defecting to the banner of El Hassan.

He threw his empty Tommy-Noiseless to the side. All he wanted now was sleep, the surcease of a few hours of oblivion.

Isobel, her face wan from the horror of the agony of the combat whose result was everywhere visible, was picking her way through the wreckage with Cliff Jackson.

El Hassan looked at her absently. Whatever message she bore held little interest to him.

Cliff said, "India has recognized El Hassan as legal head of state of all North Africa. It is expected that Australia will follow before the week is out."

El Hassan nodded. For the time, not caring.

Isobel said, "We have other word. It came by messenger." She closed her eyes in pain and handed him a small box.

He opened it and recognized the ring on the enclosed finger. He looked up at them.

Cliff Jackson growled low in his throat. "Elmer Allen. He's been captured by a leader of the Ouled Touameur clan of the Ouled Allouch tribe. You know this Abd-el-Kader?"

El Hassan was staring down at the finger, his mind slowly clearing of its fatigue. "He belongs to the Berazga division of the Chaambra confederation. I had a run-in with him a few months ago and had him jailed. He's nothing but a desert bandit on the make."

Cliff said, "He's escaped, has thrown his weight behind the Arab Union, proclaimed himself the Mahdi and is uniting Algeria and parts of Morocco and Tunisia like a wildfire. The marabouts and Shorfa are backing him."

"Proclaimed himself the Mahdi?" Isobel said in question.

El Hassan turned to the girl and took a deep breath. "The original Mahdi was the holiest prophet since Mohammed and according to the more superstitious Moslems, he's still alive. According to Islamic tradition, he periodically shows up again in the desert and makes various predictions. When he does, it almost always winds up with a jehad, a holy war. Don't you remember in history the anti-British Mahdi at Khartoum, the killing of Chinese Gordon and so forth? That Mahdi was the son of a Dongola carpenter and he managed to conquer two million square miles in two years."

"But, what has this got to do with this Abd-el-Kader?"

"He's evidently proclaimed himself sort of a reincarnation of the original Mahdi. He's out to do the same thing we are-to unite North Africa. But in his case he doesn't exactly have the same dream and he's working under the green ensign of the Pan-Islamic Arab Union."

"And has Elmer Allen captive."

"Yes, he has Elmer." El Hassan's tone of voice turned sharp. "Cliff, go get Bey. Tell him we're forming a flying column and heading north."

Cliff was gone. El Hassan turned back to the girl. "You know, Isobel," he said softly, slowly, "in history there is no happy ending, ever. There is no ending at all. It goes from one crisis to another, but there is no ending."

www.ingramcontent.com/pod-product-compliance
Lightning Source LLC
Chambersburg PA
CBHW051243170626
46809CB00004B/1456